PRAISE FOR BETTE LEE CROSBY'S NOVELS

THE SUMMER OF NEW BEGINNINGS

"Once again Crosby has written a beautiful story filled with loving, caring—and sometimes a little flawed—characters who struggle to end up with the lives they are meant to live."

—*The Book Bag*

"A heartwarming story about family, forgiveness, and the magic of new beginnings."

—Christine Nolfi, bestselling author of *Sweet Lake*

"A heartwarming, captivating, and intriguing story about the importance of family . . . The colorful cast of characters are flawed, quirky, mostly loyal, determined and mostly likable."

—*Linda's Book Obsession*

"Crosby's Southern voice comes through in all of her books and lends a believable element to everything she writes. *The Summer of New Beginnings* is no exception."

—*Book Chat*

THE TWELFTH CHILD

"Crosby's unique style of writing is timeless and her character building is inspirational."

—Layered Pages

"Crosby draws her characters with an emotional depth that compels the reader to care about their challenges, to root for their success, and to appreciate their bravery."

—Gayle Swift, author of ABC, Adoption & Me

"Crosby's talent lies in not only telling a good compelling story, but telling it from a unique perspective. Characters stay with you because they are simply too endearing to go away."

—Reader Views

BABY GIRL

"Crosby weaves this story together in a manner that feels like a huge patchwork quilt. All the pieces and tears come together to make something beautiful."

—Michele Randall, Readers' Favorite

"Crosby is a true storyteller, delving into the emotions, relationships, and human dynamics—the cracks which break us, and ultimately make us stronger."

—J. D. Collins, Top 1000 reviewer

SILVER THREADS

"*Silver Threads* is an amazing story of love, loss, family, and second chances that will simply stir your soul."

—*Jersey Girl Book Reviews*

"Crosby's books are filled with love of family and carry the theme of a sweetness for life . . . You are pulled in by the story line and the characters."

—*Silver's Reviews*

"In *Silver Threads*, Crosby flawlessly merges the element of fantasy without interrupting the beauty of a solid love story . . . sure to stay with you beyond the last page."

—Lisa McCombs, *Readers' Favorite*

CRACKS IN THE SIDEWALK

"Crosby has penned a multidimensional scenario that should be read not only for entertainment but also to see how much, love, gentleness, and humanity matter."

—Gisela Hausmann, *Readers' Favorite*

A Year *of* Extraordinary Moments

A Year *of* Extraordinary Moments

A
MAGNOLIA
GROVE
NOVEL

Bette Lee Crosby

LAKE UNION
PUBLISHING

Text copyright © 2018 by Bette Lee Crosby

Published by Lake Union Publishing, Seattle

www.apub.com

Amazon, the Amazon logo, and Lake Union Publishing are trademarks of Amazon.com, Inc., or its affiliates.

ISBN-13: 9781503904705
ISBN-10: 1503904709

Cover design by Rachel Adam Rogers

Printed in the United States of America

In loving memory of
Virginia Ann Wilson
You were taken too soon
but will forever be remembered.

1

Alice DeLuca

I'm an old woman now and not long for this world, but I'm not afraid of dying. What I am afraid of is leaving behind a grandson who will follow in his mama's footsteps. I'd like to believe that in the years she's been gone my Dorothy has straightened herself out, but inside my heart, I fear this may be little more than wishful thinking.

There is an old adage that says a child's ways can be formed by either nature or nurture. In Dorothy's case, it was a bit of both. She had her daddy's genes and was the spitting image of him in more ways than a person could count: dark hair, long-lashed eyes capable of looking a hole through you, and a stubborn streak a mile wide. Just like Joseph, she'd set her mind to something and then have it her way, come hell or high water. Instead of correcting such behavior, he applauded it.

"A bit of mischief takes the sting out of life," he'd say when she told us of shenanigans like sneaking in the side door of the Rialto to watch a show without paying or thumbing a ride out to the fairgrounds with a perfect stranger.

I'd scowl and tell her such things were not at all good ideas, but she chose to listen to her daddy. Joseph and I had just the one child, and since she turned out as free-spirited and irresponsible as him, that was probably a blessing.

I know you're wondering how it was I married such a man; there were times when I wondered it myself. But when we met, I was barely seventeen. Joe was two years older than me and as handsome and charming as a man could possibly be. The first time he pressed his mouth to mine, my knees turned to jelly, and there was no resisting him.

Once it became obvious I was expecting a baby, my daddy marched himself over to the DeLuca farm and had a heart-to-heart talk with Daddy DeLuca. That same day, Joe's daddy demanded he do the honorable thing and marry me. There was no wishy-washy discussion about it; a week later, Joe did what his daddy told him to do.

That was fifty years ago. Back then folks thought having a baby out of wedlock was something to be ashamed of. Nowadays they say it's socially acceptable, and maybe it is for the parents, but what about the baby? You can argue this for a month of Sundays, but as far as I'm concerned, a child still needs a mama and a daddy.

The thing I regret is not being more like Daddy DeLuca when Dorothy came home with a toddler and no word of who the father was. I started to say she needed to think about the baby and get her life back in order, but Joe stopped me.

"Butt out," he'd said. "It's her life, and if she doesn't want to be tied down by marriage, she shouldn't have to be."

Hearing the regret in his words, I realized he was thinking of himself as much as he was thinking of Dorothy. Joe didn't think I knew, but I did, and it pained my heart to know he felt the same about marrying me. Like every young woman, I wanted to believe that the man I was going to spend the rest of life with was marrying me because he loved me like I loved him, not because it was something his daddy made him do.

For the next ten years, I held my tongue and didn't say a word as Dorothy shuffled poor little Dominic from town to town, looking for her "inner self." That inner self was all she cared about; she didn't give a fig about the boy's education and upbringing. Two years after Joe died, she came home, and for a while I thought maybe she'd come to her senses and would be ready to take on the responsibility of motherhood. I was wrong. She stayed for a few months, then took off for California and left twelve-year-old Dominic with me.

"I'll send for him as soon as I get settled," she'd said, but she never did.

Once in a while we'd get a postcard saying she was in one place or another, but there was never any mention of coming back to claim her son. It's little wonder he grew up with a chip the size of a sapling on his shoulder and his mama's irresponsible attitude. Dorothy's daddy stopped me from insisting she settle down and make a family for her boy, but Joe's gone now, and this time I'll do things the way I see fit.

Only God knows whether I've got a month, six months, or a year left on this earth, but I promise you this: I'm going to use every last day I'm graced with to make sure Dominic doesn't follow in his mama's footsteps.

2

Philadelphia

Three and a half years ago, Dominic DeLuca left Magnolia Grove, Georgia, for the second time, and that's when he swore he'd never return. Never mind his grandma still lived there and was getting on in years. As far as he was concerned, the town held nothing but bad memories. When he allowed himself to think about it, he could still picture his mama's car disappearing in the cloud of dust she'd kicked up as she'd sped down the road. He'd called out to her, but there was no way of knowing whether she'd heard him, because she'd never glanced back.

And then there was the thing with his ex, Tracy. She'd turned her back on him the same as his mama had.

"I never want to see you again," she'd said, which was fine as far as Dominic was concerned. He couldn't abide her uppity sister and had no need of a kid who'd been trouble from the day he'd been born almost five years ago.

He hadn't spoken to Tracy for over three years, not since that Thanksgiving Day when they last saw each other, and he had no intention of ever doing so. He'd been the one to reach out last time; there was no way he'd do it again. Sure, that day he'd had a few drinks to bolster his courage, but she'd turned it into an issue. Instead of being happy about his offer to get married and be a real daddy to Lucas, she'd pounced on him, calling him a drunk. He didn't need that kind of shit; not now, not ever.

Yeah, they'd been good together, but that was in the early years before she'd had the kid. Once Lucas came along, everything changed. The good times were gone. The only interest Tracy had was Lucas, and she was forever talking about how he needed this, that, and the other thing.

"What about me?" Dominic had asked. "What about my needs?"

That was something for which she'd had no answer. Little wonder he'd decided to take his pleasure elsewhere.

Dominic's cell phone was bulky in his pocket, so he left it lying on the shelf while working. It rang when he was at the far end of the bar pouring a double bourbon for Willie Edwards. He caught the familiar sound of the ringtone, but with one thing and another, he forgot to check for missed calls.

It was two hours later when the phone rang again, and Dominic answered. There was a fragile sound to his grandma's words as she asked how he was. It was so like her to ask about him. It had always been that way, almost as if she was trying to make up for what had happened. After he'd complained about working too hard, she moved on to give him the news.

"The cancer is back," Alice said softly. "I've been to Dr. Willoughby, and the tests confirm it."

Dominic stood speechless for a moment. He'd always known this was a possibility, but he'd never really expected it to happen. His grandmother seemed so strong, so in charge of life. Twice before, she'd beaten it, and he wanted to believe she would do it again.

"So . . . what's it going to be, chemo or—"

"Nothing," she said and gave a frail laugh. "This time it's too late. I've got five, maybe six months, but it's unlikely to be longer."

He inhaled sharply but said nothing.

"I know how you feel about Magnolia Grove . . ." She hesitated, as if considering what she was going to say next, then went on. "I was hoping you could come home and spend some time here. Someone will need to take care of things—details, final arrangements, the house—"

"What about Mama?"

Several moments ticked by before Alice spoke again. "I haven't heard from Dorothy for almost fifteen years." A labored sigh rattled up from her chest. "I doubt she'd come home even if I could get in touch with her."

It was a hard truth to accept, though now, it came as no surprise. The woman who claimed to be his mother was off somewhere, busy with something else. Unavailable. The resentment of those years rose in him like a storm brewing.

"Figures," he said sharply. "I'm not exactly eager to see her anyway."

They spoke for several minutes; then Dominic said, "I'll be there in a week, maybe less."

"Good." The relief in her voice was clear. "I'm really looking forward to seeing you."

After hanging up, Dominic thought about what he had to do. He hated the idea of returning to Magnolia Grove, but after all Alice had done for him, he had to go. He was the only one she had, just as she was the only one he had. Once Alice was gone, there would be no one; an absentee mama who couldn't be found didn't count.

That thought lodged itself in Dominic's chest like a huge chunk of granite.

"Hey, there," Willie called out. "Did you not hear me ask for a refill?"

"Yeah, I heard." Dominic took a bottle of bourbon from the back bar and poured a generous amount over the ice in Willie's glass. He pushed the drink across the counter, then poured a second one for himself. Figuring this would be his last night of working at Rosie's, he decided to make the most of it.

"Cheers," he said in a flat voice.

He lifted the glass to his mouth and chugged down the pain-dulling elixir. That drink was followed by another and then another. By the time the bar closed at 2:00 a.m., he'd lost count.

Once the last patron stumbled out and Dominic flipped the lock on the front door, Rosie sauntered out from the back office. She had twenty years and a good thirty pounds on Dominic but was still pleasing to look at.

"Pour me a double," she said and wriggled onto a stool.

He set two glasses on the bar and poured heavily.

It wasn't unusual for Dominic to have a drink or two during the evening. Every so often, the house bought a round for customers, and they in turn bought him one. Supposedly it was good for business, but this was the first time he'd ended up totally sloshed.

Rosie noticed. "Looks like you've already had enough," she said. "Maybe you ought to lay off."

Dominic pushed her glass across the counter and pulled a swig from his. "Don't sweat it. I'm fine. I can handle myself."

A look of annoyance settled on her face. "Yeah, well, from where I'm sitting, you look pretty damn smashed. I say we call it a night." She downed her drink, slid off the stool, and started back toward the office.

"Wait," he called out. "There's something I gotta tell you."

She stopped and turned back. "If it's an apology, I don't want to hear it."

"It's not that," he said, shaking his head. "I gotta go home to Georgia, and I need some time off."

"How much time?"

"A few months, maybe five or six."

"No way," she snapped. "I can cover a few days, possibly a week, but I can't give you longer than that."

"I need more time. My grandma's dying, and I'm all she's got. Somebody's got to be there to take care of things."

"I'm sorry, Dominic. I really am. But I've got a business to run."

"Grandma raised me; I owe her. I've gotta be there—"

"Look, if you can't settle your affairs within a week, then I'm sorry, but I'll need you to take your stuff and clear out."

"Fine by me!" he snapped.

As he stumbled out the back door leading to the one-room apartment above the bar, he snagged another bottle of bourbon and carried it up with him.

When Dominic awoke, the sun was already high in the sky. His head felt as if an elephant had stomped on it, and he could barely lift his eyelids. His first thought was only of the pain; then he remembered the phone call.

"Shit," he mumbled and tried pushing himself up from the bed. The pounding in his head grew worse. He sat there for several minutes, then dropped back onto the mattress. His inclination was to say *screw everything* and just go back to sleep, but he couldn't do it.

He hated Magnolia Grove. Hated the steamy summers and the nauseatingly sweet smell of jasmine. Hated the slow drawl of nosy neighbors. Hated the thought that everyone knew everyone else's business.

Most of all he hated Lucas, the kid who'd ruined the good life he'd once had with Tracy. After Lucas was born, everything changed. If it weren't for the kid, they might have worked things out, but no, Lucas always came first. Maybe it was wrong for a father to hate his son, but it was what it was.

The thought of going back caused all those memories to resurface, and not one of them felt good. If it had been anyone else, he wouldn't have gone. He would have flat-out said no and left it at that. But he couldn't do that to his grandma. She was the one person who genuinely cared about him. Try as he might, he couldn't blame her for what his mama did.

It was nearly noon when Dominic finally pulled himself from the bed and set a pot of coffee on to brew. The milk in the fridge was sour, so he drank his coffee black. After he'd downed two cups, he gathered his belongings and stuffed them into a large trash bag.

Surprisingly enough, after being there for almost three years, he had a small amount of stuff—clothes mostly, a hockey stick he hadn't used in over a decade, and a basketball sorely in need of air. The television, the furniture, even the clock radio all belonged to Rosie. The one-room furnished apartment came with the job, but after what had transpired last night he'd have neither.

Dominic poured the last of the coffee in his WORLD'S BEST BARTENDER mug and finished it off. The mug had been a gift from Rosie, so it officially belonged to him. He thought about taking it, then decided not to. He set the cup in the sink and looked around to make sure he hadn't forgotten anything.

Chances were he wouldn't be coming back, not to Rosie's anyway. Philadelphia maybe, but maybe not. He'd heard good things about New Jersey and was thinking of giving it a try. There was a possibility he could end up in any one of a dozen different places, but one thing he knew for certain was that he wouldn't be staying in Georgia. Not after his grandma was gone.

Dominic slung the overstuffed black trash bag across his shoulder and started down the stairs. By the next afternoon, he'd be back in Magnolia Grove. That thought was a lot heavier than his bag of belongings.

3

Magnolia Grove

On the day Meghan Briggs married Tom Whitely nearly two years ago, she'd had absolutely no regrets. True, her breath had caught in her throat when the pastor asked for the rings and Tom gave a long low whistle. For a moment, she'd thought he'd forgotten them or, worse yet, misplaced them altogether. Then she'd noticed the grin on Tom's face as he looked down the aisle. Seconds later, Sox had trotted in with the handle of a small white basket in his mouth. It seemed everyone but Meghan had known her rescue dog was to be part of the ceremony.

When Tom slid the ring onto her finger and promised to love her forever, Meghan had been certain that nothing, absolutely nothing, could stand in the way of their happiness.

For almost two years now, that had held true. Meghan had continued her online studies, gotten her veterinary technician's license, and worked alongside Tom in what was rechristened the Kindness Animal Clinic. The Saturday after she received her license, Tom placed the certificate into a gold leaf frame and hung it alongside his in the examination room. He suggested they celebrate by going out to dinner.

"I thought maybe you'd like to drive over to Benson. I heard the Candlewick Lounge has a great piano player."

"Or we could go to the Garden," she replied. "Anna has a guitar player now, and with the weather being so great . . ."

Tom grinned, the same easy grin she'd fallen in love with. "I'm sure going to the Garden has nothing to do with Sox," he teased.

"He might have influenced me a little. I just thought—"

"That if we sit on the patio, Sox can come along, right?"

"Well, he could, but he doesn't have to."

Tom's laugh had a way of spreading throughout the room and catching her up in it. When he started to chuckle, she couldn't resist joining in.

"Okay, okay," she said between giggles. "It's true; I wanted Sox to come along. After all, I would never have met you if it weren't for him."

He playfully tugged her into his arms and kissed her mouth. Keeping her locked in his embrace, he whispered, "Sometimes I think you care more about that dog than you do me."

She tilted her face up to his and pretended disbelief. "How can you say that? You know darn well I love the two of you equally!"

They both laughed.

It was early May, the time of year when the days were long and the blistering heat of summer had not yet descended on Georgia. Knowing they would have Sox with them, Tom called ahead, and Anna saved the corner table on the back patio.

When they arrived, she greeted them and asked, "Is this the anniversary?"

"No," Tom replied. "That's next month. Tonight we're celebrating Meghan's graduation. She's become a full-fledged veterinary technician."

With a squeal of delight Anna said, "Molti complimenti!" She pulled Meghan into a bear hug, then kissed both cheeks. "For you I am much happy!"

She scurried back to the kitchen and returned with a bottle of champagne and a steak bone that had a decent amount of meat left on it. She passed the bone down to Sox, then filled three glasses. "This night you have special celebration!"

"Absolutely!" Tom raised his glass and toasted Meghan. "Congratulations again, sweetheart. I'm so proud of you."

Anna nodded as he spoke. "Yes, is right for husband to be proud." After a few sips, she gave Meghan a single-arm hug and disappeared back into the kitchen.

True, tonight was special, but every night at the Garden was special. It was where Tom and Meghan had spent their first evening together, where he'd told her that her eyes sparkled in the moonlight and she'd felt the warmth of his hand touching hers.

As Sox lay gnawing on his bone, Tom looked across the table, and his eyes lingered on hers. A soft sigh drifted up from his chest, and he said, "When you first came into the clinic with Sox, I never dreamed that one day I'd be lucky enough to have you as my wife and partner."

"I'm the lucky one," Meghan replied; then she stretched her arm across the table and tucked her hand into his. The touch of her fingers against his soft palm warmed her heart with happiness, the kind of happiness that remains long after the moment has passed.

As the evening wore on, the sky turned to purple and the scent of night-blooming jasmine filled the air. They ate and then sat drinking cappuccinos as they had the first time.

Even after being married for almost two years and working together every day, there was no shortage of words. There were always new thoughts to discuss, secrets to share, plans to make.

For nearly two years they'd worked to build the business, and during that time, Meghan had somehow managed to juggle her hours at the clinic with studying and helping her sister, Tracy, manage the *Snip 'n Save* coupon magazine. As much as Meghan enjoyed the clinic, she couldn't let go of the *Snip 'n Save*. Her heart simply wouldn't let her forget all those years she'd worked alongside her daddy. With him gone, the magazine was the only piece of that life she could hold on to, and she was determined to do it. Now that the state exam was out of the way and she had her license, she'd have more free time. Hopefully she and Tom could start a family; if not this year, then next for certain.

As the shadows of the tall pines fell across the lawn, a rush of chill air crossed Meghan's shoulders, and she shivered. At the same moment, Sox stopped chewing on the bone he'd already licked clean. With his ears pushed back he lifted his snout, sniffed the air, then pushed himself up against Meghan's leg and settled down.

"It's getting late," she said. "We probably should get going."

Instead of taking the shortcut through the restaurant out to the walkway, they went down the patio steps and circled around the building. As they crossed over to where the car was parked, Tom pressed the remote to unlock the door, then opened it for Meghan. Walking around toward the driver's side, his back was turned to the road when a car lumbered along.

Meghan saw it and gasped. As Tom slid into the driver's seat, she asked, "Did you see that?"

"See what?"

"The car that just went by."

"Not really. Why?"

Meghan thought she'd seen the old Buick with the single blue fender, but it was dark, and she couldn't be certain. She shook her head. "It's nothing, I guess."

Tom knew better. He heard the edginess in her voice and saw the way her neck had suddenly stiffened.

"What's wrong?"

"Nothing. I thought I saw . . ." She left the remainder of her thought unsaid. It had been over three years, and Tracy hadn't heard from Dominic.

"Thought you saw what?"

Meghan peered past Tom, looking down the road as if she expected the car might still be there. It wasn't.

"I thought I saw a car with a blue fender, like the one Dominic used to drive."

Tom remembered the old car with a patch of tape on the back window and the front fender replaced by a blue mismatch that looked like it had been snatched from the junkyard.

"There's no way," he said. "I doubt that car is still running, and there probably isn't another one like it."

"I guess you're right."

She eased back into the seat as he pulled out of the parking lot, but a feeling of apprehension had already settled into her chest.

4

Meghan Whitely

I know it probably wasn't Dominic in that car, but I can't help feeling scared. Not just for myself; I'm scared for Tracy. She says she's over him, but I'm not sure that's true. Last month when we were downtown shopping, we saw a guy turning into the pizza place, and from the back, you'd swear it was Dominic. Same slicked-back hair, same swagger.

Tracy almost tripped over her own feet trying to get a better look. She pretended to be glad when we saw it wasn't him, but even as she was saying how relieved she was, I could see the disappointment on her face.

Every now and then she'll mention his name in passing. She says things like, "Lucas has Dominic's smile, don't you think?" The way she says it, I can tell she's wishing he'd find it in his heart to love Lucas and want them to be a family.

If that happened, she just might take him back, but why is beyond me. He's a liar and a cheater. Not only that, but he'd be a terrible daddy, and Lucas deserves better, especially after all he's gone through.

I flat-out asked Tracy if she'd ever consider going back to Dominic, and at first she said, "No, absolutely not." Then five minutes later she said, "Not the way he behaves now." When she said that, I began to wonder what would happen if by some miracle he did change.

The thing is, it's no secret that Dominic hates Magnolia Grove. If he and Tracy did get back together, he'd want to move her back to Philadelphia. That scares the life out of me. Mama and I would miss her and Lucas something fierce, not to mention, what would happen to the Snip 'n Save?

As much as I love working with Tom at the clinic, I'd have to give it up. I'm never letting go of the Snip 'n Save; *Daddy bought it and built it up, and it's the only piece of him I have left.*

5

The Question

On Saturday night, sleep was almost impossible to come by for Meghan. She was now certain she'd seen Dominic's car, but what she didn't know was if he was passing through or had come back to try and work things out with Tracy. If it was nothing more than a short visit with some of his old buddies, Meghan didn't want to stir things up by saying she'd seen him. Dominic was an issue better kept out of sight and out of mind.

A ribbon of pink was already edging the horizon by the time she finally fell into a restless sleep, and even with Sox curled against her side, she tossed and turned. When she woke, she dressed in cut-offs and a T-shirt, then told Tom she had to run over to her mama's house to help Tracy with a few *Snip 'n Save* issues.

A look of disappointment swept across his face. "Do you have to go now? I was hoping we'd take Sox for a run, then have breakfast at that new coffee shop on Grant Street. They have outdoor tables and . . ."

Meghan already had the car keys in her hand and one foot out the door, but she stopped and turned back.

"I guess it can wait," she said and dropped the keys into a catch-all bowl on the hall table.

She whistled for Sox, snapped the leash onto his collar, and then off the three of them went. Running was good. It cleared her mind.

They started out slowly, with Sox stopping to sniff a fire hydrant and a few trees, but once they rounded the corner onto Elroy Street, they picked up the pace. Sox took the lead with Meghan and Tom following close behind. As they passed the bungalow houses on Lakeside, they fell into step with an evenly matched stride. There was no need to say turn here or there; their bodies moved together.

The rhythmic slap of sneakers against the sidewalk brought a sense of order to Meghan's mind. Once she thought it through, it seemed possible the whole Dominic sighting was nothing more than a silly mistake. It had been dark, the streetlight had been out, and she'd only gotten a glimpse of the car. Perhaps the fender wasn't blue but that gray primer used before painting. Any number of cars had dents that needed to be fixed or fenders that had to be replaced.

As they crossed over onto Hillcrest, Meghan heard the sound of angry voices coming from an open window. She thought of the Thanksgiving afternoon when they'd last seen Dominic. Angry words had been hurled in both directions, and when Dominic turned violent with Tracy, Tom had stepped in. The image of Dominic sprawled out on the front lawn came to mind, and she remembered how he'd screamed obscenities and threatened to get even. For months they'd worried about what he might do, but now, after three years, no one thought of it anymore.

They'd forgotten, but had Dominic?

By the time they turned onto Grant Street, Meghan's shirt was soaked with perspiration, and her stomach had begun to rumble. She sniffed the rich aroma of coffee in the air and said, "I'll grab a table and wait here with Sox."

She plopped down into the chair. The outside seating area was almost full, but she saw no one she knew. A few elderly couples, a group of teenage girls, and two young men who looked like they'd just come from the gym.

Back when she worked beside her daddy at the *Snip 'n Save*, Meghan had thought she'd known everyone in town. Not any longer. Magnolia Grove had grown so much in the last six or seven years that sometimes it seemed almost unrecognizable. At one time, there had been only a handful of farms spread out beyond the city limits, but after the highway went through, fast food places had sprung up. Housing developments and strip malls had followed soon after.

The previous year, there had been a referendum on the ballot asking voters to decide whether the area outside the city limits should be incorporated into the city. It had passed, and overnight Magnolia Grove had become twice the size it once was.

Tom poked his head out the door of the coffee shop and called, "They're all out of croissants; do you want a bagel?"

Meghan nodded. "And bring back a cup of water for Sox."

It was late afternoon by the time Meghan arrived at the Briggses' house. Lila was in the kitchen.

"Hi, Mama," Meghan said and kissed her cheek.

Looking a bit surprised, Lila raised an eyebrow. "What are you doing here on a Sunday? I thought you and Tom would be enjoying the day together."

"We took Sox for a run this morning. This afternoon Tom wanted to watch a baseball game, so I thought I'd pop over for a visit."

Lila pulled a dog biscuit from the treat jar and held it out for Sox. As soon as Sox barked, Lucas came running into the room.

Meghan squatted to give him a hug. "How's my little man?"

"Aunt Meyan!" he exclaimed as he wrapped his chubby arms around her neck. "Me play wif Sox, ohay?"

"Yes, it's okay," Meghan said and laughed.

"Meyan" was how Lucas pronounced her name. Although he'd been born deaf, a cochlear implant enabled him to hear, and he was now learning to talk. Despite the speech class twice a week and ongoing therapy, his speaking age had not yet caught up to his actual age. That would take another year, possibly two. He still had problems with certain sounds and tenses. In time he'd move past that, but for the moment he was doing great. He was able to name colors, connect words, and ask an endless amount of questions. When he started asking why this and why that, it was hard to believe the only sounds he heard came through a cochlear implant.

Lila smiled. "Lucas has been helping me make cookies."

"I can see that." Meghan ruffled his hair, gave him a peck on the cheek, and brushed a smudge of cookie dough from his chin; then she stood and turned to her mama.

"Where's Tracy?"

Lila slid the tray of cookies into the oven. "Back in the office."

"I'll go say hello," Meghan replied and started down the hall.

It was exactly seventeen steps from the kitchen to the sewing room that over a decade ago had become the *Snip 'n Save* office. Meghan knew it all too well. The worn spot in the hallway carpet marked a pathway she'd walked for almost three years. Now she'd turned over most of the responsibilities to Tracy. Most, but not all.

She couldn't bring herself to let go completely. When it came to the *Snip 'n Save*, Meghan was like a kid hanging tight to a balloon, fearful that loosening her grip would allow it to float away and be lost forever. She was determined not to let that happen.

Poking her head in the door, Meghan asked, "Am I interrupting anything?"

Tracy looked up from the computer and smiled. "Of course not. Come on in."

"Sorry to bother you on a Sunday, but there are a few *Snip 'n Save* things I wanted to touch base on. I noticed a lot of the billing for this month hasn't gone out yet, and the Memorial Day layout—"

"Yeah, I know, I'm a bit behind."

The old familiar worry about Dominic picked at Meghan's mind. "Any particular reason?"

Tracy gave a sheepish nod. "I planned to catch up on the billing yesterday, but Lucas and I spent the day in Barrington, so I never got around to it."

The mention of Barrington brought a smile to Meghan's face. "Barrington, huh? You see Gabriel Hawke?" From the start, Meghan had suspected Gabriel would be a perfect match for her sister.

"No. We weren't at the school. Lucas had a playdate with Chloe's son. We took the kids to the park, then lunch at McDonald's."

Meghan's smile dissolved into a look of disappointment. "You could have at least stopped by his office to say hi."

Turning back to the computer with an impatient huff, Tracy said, "Don't start. I've already told you I'm not ready."

"I'm not starting anything. Gabriel's a great guy. All I'm saying—"

"I know what you're saying, but you can forget it. Gabriel's a friend. That's it."

"Seems to me that if you were open to the thought, he could be more than a friend," Meghan blurted out. "Lucas is really crazy about him and—"

"I don't want to talk about it," Tracy said, keeping her eyes locked on the screen.

"Why do you refuse to see the obvious? Is it because you're still hung up on Dominic?"

"I'm not going to waste my time talking about such nonsense," Tracy snapped.

Meghan was reluctant to mention the possibility that Dominic might be back in town, but she couldn't stop herself from asking, "Is it really nonsense, or have you heard from Dominic recently?"

Tracy looked at her with an angry glare. "No, I haven't. He hasn't called, and I certainly have no intention of calling him." There was a momentary pause, then she added, "Anyway, what I do or don't do is none of your business!"

Almost a full minute of silence passed before Meghan responded.

"I'm sorry. I wasn't trying to pry into your business, but I love you, and I really want you to be—"

"Don't worry, I'm fine. Right now, Lucas is the only man I want in my life, so stop asking about anyone else."

Meghan started to leave, then turned back. "Okay, but if anything changes or you need someone to talk to, call me."

"I will," Tracy replied without looking up.

6

Tracy Briggs

Meghan means well and is trying to be helpful, but sometimes I wish she wouldn't. I know she loves me, but she makes me feel like she's always right and I'm always wrong. Granted, it may be true, but it's no fun coming to grips with that truth.

Sure, I make mistakes; everybody does. The only difference is that the ones I make are monumental. It's easy to look back and say I should have known Dominic was never going to marry me, but I was eighteen and crazy in love.

Love makes people act stupid. Even if you start out smart and think you've got the world by the tail, you still never know where you're going to end up.

It may have been stupid for me to move to Philadelphia with Dominic, but I can't find one ounce of regret in my heart for it. Even knowing what I know now, I'd do it all over again. Why? Because of Lucas. Having him brings me more joy than I ever dreamed possible. Sometimes when I'm working, he'll come waddling back to the office just to give me a hug. Not even having a hunky movie star in love with you is as good as that.

The one thing I do regret is that Lucas doesn't have a daddy to love him. I try to make up for it by loving him twice as much, but that's about all I can do.

I realize Meghan's got a point. Gabriel is a good man, the kind of man who'd make a great daddy for Lucas, except right now, my heart isn't ready. Dominic and I are through. I've accepted that. But I'm still falling out of love with him.

Falling out of love is a lot harder than falling in love. When you fall in love, everything is beautiful—flowers bloom, music plays, and every star in the sky is winking at you. But falling out of love is like finding yourself in a pitch-black tunnel. At first you think in time you'll get through it, and then you realize how terribly long the tunnel is. I'm starting to see pinpricks of light ahead, so I might be coming to the end, but I'm not there yet.

Gabriel's a good man, no doubt about it. That's why I've got to wait until I'm at the end of this tunnel and standing in the light of day before I let myself even think about falling in love. Gabriel deserves a woman who can love him with her whole heart, not someone who's just looking to give her boy a daddy.

7

The DeLuca Farm

The night Dominic arrived back in Magnolia Grove, he visited some of his old haunts and had more than a few drinks. It was well after midnight when he turned onto the dirt road leading to the DeLuca farm. It had been over three years since he was last here, but even in the dark of night he could see nothing had changed. In the distance there was the familiar screeching of birds down by the pond, most likely fighting over a fish, he thought, as he moved past the barren peanut fields. The old Buick bumped through ruts that had been there since before he was born, then came to a stop in a clearing beside the house.

The porch light was on; she was expecting him. She'd probably been waiting up for him ever since their phone call.

He climbed from the car, hefted the large plastic bag onto his shoulder, and started for the house. The door was unlocked, just as he knew it would be. She never locked it. Why bother when there was almost nothing worth stealing? An old, boxy television or a thin, worn wedding band wouldn't bring enough to pay for the gas it took to drive out here.

He still hated this place, hated it just as much as he had all the years he'd lived here. The only reason he'd come back was because she'd asked him to—not just asked but begged. She was the one good thing he'd had in his life. The only one.

He pushed open the door and called out, "Grandma, I'm home."

Alice was sitting in the oversize club chair with her head dropped onto her shoulder. She'd been dozing, but the sound of his voice woke her. She pulled herself to her feet and hurried over as fast as she was able. Reaching up, she stretched her arms around his neck and gave him an affectionate hug.

"Oh, how I've missed you." She traced her fingers along his cheek and smiled.

"I've missed you, too." He meant it, even though years had gone by and he'd seldom picked up the phone to call her.

She seemed smaller than he remembered, more bony, and birdlike. Her hair was snow white now, thin and sparse as a baby's. He hated seeing her this way and for a moment regretted coming home.

It would have been better to remember her as she once was.

"There's beef stew on the stove," she said. "I'll heat it up while you bring in the rest of your things."

"I don't have a whole lot," Dominic replied. "This is it."

She eyed the plastic bag with a furrowed brow.

Alice noticed that when Dominic sat at the table, he chose the same chair he'd sat in all those many years.

"Sit in Granddaddy's chair," she said. "It's got a cushion."

Even though Joe had been gone twenty years, the big chair was still called "Granddaddy's chair."

"No, thanks." Dominic stayed where he was, in the straight-backed chair with a woven rush seat. Alice knew he wanted nothing of his granddaddy's. He'd disliked the man almost as much as he disliked his mama, claiming they were two of a kind—self-centered people who snapped up the best of everything for themselves.

She scooped an ample helping of stew into the bowl and set it in front of him, along with a basket of bread and a crock of butter. "Would you like some milk?"

Dominic shook his head. "No, but I could go for a beer."

"You know I don't believe in—"

Dominic heaved a sigh. "I know, Grandma, I know."

Alice DeLuca was a bona fide Bible-thumping teetotaler and member of the Light of the World Congressional Church. After sitting in the third pew and listening to Brother Browne's fiery sermons for more than fifty years, she'd come to the conclusion that demon rum was to blame for most of life's problems, including Dorothy's total lack of responsibility.

For as long as anyone could remember, she'd made no secret of her disdain for drunkards. The night Joe died she'd gathered up his stash of whiskey, opened the bottles, and poured every last drop down the drain. She'd hoped it would keep Dominic from straying onto the same pathway of destruction.

Unfortunately, it hadn't. Once he was old enough to walk into a liquor store and plunk down the price of a bottle, he'd come home wearing the stink of alcohol. Then, to make matters worse, he'd gone to work in a bar.

Now here he was, barely one foot in the door and already wanting a beer.

Several moments of silence passed, but with the issue at hand weighing heavily on her mind, she decided to go ahead and broach the subject.

"I hope you're planning to see Tracy Briggs while you're here."

He lowered the spoon and glared at her. "I'm not."

"You should. It's the right thing to do."

He pushed the bowl of stew back as if it had suddenly grown cold. "And why, exactly, is it the right thing to do?"

"Because of your son."

27

Dominic bolted out of his chair and began to pace the far end of the kitchen.

Without turning to face her, he ranted, "What makes you think Tracy's kid is mine? Did she tell you that? Because if so, she's a liar!"

"You know I've never met the girl," Alice said. "You never brought her home, and it wasn't until after you moved to Philadelphia that I learned the two of you were serious."

"So Tracy went to Philadelphia with me. That doesn't mean—"

Cutting him off, she said, "Dominic, please. When the Briggs girl returned to Magnolia Grove, it was just her and the boy; and he's the right age . . ." Alice let the remainder of her thought drift off, and she gave a disheartened sigh. "This town may be a lot bigger than it was when you lived here, but it's still a small town, and rumors get around."

Dominic threw up his hands and gave a sardonic laugh. "A rumor? You think I'm the daddy of her kid because of some bullshit rumor?"

Fingering the narrow gold band she still wore on her left hand, she shook her head slowly. "I don't think it's just a rumor, Dominic. The boy was pointed out to me at the market. He was with his mama."

Dominic's face went slack for a moment, then his mouth curled into a snarl. "Why should I have to prove myself to you, Grandma? I'm your own flesh and blood. Can't you just take my word instead of jumping to conclusions because you saw a kid who you think looks like me?"

Her face grew pale and her eyes moist. "I remember how it was with your mama, Dominic, and I don't want you to hurt that boy the way she hurt you."

"Mama didn't hurt me," he snapped. "You think I gave a rat's ass when she took off and left me here? Well, I didn't! 'Good riddance'— that's what I was thinking when I watched her drive off!"

Alice remembered it differently. She remembered the way he'd sat on the front step for days, looking down that long dirt road as if he'd expected to see her car coming along any minute. Perhaps if she reminded him of that . . .

The thought lingered for sever
and said, "After all that driving
old room, so it's waiting for you
    With no further mention of his
his grandma's cheek and turned toward ⸲
    "Good night," he called down from the ⸲

8

Dominic DeLuca

I ask for one lousy beer, and Grandma goes off on me. Obviously it wasn't just the beer; she was fired up about Tracy and the kid. She claims she saw the kid and that's how she knew, but I doubt it's true.

I never told Grandma about Tracy or the kid because I knew she'd start pushing me to get married and do the right thing. Right thing, ha! After the way Tracy treated me, I don't owe her or the kid anything.

My bet is Tracy's been here. She probably laid it on thick about how Lucas needs a daddy and she needs support money. As far as I'm concerned, she can just whistle up a tree for it. You can't get blood from a stone, and right now I'm worse off than a stone. I don't have any money, and I sure as hell don't have a way to get any. You think if I had money I'd be driving around in that shitpot car? No, sir. I'd buy me a nice convertible and ride through town with the top down.

What I should do is tell Grandma this isn't all on me. I should explain I already offered Tracy the chance to come home to Philadelphia with me. Shit, I even said I'd marry her and take the kid, but she damn near spit in my eye. Then while I was trying to reason with her, Meghan's crazy-ass boyfriend came from out of nowhere and decked me.

I can tell you right now, there's no way in hell I'm opening myself up to another round like that. If Tracy wants me, she's gonna have to *come crawling on her hands and knees; then maybe I'll take her back. But it's no guarantee.*

As far as I'm concerned, the thought of us getting back together is a dead issue. We're over and done with. Tracy wants no part of me, and I sure as hell won't be held responsible for a kid I haven't seen in over three years.

I'd like to believe Grandma will take my word on this and leave it be. Knowing how she is, though, I'm guessing she'll have something more to say. But I'll wait and see. If she brings it up again, I'll just go along with her and pretend I'm thinking it over. Given the condition Grandma's in, she doesn't need more aggravation; she got enough from Mama and Granddaddy to last a lifetime.

9

A Question of Time

The rooster crowed just before the break of dawn, but Alice was already awake. She hadn't slept well and was lying there waiting to hear him squawk. She climbed out of bed, eased her feet into a pair of worn slippers, and pulled on the bathrobe lying on the chair.

Stepping softly so she wouldn't wake Dominic, she hurried downstairs and stoked the fire in the furnace, then added a few scoops of coal. The chill would be gone from the house by the time the sun crested the horizon, and before noon she could slide the windows open to let the spring breeze freshen the house. Only in the predawn mornings was there a damp frigidness that settled in her bones. As she sat at the kitchen table with a cup of watered-down coffee, she tried to remember if it had always been this way or just this past year.

Last year she'd tamped down the furnace the week after Easter, sometime in April. Now here it was May, and she was still getting the shivers.

It's because I've lost all this weight.

Her hand trembled as she lifted the cup to her mouth. Dr. Willoughby had warned this would happen.

"You'll grow weaker and need someone to care for you," he'd said.

At first she'd been reluctant to believe such a thing could happen. She'd always been a strong woman, someone who could chop firewood or wring a chicken's neck without getting squeamish. But it had crept up on her. A bit of nausea in the morning, a loss of appetite, the dizziness of having risen too rapidly, then the dreaded weakness that forced her to sit and rest after each small chore.

Now she wondered how long she had left. Six months, if she was lucky. Six months was such a small amount of time, especially if one wanted to correct the mistakes of a lifetime. She thought of Dorothy, and a heartsick longing for her missing daughter made her eyes grow moist. She wondered for the thousandth time if there was something more she could have done, something that would have kept Dorothy in Magnolia Grove with a family who loved her and would see to her needs.

Her last postcard had come almost fifteen years ago. Days had turned into weeks, and weeks into years, and now there was no way of knowing if Dorothy was dead or alive. That was perhaps the most painful part; the sleepless nights of imagining her sick with no one to care for her or, worse yet, facedown in a ditch along some godforsaken road.

Suddenly the coffee tasted too bitter. She poured the remainder down the sink, then headed for the back door. Stopping in the mudroom long enough to pull on a pair of rubber boots, she moved across the yard to the chicken coop. Five chickens and Henry, the rooster, were all that was left of the farm. At one time there'd been two cows and a vegetable garden on this side of the pond; beyond that, acres of leafy, green peanut fields. Now it was mostly all scrub brush and tangles of vines that had lived and died with no one to tend them.

She closed her eyes for a moment and tried to see the place as it would be once Dominic took over. Everything would grow again, and hopefully one day Dorothy would return to find her son and his family thriving in the house that she herself had grown up in.

With that vision fixed in her mind, Alice filled the water pan. Then she poured a generous amount of seed into the feed trough and started back to the house, knowing she'd come up with the best possible course of action.

By the time Dominic woke, Alice had gone through the plastic bag he'd carried in and laundered most of his clothes. She'd intended to simply fold and stack them so they wouldn't wrinkle, but when she caught the odor of bourbon and stale smoke in his jeans and T-shirts, she turned the washer's setting to "heavy-duty." Afterward, she hung everything on the line outside to dry.

Dominic thumped down the stairs wearing sweatpants, his chest bare and face not yet washed.

"Have you seen my bag of clothes?" he asked.

"I washed them." She pulled out Granddaddy's chair and gestured for him to sit. "They'll be dry by the time you have breakfast."

"I'm not really hungry, but if you've got coffee . . ." He edged past Granddaddy's spot and sat in the straight-backed chair.

Alice handed him a mug of coffee, then cracked two eggs and dropped them into the frying pan.

"You don't have to be hungry to enjoy these. They're fresh today." She set the griddle atop the stove and laid out several slices of bacon.

"You don't have to go to all this trouble, Grandma. I said—"

"I heard what you said," she replied. "But obviously you've forgotten how good a farm-fresh breakfast tastes. Why, when your granddaddy was alive, he put away four eggs and a stack of pancakes every morning, along with whatever bacon or ham there was to be had."

She flipped the eggs over, then a few seconds later lifted them from the pan and set the plate in front of him.

Once Dominic began to eat, she slid into the chair across from him. "Now, don't those taste good?"

He gave an acquiescing nod, then reached into the basket she'd placed on the table, helped himself to a piece of toast, and dipped it into the runny yolk.

"A good breakfast gives you strength to do your day's work. During planting season, your great-granddaddy, Grandpa Joe's daddy, used to start out with six or eight eggs. Of course, back then, the henhouse was full, and every chicken was a good layer. These five I've got are well past their prime, and they don't lay but two or three eggs a week."

"Well, you didn't have to give them to me, Grandma."

"I wanted to. Besides, my stomach doesn't take kindly to eggs anymore. I give most of them to Charlie Barnes to thank him for helping me out around here. Ever since your granddaddy died . . ." She let the words trail off, because there was no simple way to explain her relationship with Charlie.

"He's Granddaddy's friend, right?" Dominic continued to eat. "I'm surprised he's still coming around."

"Charlie's always been a friend to both of us."

Alice could have said more. She could have told him how Joe and Charlie had grown up together, each one looking out for the other, but she didn't. She'd planned this talk carefully and needed to get back to telling the story that would help Dominic see the importance of her plan.

Without lingering on thoughts of Charlie, she continued. "Did you know your great-granddaddy built this house?"

"Yeah, you told me that years ago."

"Well, having a house like this is something to be proud of. Daddy DeLuca used to say there wasn't a sturdier house in all of Georgia. He built it that way, knowing it would be passed from one generation to the next."

35

She looked across and studied Dominic's expression. It was as blank as a white bedsheet hanging on the line. She was going to tell how Daddy DeLuca set the windows in place with his own two hands and how the oak for the mantel came from trees that had grown right here on the land, but after seeing Dominic wasn't the least bit impressed with the history of such thoughts she jumped to the end.

"With your mama missing, you're the last of our family," she said. "When I pass on, this farm will go to you."

Dominic looked up, wide-eyed. "Me? What am I supposed to do with a farm?"

"I was hoping you'd live here. Raise a family."

"Grandma, there are no good jobs here. I make twice as much money tending bar in Philadelphia. More than I could ever make here."

"You wouldn't need a job. You could work the land like your grand-daddy did. Peanuts are an easy enough crop to grow, and they bring in good money."

Dominic groaned. "I don't know a thing about farming."

"You'll learn. It's not all that hard." She gave a small chuckle. "When it comes to growing things, the sun and rain do most of the heavy lifting."

Dominic gave an impatient huff and rolled his eyeballs. "Grandma . . ."

"Hear me out," she said. "There's more than just yourself to think about. You have a son, and one day he'll be the one to inherit this house."

"I told you, that kid ain't mine, and I don't want to talk about it anymore!"

"Well, we're going to, whether you want to or not. You have a responsibility to the boy and his mama. It's time you got married and settled down. You can live here on the farm."

"Hold on a minute! First off, I'm not ready to get married. Second, Tracy Briggs doesn't want me any more than I want her, so you can just forget about her and the kid."

Alice gasped as a sudden pain hammered her. She lowered her face and leaned forward, clutching her chest.

Dominic stood so quickly that his chair toppled over. In two long strides he was by her side. He wrapped his arm around her shoulders.

"Grandma, are you okay?"

She gave a feeble nod. "Get me a glass of water, and hand me that bottle of pills on the counter."

Dominic kept his eyes on her as he grabbed the prescription bottle and then held a glass beneath the tap.

"How many?" he asked.

She held up one finger.

As he handed her the pill he stood beside her, his hand on her shoulder. He remembered her being sturdy. Now she seemed to be all bones with a tissue-thin layer of skin covering them.

"Should I call the doctor?" he asked.

She shook her head slowly, almost as if the effort were more than she could handle.

"There's nothing he can do. Help me into the parlor, and I'll rest in your granddaddy's chair for a while."

He all but lifted her from the chair, and they walked toward the front room, his arm braced against her back, her shoulder leaning into his chest.

"I'm sorry, Grandma," he said. "I didn't mean to upset you."

As he eased her into the oversize recliner, she rubbed her fingers along his arm the way she'd done when he was a boy.

"Dominic, I love you the same as I loved your mama, but I don't want you to make the same mistakes." She looked up, her eyes on his face as she spoke. "Please promise me you'll do the right thing."

Dominic felt the weight of her request settle on him and waited for a long moment. "Grandma, I swear that kid isn't mine. Tracy Briggs has no interest in me, so why would you ask me to—"

Another pain shot through her chest, and she cringed as she folded into it.

"Grandma, are you all right?"

She lifted her eyes and nodded ever so slightly. "This pain is nothing compared to the heartache of knowing you're following in your mama's footsteps. Please promise me that you'll do right by that boy; then I'll be able to rest in peace when I leave this earth."

Dominic turned away and buried his face in his hands. "Don't—"

"Please . . . ," she repeated.

He hesitated for a moment, then turned back. "Okay . . . I promise."

"Thank you." She gave a heavy sigh and lowered her gaze.

10

Alice DeLuca

I suspect Dominic is lying, just as I suspected it the hundreds of times Dorothy stood in front of me and told tales to my face. Lies can slide out of a person's mouth silky-smooth and sounding sweet, but look closely and, more often than not, you can see the truth in their eyes.

After Dominic went out yesterday, I sat in Joe's recliner, thinking about Daddy DeLuca building this house with all those great hopes and dreams and how nobody but him saw the same vision. He thought we'd raise a family here, but even though we were living in this nice house, Joe was always itching to be somewhere else. I used to hope and pray one day he'd get to be more like his daddy, but it never happened.

Now I've moved on to hoping there's a bit of Daddy DeLuca in Dominic. I can't say for sure there is, but it's what I want to believe. Sometimes the right path is smack in front of a man, and he can't see it because he's busy looking at other things. I think that's the problem with Dominic. All he needs is someone to show him the right path, and if I don't do it, who will?

Living here on the farm is something to be appreciated, not pushed off. When you're young and the only thoughts in your head are of running wild and partying, it can be hard to see that. I'll admit, I might be overly opinionated about the evils of drinking, but a man losing himself *in a bottle of whiskey is the same as giving up on life, and I don't want that to happen to Dominic.*

Joe and I weren't always happy with one another, but that's true of most any married couple. One way or another, we always worked it out. Daddy DeLuca saw to it that we had a good life. We never went hungry, and we had a warm bed to sleep in. Those things are blessings to be counted.

Yes, I'm Dominic's blood kin, but the truth is, I can feel for the Briggs girl. I've stood in those same shoes and know the heartache it brings. Opinions about what's socially acceptable may have changed, but the feelings inside a woman's heart are the same as they were the day Eve landed on this earth. No woman wants her baby to be without a daddy.

Both my daddy and Daddy DeLuca saw to it that I didn't have to go through such a thing; now it's up to me to make sure Tracy Briggs doesn't have to, either.

I made the mistake of being too easy with Dorothy. I never got in her face and stood firm about what was right and what was wrong, and look what happened. This time will be different, God willing.

Regardless of what Dominic says, I believe that boy is my great-grandson, and if he is, I want to hug him to my chest and tell him I love him before I leave this earth. The boy deserves to know he's got family. If the Good Lord grants me enough time, I'll make sure Dominic does the right thing.

11

Back to Barrington

On the following Wednesday, Tracy drove back to Barrington for Lucas's speech therapy class. By then she'd forgotten about her discussion with Meghan. The thought of comparing Gabriel to Dominic was preposterous anyway. It was like comparing an apple to an orange; they were that different.

Gabriel was a good friend; Dominic was a bad memory.

On the forty-minute drive, Tracy played the sing-along CDs Lucas enjoyed. They were practice therapy, disguised as fun.

"Ten wittle monkeys jumping on the bed . . ."

Listening carefully, Tracy heard his wispy *w* in the word *little*.

"It's *little* monkeys," she said, emphasizing the *l*. "Touch the tip of your tongue to your top teeth, then let it come down as you say 'lit.'"

"Wit," Lucas replied, then went back to singing, "Nine wittle monkeys . . ."

Tracy gave a wistful sigh. "We'll ask Miss Margaret to help you with that sound in class today; how's that?"

Lucas nodded happily. "I wuv Miss Marwhet."

Ten minutes later, they pulled into the parking lot of the Hawke School for Deaf Children. She unbuckled Lucas's safety belt, and he scampered toward the walkway. Just inside the lobby, they ran into Gabriel.

"I was hoping to see you this morning," he said. "Are you free for lunch?"

"Sure. I'll stop by your office when Lucas finishes class."

"Sounds good."

They walked across the lobby together; then he turned toward his office, and she headed down the hallway toward the classroom.

Having lunch together was nothing out of the ordinary. They'd been doing it off and on since Meghan had all but dragged Tracy into the school to meet Gabriel.

Almost a decade earlier, Gabriel had lived in Magnolia Grove; that's where Meghan had first met him. On a summer evening that was too hot for anything but walking around the neighborhood, Meghan came home and told Tracy how she'd heard the sweet strains of a guitar and followed the sound. Back then, the Hawke family had attended the same church as the Briggses, and most everyone had known Gabriel was born deaf. But there he was, sitting on his front porch, strumming one melody after another. He and Meghan had chatted for a few moments; then he'd invited her to sit with him, and she had.

She'd been only fifteen, and he not yet twenty, but even so, she'd realized that a deaf man capable of making such beautiful music was someone special. That evening as she'd walked home, the memory of Gabriel Hawke had settled in her heart and stayed. When the family first learned Lucas was deaf, Meghan had remembered Gabriel and had known he was the one person who'd be able to help them.

"If anyone can understand Lucas's problem, it'll be Gabriel Hawke," she'd told Tracy, and it had turned out to be true.

It was here, in the Hawke School audiologist's office, that Lucas had heard his first sounds. When the world was a scarier place and Tracy couldn't say for certain whether Lucas would ever hear or speak, Gabriel had stood beside her. He'd guided her through the maze of decisions to be made and held her steady when she'd felt like toppling from the weight of it all.

Now, over three years later, there was no question he was Tracy's most treasured friend.

Gabriel was waiting when Tracy tapped on his office door. They went in her car so they wouldn't have to switch Lucas's car seat. As they settled into a booth at the Bluebird Café, the waitress handed Lucas crayons and a placemat to color.

For a while the conversation was nothing more than the usual small talk. He asked about the class, and she told of how they were working on the differentiation of words starting with the letter *T*. But as one thing led to another, Tracy noticed Gabriel seemed distracted. She'd watched him slide the saltshaker from one side of the table to the other three times, which was strangely out of character.

"Is something wrong?" she asked.

"No, nothing." He replaced the saltshaker alongside the pepper, then looked square into her face. "I've been named the county's humanitarian of the year."

Tracy gave a wide-eyed grin. "Wow, what an honor! You must be so proud."

"I am." He stared at the saltshaker with that distracted look still on his face. "The thing is, the awards dinner is this Saturday evening, and it's black tie." He glanced up with a hopeful expression. "I'd like you to be my date."

Tracy's grin stretched wider. "I'd be thrilled! Wow, a black-tie dinner."

The delight that shivered along her spine surprised her. She had thought she wasn't ready to date; she'd told Meghan as much, that

Gabriel was a friend, nothing more, and she'd meant it. But now, here she was, as giddy as a high school girl being invited to the senior prom.

When she began to ask questions about both the award and the event, a look of satisfaction settled on Gabriel's face. He finally picked up his grilled cheese sandwich and started to eat.

On the drive home Tracy called Meghan.

"I've got some exciting news, but I'm not telling you unless you promise not to say 'I told you so.'"

Meghan laughed. "But you know I love saying that."

"Fine, then I'm not telling you."

"Okay, okay, I promise. Now what's the news?"

"Gabriel has asked me out on a date. A real date, not just lunch or us taking Lucas to the movies. It's a formal dinner where he's the guest of honor!"

"I knew this was going to happen!"

"You knew the county was going to name him humanitarian of the year?"

"No, but I knew that sooner or later you two would get together."

"You promised not to say—"

"I didn't. I just said that given the way he looks at you, any fool could see . . ."

As Tracy rounded the corner of Washington Street, her mouth was curled into a gigantic smile.

"I'm going to need some help finding a dress."

"And shoes," Meghan added.

Before Tracy turned into the driveway, she and Meghan had planned a sisters' day of shopping.

12

Getting Ready

On Friday, Meghan arrived early at her mother's house. She'd brought Sox with her, and the moment she opened the front door, he bolted in. Sniffing out Lucas, the dog ran from room to room until he found him, then the romp and play began. In the blink of an eye, boy and dog became one squiggling, laughing, impossible-not-to-smile-at ball of fun.

Meghan eyed Tracy with a crooked grin. "Look at how cute they play together. Don't you think it's time Lucas had his own dog?"

Lucas stopped tugging on his end of the rope Sox had retrieved and turned to Tracy.

"Pwease, Mama, pwease?"

"Sometimes you hear more than you're supposed to, Lucas, but I'm not complaining." Tracy playfully ran her hand through his hair. "Okay, I'll consider the possibility of getting a dog."

Meghan snickered. "Possibility or probability?" she asked, using their daddy's oft-repeated adage. It was a memory she held dear. *Possibility*, he'd told her, meant there was only a slender chance of something happening, whereas *probability* meant the likelihood was far greater.

Seconds later the romp and play started up again, so Tracy grabbed her handbag, and the two sisters headed off to go shopping. All morning they roamed from store to store with Tracy slipping in and out of dresses that ran the gamut from frothy ice cream–colored frocks with layers of tulle to a scarlet-colored ball gown. Shortly after eleven they stopped for coffee.

Sitting across from one another, they talked and laughed as they hadn't for many months. As she caught the sparkle in Tracy's eye, Meghan wondered why she had been foolish enough to think Dominic might be back in the picture.

"It's good to see you so happy," she said.

Tracy took a sip of her coffee, then leaned into the conversation and confided, "This'll be my first formal dinner, and the first real date I've had in ages, so I really am excited."

"And it's Gabriel!" Meghan teased. "No wonder you're excited. This could lead to something—"

Tracy shot her a say-no-more look.

There had been other occasions—prom, the homecoming dance, the senior farewell—but Tracy had opted out of them all. Back then, she'd said they were uncool; now it seemed apparent that she felt differently.

"Come on, tell the truth," Meghan prodded. "You're really into Gabriel, aren't you?"

Tracy turned her face to the side and peered out the coffee shop window as if she'd not heard the question. When she turned back, she grinned and asked, "What about my hair? Wear it up or down?"

Typical Tracy, Meghan thought, and laughed. "Wear it up," she said. "I've got one of those sparkly clips. I'll style it for you."

Three shops later, they walked into the Madison Boutique, and Tracy spied a tea-length black chiffon dress hidden behind the others. She lifted it off the rack and headed for the dressing room. The moment she slipped it over her head she had a feeling, and when she turned to view herself in the mirror, she knew for certain. This was *the dress.*

It seemed as though there was some kind of magic woven into the gossamer fabric. A magic that somehow made her look . . . well, prettier. In the span of a single breath, she had taken on a more carefree appearance. Gone were the frown lines that usually ridged her forehead. The girl in the mirror had eyes that looked like melting chocolate and highlights in her hair she hadn't noticed before.

She lifted her hair, held it atop her head, and turned to Meghan. "What do you think?"

Meghan smiled. "You look absolutely gorgeous!"

"Gorgeous?" She again eyed herself in the mirror. "That's a word I never thought of as describing me, so I guess this really is a first."

Friday evening, Gabriel called, and for a moment Tracy's heart stuck in her throat.

I hope he isn't going to cancel.

"About Saturday night," he said.

In that split second before he continued, Tracy's heart plummeted into her stomach.

"I was thinking it might be easier if I pick you up rather than having you drive to Barrington."

She breathed a sigh of relief. Their date was still on. "That's very sweet, but it's a lot of driving back and forth for you, isn't it?"

"Since it will be a late night and everything, I thought maybe you could stay over."

A slightly awkward pause followed, then he quickly added, "My apartment has a guest room."

"I would hope so!" she replied, laughing.

13

The Event

Saturday evening, Gabriel rang the doorbell at six thirty on the dot. He'd arrived ten minutes earlier and driven around the block several times so as not to seem overly eager. He kept reminding himself that they'd been out together a number of times, that there was nothing to be nervous about, but still he sensed this evening would be different. It wasn't an evening where they'd be wearing jeans and sharing popcorn at a movie. It wasn't an afternoon where Lucas would tag along; this was an actual date.

Lila opened the door, and he stepped inside.

"Tracy will be down in just a moment," she said. "Have a seat. Would you like something to drink while you're waiting?"

Gabriel dropped down into the club chair closest to the door. "Thanks, but I'll pass on the drink. I'm driving."

"I meant a glass of water or iced tea," Lila replied, smiling. "But it's nice to know that you'll be taking good care of my daughter."

Gabriel's face reddened. "That's something you can be sure of."

Before he had the chance to say anything more, he glanced up and spotted Tracy coming down the stairs.

He stood more suddenly than he'd meant to and almost bumped into Lila. "Sorry," he said without taking his eyes off Tracy. He'd always thought her beautiful, but he was not prepared for this.

"Wow," he exclaimed. "You look amazing!"

A blush of color appeared on Tracy's cheeks, and she gave an appreciative smile.

On the drive back to Barrington, the conversation flowed freely, and this time it had nothing to do with Lucas or the school.

"It's strange seeing you all dressed up in a tux." Tracy looked across and smiled. "You look great. Not that you don't look great other times, but tonight is, well . . . kind of special."

He grinned like a schoolboy. "It's something I've looked forward to for a long time."

"The humanitarian award?"

He gave a sideways glance with that grin still tugging at his mouth. "No, not the award. Our first real date. I've been hoping this would happen since the day I met you."

"Really?"

"Yes, really." He nodded. "And have I mentioned that you look amazingly beautiful tonight?"

She laughed. "Yes, five times."

In what seemed far too short of a time, they pulled up in front of the banquet hall, and the valet popped open Tracy's door. Gabriel stepped out, handed the attendant his car keys, and looped his arm through Tracy's as they walked across the foyer.

The cocktail party was already underway. As a waiter passed by, Gabriel lifted two glasses of champagne from the tray and handed one to Tracy.

He touched his glass to hers and whispered, "Here's to the prettiest girl in the room."

After a few sips of champagne, they made their way through the hall, and Gabriel introduced her to some of his colleagues. They'd just begun to talk with Dwayne Morrison, editor in chief of *Georgia Life* magazine, when the lights flickered, and everyone turned toward the ballroom where dinner was to be served.

Once the dishes were cleared, the master of ceremonies stepped to the microphone and began the program. He informed the audience that tonight they were honoring three of the county's most influential citizens.

The first was a businessman who'd refurbished an entire block of small shops along Greene Street. Everyone applauded as he talked of his plans to continue the expansion with a gourmet restaurant in the Keystone Building.

When the applause ended, the emcee stepped to the microphone. He pulled a sheet of paper from his breast pocket, scanned the printed bio, then began to speak.

"Many of you know Gabriel Hawke as a member of our business community, but are you aware that his school, the Hawke School, is regarded as Georgia's finest learning institution for hearing-impaired children? Because of the hard work and dedication that built this school, thousands of children who might have suffered through a life of silence can now hear and speak. That, my friends, is a true humanitarian effort." He raised his arm and waved Gabriel to the platform.

As Gabriel approached, the emcee said, "On behalf of the Georgia Communities at Work Organization, I am proud to present you with our Humanitarian of the Year Award." He handed Gabriel an engraved crystal obelisk and shook his hand.

There was a round of applause, then Gabriel stepped to the microphone. Instead of expounding on the growth of the school or the number of children who had passed through, Gabriel's response seemed to be drawn from the depths of his heart.

"Imagine what it would be like to never hear your loved one's voice, or the song of a bird, or the drip of a faucet . . ."

His voice was deep and filled with emotion. As he spoke, the whispers of conversation circling the room fell silent, and all eyes were on him. He explained that he, like many of the children attending the school, had been born deaf.

"It's impossible to understand the challenges of deafness unless you've experienced them. Deaf children live in a world all their own, isolated from friends, siblings, parents. It's as if they're surrounded by a glass bubble. They can see out but not be a part of anything. Without today's technological advances and proper training, a deaf child is destined for a lifetime of silence, and silence can be very lonely."

He went on to detail the difficulties of learning to speak and differentiating the sounds of one word from another. As he spoke, Tracy pulled a tissue from her bag and dabbed her eyes.

Toward the end of his speech, he thanked those who had helped him build the school and the dedicated teachers who worked with him. When he told of the overwhelming joy that came from witnessing a deaf child hear for the first time, his voice became softer, and his eyes glinted. As he stepped back from the microphone, there was a thunderous round of applause.

Tracy's heart swelled to twice its normal size, and a cloud of tears blurred her vision. When he returned to the table, she reached over, took his hand in hers, and held it as they listened to the third award presentation to Jennifer Morales, a ten-year veteran of the first responders team who had, in the past twelve months, saved three lives because of her skill and quick thinking.

When the speeches ended, the band returned to the platform, and couples began to step onto the dance floor.

Gabriel stood and offered Tracy his hand. "Shall we?"

She nodded and slid into his arms.

The band played "You Are the Best Thing." As they swayed to the music, he held her close enough to feel her heartbeat.

"This is nice," he whispered.

"Yes, it is," she replied, then nuzzled her head to his chest and sighed.

When Gabriel pressed his hand tighter against her back, Tracy didn't resist.

In time, the band moved into more upbeat tunes like "Don't Look Down" and "Happy"; still, they remained on the dance floor. When the hour grew late and the bandleader announced the last song, the music transitioned to something soft and dreamy, a song neither of them knew. Still, they danced. When the band struck the last chord, the two stood in place for a moment; then she tilted her face up, and he brought his lips to hers.

Right then, Tracy knew their relationship would never again be the same. Her back stiffened, and she wondered if he also had felt something.

"I'm sorry," he said. "I shouldn't have—"

She touched her index finger to his mouth and shushed him. "Don't be sorry," she whispered. "I'm not."

———— ⚬☙⚬ ————

On the drive back to the apartment, they said very little.

"Are you okay?" Gabriel finally asked.

"Yeah, sure, I'm fine. What about you?"

He laughed. "I'm fine, too."

Tracy had said "fine," but inside her chest, there was a niggling concern that the remainder of the evening would lead to something she wasn't prepared for. When they arrived at the apartment, he carried in her overnight bag and set it in the small bedroom to the right of the master suite.

She couldn't honestly say if that was what she wanted or not. For the past year, she'd told herself it was too soon, but tonight something inside of her had stirred. Something she'd almost forgotten.

"How about a nightcap?" he asked.

"I'd love one."

She followed him into the kitchen and watched as he set out two glasses, dropped ice into them, and splashed Bailey's Irish Cream over the cubes. They carried the drinks to the living room and sat on the sofa, with barely a sliver of space between them. For a while they talked of the evening, happily reminiscing.

When the mantel clock chimed, she was reminded of the time. "I can't believe it's already two o'clock."

Gabriel stood, then bent and offered her his hand. "I guess it's time to turn in; I know you must be tired."

"I'm not that tired." Tracy rose and playfully tilted her face to his, inviting another kiss.

He held her for a moment, then brought his lips to hers. It was a soft, easy, loving kiss that she felt take hold of her heart. It was a kiss given without words, but it spoke volumes and told of a love that could last forever.

Suddenly, an unbidden thought of Dominic flashed through Tracy's mind; it was there one second and gone the next. She wanted to let go, toss caution to the wind, and give herself to Gabriel, completely and without restraint, but the past was stuck to her like a speck of lint clinging to a black skirt. It refused to be plucked loose or left behind.

As they turned and started hand in hand toward the bedrooms, Tracy found herself wondering if perhaps they could have a future together. She looked up at him and smiled. *Possibly yes.* But first, she had to let go of the past, and that was not an easy thing to do.

In the tiny hallway between the two bedrooms, he stopped and took her in his arms. "Tracy," he whispered, his voice faltering, then giving way to a soul-deep sigh. He held her close, his hand strong against her back, his breath heavy in her ear. Then without saying anything more, he stepped back.

"Is there something . . ." Tracy met his eyes but left the remainder of her question unspoken.

"Get some rest," he said. "I'll see you in the morning." He leaned in and tenderly brushed his lips across her cheek.

She hesitated for a heartbeat, then reluctantly turned toward the guest room.

When she looked back, he had already closed the door to his room.

14

Tracy Briggs

Last week when Meghan said Gabriel could be more than just a friend, I'd told her I wasn't ready. All along I've felt our friendship was so special I didn't want to ruin it by getting involved in something more and then having it not work out. But now I've got mixed feelings. Just knowing Gabriel is in bed a few steps down the hallway, I'm tempted to run down there and jump in beside him. I won't, of course.

First of all, my doing something like that would totally shock him. Second, I learned my lesson after doing almost that same thing with Dominic. It's too easy to get carried away when you're caught up in the moment.

The weird thing about all of this is that Gabriel and I have gone out a bunch of times before. We're friends. We've gone to the movies and ball games, and he's been to dinner at the house. We even have lunch together at least two or three times a month.

Now everything is different, and I don't know if it's good or bad. Last night, when Gabriel kissed me on the dance floor, I felt it clear down to my toes. It was like I'd never been kissed before. A kiss like that isn't something you can forget.

I'm excited about where we might go from here, but I'm also scared.
A while ago I said falling out of love is harder than falling in love,
but now I can see that neither is simple. Especially if your life is tangled
up in strings of the past.

15

The Truth of Friendship

Alice DeLuca knew that of all the people in the world, the one she could always count on was Charlie Barnes. He'd been her friend and confidante since the day Joe died. Their relationship could have easily been far more, were she able to forget the years of him being her husband's best friend.

In the days following Joe's funeral, when the thundering sobs had caused her body to tremble and she could do nothing to lessen her grief, Charlie had remained at her side. He'd curled his arm around her shoulders and sworn she would never be alone.

Back then, the loneliness had been like a shadow stuck to her soul. It never left; not during the day and definitely not during the seemingly endless nights.

"No matter what you need, I'll be here for you," Charlie had promised. "I was Joe's friend, and I'm yours as well."

For all these many years, his promise had held true.

Although it was not something Alice would admit, there were times she wished Charlie had come into her life earlier. Before Joe. Before she'd had no alternative but to get married. On the rare occasion when she had such a thought, she'd remember Dorothy and Dominic. They were part of her and part of Joe. Without him, she would not have them, and she could never wish them away. With the weight of too many memories and too much guilt holding her back, she and Charlie went from year to year simply being friends.

Regardless of what needed to be done, she could trust Charlie would take care of it. He was the one who showed her how to invest the insurance money and set it up so there would be a lifetime income. That first winter when the furnace broke down, he came and fixed it. The following summer, several storms roared across Georgia and tore the limbs from trees, but Charlie came with a chain saw and cleared away the debris. He fixed pipes that sprang leaks, climbed onto the roof to hammer loose shingles back into place, and listened to the things that troubled her heart.

"How can I ever thank you?" Alice said.

Charlie claimed such a thing wasn't necessary, and no matter how much she insisted, he never took anything more than a home-cooked meal and a basket of fresh eggs.

The year Dominic dropped out of high school, Alice asked Charlie to get him a job at the power company, and he did. He'd told the foreman, Albert Henniker, that Dominic was both dependable and trustworthy. That summer, Dominic moved out of his grandma's house and into the apartment he shared with a beanpole nicknamed Broom. Before the year was out, Dominic had missed four straight days of work without bothering to call in, and he got fired.

Of course, Albert Henniker took Charlie to task for making such a misguided recommendation. He'd looked across the desk and said, "I'm extremely disappointed in your judgment of character."

Two weeks later, Charlie was moved from group supervisor to a spot in vehicle maintenance. Although the incident was like a burr stuck to the seat of his trousers, he'd never once mentioned it to Alice. When she talked about Dominic, he nodded cordially, then changed the subject as soon as there was an opening.

Shortly after Dominic had moved to Philadelphia, Charlie's relationship with Alice went from meeting once or twice a week to meeting every day. He'd recently retired and had plenty of time to kill, so he'd stop by early in the morning, claiming he'd noticed a squeaky door or a loose tile. He'd fix that one thing, then stay for the rest of the day. In the afternoon they'd sit at the kitchen table, sipping sweet tea or lukewarm coffee, and it seemed there was always something to talk about. When he told stories of working at the power plant or being in the army, Alice leaned forward and soaked up every word.

That summer, on a day when they'd taken in a show at the Rialto and then stopped for dinner at the Red Rooster, Charlie said there was something they needed to talk about.

"I'm alone and you're alone, Alice," he said. "That's not the way God intended it to be. There's no reason why we—"

"Don't." She touched her fingers to his mouth. "You were Joe's best friend. It's wrong . . ." She never finished that statement because she couldn't honestly say why it was wrong, but on the nights when she allowed herself to imagine Charlie's touch, the kind of touch a husband and wife share, the nightmares came at her like a screeching hawk. She'd dream of Joe at his angriest, his dark eyes hooded and his mouth drawn tight. In the morning she'd awaken, firm in her resolve to keep things just as they were.

Now that Dominic had returned, Charlie stopped by far less often, only twice in the three weeks he'd been there. Knowing there was no love between the two men, Alice began to worry that the sight of Dominic's car sitting in the driveway had something to do with this change.

After three days straight without even a call, she telephoned him. "I've missed you," she said.

Charlie was slow in answering. "I've missed you also, but figured maybe you needed a few weeks to visit with your grandson. I didn't want to butt in."

"Butt in?" Alice laughed. "You could never . . ."

"Well, I was just on my way out to get some lunch and the news-paper, if you're sure I'm not—"

"I've got ham salad already made in the refrigerator, so come on over."

Fifteen minutes later, Charlie was at the front door.

Alice opened it and smiled. Before he had a chance to say anything, she held her finger to her lips and made a shushing sound.

"Let's sit in the kitchen," she whispered. "I don't want to wake Dominic."

Charlie followed her through to the back of the house, then dropped down in the large cushioned chair. She poured two glasses of sweet tea and sat across from him. Charlie glanced up at the kitchen clock.

"It's almost two thirty. Is he sick?"

She looked over with a quizzical expression.

"Dominic," he clarified. "You said he was sleeping."

"Oh, that." She blushed with a touch of embarrassment. "No, he's not sick, but it was a late night."

A scowl of disapproval settled on Charlie's face.

"I think he was talking to some friends about a possible job," Alice explained.

"In the evening maybe, but at night?"

She nodded and avoided his eyes. "Is your tea sweet enough?"

"The tea is fine. What kind of job?"

She slumped back in the chair and heaved a sigh. "Bartending."

"But you don't—"

"I know, I know. He said he's looked everywhere, and there's noth-ing he's qualified for except . . ."

"Bartending?"

She lifted her eyes and gave a chagrined nod.

Given his past experience with the boy, Charlie couldn't hold back.

"That's a flat-out lie!" he said. "There's a HELP WANTED sign in the window of the Texaco station down by the highway. Ed needs someone to work the evening shift."

"Maybe Dominic doesn't feel qualified."

"It's sitting behind the register at a gas station. How can he not be qualified?"

Alice didn't have an answer, so she sat there feeling foolish. It was a feeling she didn't appreciate, and before long, it was pushing up against her thoughts. She stood, excused herself, then tromped up the stairs.

Without bothering to knock, she burst into Dominic's room, snapped up the window shade, and pulled back the blanket.

"You told me there were no jobs," she said angrily. "But the gas station is looking for help."

"Whoa!" Dominic sat up and rubbed sleep from his eyes. "What the hell?"

"Charlie told me the Texaco station is looking for someone to work evenings. A job like that could tide you over until—"

"Grandma! Gimme a break; I just woke up."

"It's two thirty in the afternoon! Get dressed and go ask about the job."

Since Dominic wasn't planning to be in Magnolia Grove that long, he hadn't actually considered getting a job, but the thought of a little extra money in his pocket was appealing. Sitting in a gas station wasn't all that hard. People pumped their own gas and usually only stopped in for a soda or a candy bar, so there'd be little to do other than keeping an eye on the place.

"Okay, I'm on it," he mumbled. He swung his legs to the floor and started for the bathroom.

Alice returned to the kitchen feeling pleased with herself. "Dominic's going to the gas station right now to apply for the job."

Charlie gave a dubious smile and didn't say a word.

16

The Job

The HELP WANTED sign had been taped to the gas station window for nearly a month and was starting to fade. The words EVENING SHIFT, once a bright red, were now a watered-down shade of pink. When Dominic walked in the door, Ed Farley was leaned back in the desk chair with his eyes half closed.

Dominic's voice startled him, and he jumped up. "Sorry," he said, clearing his throat. "How can I help you?"

"I said I'm here about the job."

"That's great. Excellent. You okay with working the evening shift?"

Dominic gave an unenthusiastic shrug and nodded.

"What about experience, and references?"

"Not from around here, but Charlie Barnes suggested I'd be good for this."

"You a friend of Charlie?"

"He and my grandma are like this." Dominic held up two fingers twisted together.

"And your grandma is . . . ?"

"Alice DeLuca."

As soon as Farley learned that Dominic was Alice DeLuca's grandson, he hired him on the spot, no application, no references.

He spent the next two hours showing Dominic around the station, explaining the credit card authorization process, showing him how to release the sticky handle on the pump in lane three, and detailing the different grades of engine oil. Once all of that was done, he tossed Dominic a set of keys with the bright-orange Farley's Filling Station fob and said, "You can close up at ten."

Then he headed home for what would be his first night off in three weeks.

At ten o'clock on the dot, Dominic switched off the lights, locked the door, and left with the twenty bucks he'd filched from the register. He headed over to Murphy's Ale House, hoping some of his old buddies would be around.

Broom was a head taller than anyone else, and with a mop of stick-straight blond hair, he was impossible to miss. Dominic spotted him the minute he stepped inside. He waved, and Broom waved back. Seconds later, Dominic was standing at the bar ordering a whiskey. He knocked that one back, ordered a second, then backed up the drinks until his twenty bucks gave out. After that, he told the bartender to run a tab.

Murphy's closed at two in the morning, and by then, Dominic and Broom were so drunk they could barely stand. Dominic climbed into his car, pulled away from the curb, then lowered the window, stuck his arm out, and yelled back, "See ya tomorrow."

Alice was in bed, sound asleep, when he finally got back to the house. After bumping his way past the sofa and lamp table, he practically crawled up the stairs, fell into bed, and slept for twelve hours straight.

The noonday sun had come and gone by the time he got up. He showered, then came downstairs, saying he could use a bite to eat before he went back to work. When he sat down at the table, Alice was full of questions about the job.

"It's good," he said. "I'm the evening manager." He pulled the keys from his pocket and jingled them as if that was proof. "I'm responsible for closing up."

Alice gave a smile of satisfaction. "I knew you'd do well. I'm very proud of you."

As he wolfed down the plate of ham and eggs, she said, "And what about the Briggs girl? Have you talked to her?"

Dominic rolled his eyes and looked away. "No, not yet, but I'm working on it."

Alice wanted to ask exactly what "working on it" meant, but before she had the chance, he was out the door.

17

Early Closing

On Dominic's third night at the gas station, a bombshell driving a canary-yellow '82 Corvette pulled into the third lane and climbed out of the car. It was almost nine thirty, and a chill had settled into the air, but she was wearing the skimpiest shorts imaginable.

After noticing her, Dominic couldn't help but notice the car. He stood at the window and watched as the woman bent over to slide the pump nozzle into the gas tank. He debated for a few seconds, then walked outside and called to her.

"Need some help with that?"

"Nah, I got it."

Dominic continued moving forward. "That pump can be tricky; shuts off for no reason."

She looked across at him and flashed a toothy smile. "Seems to be working okay now."

What little there was of the shorts appeared to be white, but, like the car, everything else was yellow: her sandals, toenails, tank top, even earrings. Standing next to her, he could see goose bumps rising on her bare arms.

"You look cold," he said.

She laughed. "I am, but I didn't want to take the time to stop and change."

He took the pump handle and gave a nod toward the convenience store. "Go wait inside where it's warmer. I'll take care of this."

"Gee, thanks." She tilted her head, smiled, then sashayed across the lot.

As Dominic topped off the tank, he saw her watching him from the office window. When the pump clicked off, he replaced the nozzle and met her inside. She'd settled into his chair, feet propped on the half-open bottom drawer.

"Want coffee?" he asked.

"Coffee?" She scrunched her nose. "Is that the best you've got to offer?"

He laughed. "If you've got time to kill, I'll close up, and we can go have a drink at Murphy's."

She gave a throaty laugh, then pushed herself away from the drawer and swung the chair around full circle. "That sounds better."

This was too good to pass up. He glanced at the wall clock: 9:45.

What the hell. It's only fifteen minutes until closing time anyway.

He pulled the keys from his pocket, snapped off the light, and let the door slam shut as they walked off.

"I'm Dominic, by the way."

"Celeste," she said.

With his thumb already tucked inside the waistband of her shorts, they headed for Murphy's. Broom was standing at the bar, but Dominic waved and passed him by as he steered Celeste toward the booths in the back.

"Less noisy," he said. After she sat, he slid in beside her. Close. So close that his leg was pushed up against her naked thigh.

He ordered a beer; she ordered a martini, two olives. Before she was halfway through her story about Wayne, the no-good boyfriend she'd left in Louisiana, her glass was empty, and she was ready for another one. By then, she'd moved on to talking about how Wayne spent his days playing golf while she was waiting tables.

Celeste plucked the olives from the second martini and popped them into her mouth. "There I was working my butt off; then Wayne tells me that since I'm making such good tips, maybe he'll concentrate on his game and go pro. That's when I decided to leave."

Dominic ran his fingers along her bare arm. "So now you're living in Magnolia Grove?"

"I ain't living anywhere. I'm on my way back to Philly."

"No shit," Dominic said with a grin. "That's where I'm from."

"I thought you owned the gas station."

"Nah, I'm just the evening manager."

When he'd come to Magnolia Grove, Dominic hadn't planned on returning to Philadelphia. He'd thought of trying someplace in New Jersey—Patterson or Little Falls—but now he pushed those places aside.

"I'm heading back to Philly, too. Not immediately, but soon."

"Oh? You looking to ride with somebody?"

"I got my own car, but if you wanna hang around for a while, maybe we could do that tag-team thing on the road. You know, have some fun."

He tipped the Miller bottle to his mouth, took a long drink, then set it back on the table.

"I'm all for fun." She scooted closer and wrapped her foot around his ankle. "I might be willing to stay for a while. It depends on what you've got to offer."

Shortly after twelve, they left Murphy's and checked into the Budget Motel a quarter mile from the gas station. Once inside the room, Dominic tossed his keys on the dresser and peeled off his jeans. It was after three when Celeste passed out from too much alcohol and not enough food.

Dominic climbed out of bed, hurriedly pulled his clothes on, grabbed his car keys from the dresser, and headed for home. It was still dark, so hopefully he would be able to make it to his room without waking his grandmother.

Once inside the house, he emptied his pockets, leaving his wallet and cell phone on the hall table, then tiptoed up the stairs. He never noticed the orange key fob was missing.

18

The Next Morning

Alice was out of bed before the rooster crowed, the same as always, and since it was Thursday, she was planning to do the wash. She emptied the upstairs hamper and gathered towels from the bath, then started downstairs. She was loading the washer when she thought about Dominic's work clothes and figured she'd toss those in also. Returning upstairs, she eased the door to his room open and scooped up the pile of clothes on the floor.

She expected his work clothes might have ground-in dirt or oil stains, so she looked them over carefully before tossing them in the washer. The only thing she found was a smudge of scarlet-colored lipstick on the shoulder of his shirt.

A smug smile curled her mouth as she spritzed a bit of Spray 'n Wash on the stain and dropped the shirt into the washer. It was nice to know that after weeks of her preaching to him about what was right and what was wrong, Dominic had moved ahead and done the right thing after all.

That morning, she baked a full tray of his favorite muffins, then mixed up a bowl of potato salad for lunch. Perhaps today would be a good time to ask Dominic if he'd like to invite Tracy Briggs and her son for Sunday dinner. The thought of meeting her great-grandson brought a swell of happiness to Alice's heart.

She was trying to decide between a pork tenderloin and roast chicken for Sunday dinner when she heard the musical sound of Dominic's cell phone. Not wanting it to wake him, she hurried into the hallway and answered with a cheery, "Good afternoon."

"Afternoon," a woman mumbled. "Is Dominic there?"

"Yes, but he's sleeping."

"Can you wake him? I've got to tell him something important."

Almost certain this was the news she'd been hoping for, she asked, "Is this Tracy?"

There was a pause, and then the woman said, "No, it's Celeste."

Celeste? "Celeste who?"

"Just say 'Celeste'; he knows me."

"From where?"

"From last night."

The cheerfulness suddenly disappeared from Alice's voice and her heart. "Last night? Are you certain it's Dominic *DeLuca* you're looking for?"

"Yeah, I'm sure. On second thought, don't bother waking him," she said. "Just tell him he left the gas station keys in my room. I'll bring them with me tonight."

Alice had a dozen questions, but before she could ask a single one, the girl was gone.

Hours later, when Dominic got up and came down for breakfast, there was nothing on the table but a pot of lukewarm coffee.

"No eggs this morning?" he said.

Slumped back in Joe's big chair, Alice just shook her head. "I'm not feeling so good today," she said.

She didn't mention the call.

19

Alice DeLuca

After Dominic left, I sat there in Joe's chair and cried as I haven't cried since I was seventeen. I don't even know the Briggs girl, yet I know what she's feeling.

All these years I've carried this secret around, too ashamed to tell, I suppose. Even after Joe was dead and buried, I never told a soul. Not my cousin Annabelle; not Charlie. Especially not Charlie. I couldn't stand it if he looked at me in that sympathetic way people do when they see a homeless person hunkered down in the doorway of some old building.

I was luckier than the Briggs girl; I had Daddy DeLuca to go to bat for me. The only one Tracy Briggs has looking out for her is me, and right now, I'm doing a terrible job of it. I know you're thinking this part doesn't make a whole lot of sense, but it would if you knew what happened before Daddy DeLuca told Joe he was expected to do the right thing.

Joe and I were dating steady for a little over six months when I missed my period. At first I thought it was just a fluke, a lack of something in my diet or maybe not enough exercise, but when the second month passed and my breasts became so tender it hurt when he fondled them, I knew what it was.

That Saturday night, I told Joe that instead of going to the movies, let's go somewhere and talk. He said The Bridge on the River Kwai *was playing at the Rialto, and he absolutely had to see it. We argued for a while, then finally compromised, going to the early show and then taking a stroll down by the lake.*

The whole time I watched that movie, I was on pins and needles, wishing that bridge would hurry up and get built. When the movie was finally over, we went for our stroll, and I told him I was pregnant.

"We've got to do something," I said, figuring he'd propose right away.

He didn't. He turned to me and said, "We?" as if he didn't have a thing to do with it.

I cried a bucket of tears that night, but Joe didn't budge an inch. He said he had plans for his life and wasn't anywhere near ready to settle down. I thought, given a day or two to see the reality of things, he'd change his mind. But a full month passed by, and he didn't even telephone.

In the third month, I started getting morning sickness, and by my fourth month, I couldn't even look at a piece of red meat. That's when Mama figured it out. She told my father, and before noon he was over at the farm, talking it out with Daddy DeLuca.

That evening, Joe telephoned me and said now that he'd had time to think it over, he'd come to the conclusion it would be best if we got married right away. I was stuck between a rock and a hard place and honestly didn't know if it was worse to be having a baby all by myself or to be marrying a man who didn't really love me.

Of course, you know the end of that story. Joe and I got married and stayed married until the day he died. We had a lot of heartaches, but we also had our share of happiness, happiness that never would have come about if it weren't for Daddy DeLuca stepping in.

Dominic is a lot like Joe. Even though he's thirty years old, he still doesn't know what's good for him. I do, and it's up to me to see he finds the kind of happiness that can carry him through the ups and downs of life.

I won't quit. Somehow, some way, I'll figure out how to get Dominic to do what's right. He may not appreciate it now, but in the years ahead, he will.

That's what I'm counting on.

20

Later That Evening

It was close to nine o'clock when Dominic saw Celeste pull into the gas station. She looked good, like she was ready to party again. He stepped outside the office and stood, smiling, as she trotted across the parking lot.

After a quick kiss on the cheek, she pulled the keys from her tote and playfully jangled them in front of Dominic's face.

"I bet you're glad to see these again."

Dominic impulsively reached into his pocket and felt for the keys. When the bulky orange fob wasn't there, he eyed her suspiciously. "Where'd you get those?"

"You left them in my room last night. Didn't you get the message?"

"What message?"

"I told your grandma to let you know I had the keys and would—"

"You talked to my grandmother?" Dominic cut in.

"Yeah, I talked to your grandma. You got a problem with that?"

Catching her caustic tone, he said, "No," but then nervously asked what it was she'd said.

"I told her you left the keys in my room, and I'd give them to you tonight."

"You didn't tell her who you were, did you?"

She huffed an exasperated sigh. "She asked, so, yeah."

"Oh, shit!"

Tossing the keys on the desk, she started toward the office door. "I don't know what kind of a problem you've got, but if your grandma is telling you who to date, I'm not about to stick around."

"Wait!" Dominic grabbed her arm. "I'm sorry. This has nothing to do with you, it's my grandma, she . . ."

Celeste turned and eyed him with a look of disbelief. "Your grandma? You're a grown man! What are you afraid of?"

"Afraid? This is not about me being afraid!" He dipped his head and grimaced. "It's my grandma . . . she . . . she's dying. It's a bad time . . ."

Celeste's expression softened. "I'm really sorry to hear that. But I don't see what it has to do with . . ." Her voice trailed off, but the agitated look remained.

Dominic pulled her into his arms, and the rigid resistance he felt at first eased a bit when he trailed a line of soft kisses along her bare shoulder.

"Let's go back to your room, and I'll tell you the whole story," he suggested.

Celeste scrunched her nose and shook her head. "I'm not in the mood. If you wanna go have a drink, then maybe . . ."

Dominic glanced at the wall clock. It was barely 9:25. Too early to close, but Celeste was not the type to stand around and wait.

"Yeah, a drink sounds good." He grabbed the keys from the desk, snapped off the light, and locked the door behind them as they left.

As they entered Murphy's, Broom was standing at the bar and waved, but Dominic avoided eye contact and steered Celeste toward the back.

"I think your friend was trying to get your attention," she said as she slid into the booth.

Yesterday she'd moved across to the far end of the bench, leaving Dominic room to sit beside her. Tonight she sat square in the center.

With no alternative, Dominic slid in on the opposite side. He smiled, and she smiled back. Not in the same way she had yesterday, but friendly enough. She was the kind of woman he liked—stacked, hot, and fun to be with—so he wanted to keep the fling going.

"You want a martini with two olives?"

She wrinkled her nose and shook her head. "Not tonight."

He ordered two beers instead, and they sat passing bits of idle conversation back and forth for several minutes, him hopeful she'd move on and forget their earlier discussion about his grandma, her obviously growing more impatient with his procrastination.

She was the one who finally broke the ice. "So are you gonna tell me what's going on or not?"

Dominic tipped his glass, drained it, then set it back on the table.

"My grandma's upset because I had this thing with a girl from town. It was ages ago," he said, "and we weren't even married . . ."

He slid the empty glass aside and leaned across the table. "I don't usually talk about it, but seeing as how we're getting close . . ."

Celeste's chilly expression didn't change.

"It happened almost seven years ago. I had a job offer in Philly, and Tracy, the girl I'd been dating, said she'd like to come along. With me trying to be a nice guy, I couldn't just say no, so she came. Next thing I know, she's pregnant and claiming the kid is mine."

"Was it?" Celeste asked.

Not anxious to explain away the truth, Dominic gave a half-hearted shrug. "Maybe, maybe not. Truthfully speaking, I think Tracy may have been fooling around with someone else. If that's the case, the kid might not be mine, so why should I—"

She glared at him, her brows pinched tight and a frown of suspicion narrowing her eyes.

"I know, it's a mess," he said, trying to look adequately despondent. "I'm not in love with Tracy and never was, but because of the kid, Grandma believes we need to get married."

"Why can't you just take responsibility for the kid?"

Dominic hesitated a moment, then said, "I wish it were that easy. I love my grandma, but she's a hard woman. Once she gets an idea in her head, it's set in stone."

When there was no response, he continued. "With Grandma practically on her deathbed, I don't have the heart to disappoint her, so I've been avoiding the issue."

Celeste's dubious expression was growing tighter by the second. Finally, she slid out of the booth and stood.

"I've had a raging headache all day," she said, "and it's getting worse. I've got to go back to my room and get some rest."

Dominic followed behind as she headed for the door. "Maybe I could massage your neck and help you get settled into a warm bath . . ."

"Afraid not," she said. "This is the kind of headache where I need to be alone." She tucked her tote bag under her arm as she walked.

"Okay, then, we'll catch up later," Dominic called out. "See you tomorrow."

"Yeah, sure," she answered without turning around. By then, she had one foot out the door.

21

Broom's Advice

After Celeste left Murphy's, Dominic felt a letdown. He'd expected the evening to go differently. He'd expected to go back to the motel with her for a repeat performance of the previous night. Instead, here he was, alone. It was too early to go home and too late to go back to the gas station. He moseyed over to the bar and stood alongside Broom.

Broom leaned his elbow on the bar and turned his back to Dominic.

"What's your problem?" Dominic asked.

Broom looked across his shoulder with a dark-eyed sneer. "My problem? You blow past without even a nod, and I'm supposed to like it?"

"Maybe not like it, but at least be understanding. You saw I was with somebody."

"Yeah, I saw." Broom turned to face Dominic. "So what happened to your friend?"

"She had a headache."

Broom laughed. "Sure she did."

"Shows what you know," Dominic grumbled. "She's staying in Magnolia Grove just 'cause she wants to be with me."

"In your dreams," Broom said and sniggered. "Looked to me like she was pretty eager to get out of here."

"You're wrong, buddy boy. She might be ticked off because of what my grandma said, but that's all it is."

Broom raised an eyebrow and shook his head. "No way. I know your grandma, and she ain't one to be causing trouble."

"Whatever." Dominic turned and signaled the bartender. "Gimme a bourbon on the rocks."

If it was another time, a time when he didn't feel quite so in need of a friend, he'd have turned his back to Broom, but tonight he needed to talk. Talking was a way to rid himself of the thoughts bouncing through his mind.

"Grandma's dying," he blurted out.

The petulant look on Broom's face disappeared. "Are you kidding me?"

"No, I'm not," Dominic said. "That's why I came back here. She claims we've got things to settle up." He lifted the bourbon, took a drink, then set the glass back down. "I wouldn't have come if I'd known this was about me marrying Tracy."

Even as he said the words, he knew they were a lie. He'd have come anyway. He'd have come simply because she asked him to. She was the one person he couldn't say no to.

"Tracy?" Broom scratched his head for a few seconds, then grinned. "Oh, yeah, Tracy. She's the one who took your car and ran off to—"

"That's her," Dominic cut in. "Grandma thinks I need to marry her because of the kid."

Broom let out a long whoosh of air and shook his head.

Dominic groaned. "Tell me about it. Grandma says she'll leave me the farm so we can live there happily ever after and the kid can inherit the place when I die." He emptied the glass and set it on the bar with a clunk.

"If she's dying anyway, just tell her you're gonna marry Tracy and let her be happy about it."

"I was planning to do that. Then Celeste called and screwed everything up."

"Too bad," Broom said. He signaled the bartender and ordered another round. "Maybe your grandma isn't too happy about you not marrying Tracy, but she's still gonna leave you the farm, right?"

Dominic turned with an angry glare. "You just don't get it, do you? I don't want that crappy farm. Grandma's the only reason I came back. Once she dies, I'm out of here for good."

"Don't be an ass. You don't have to live on the farm; you can sell it."

"The house looks like it's ready to fall down, and the fields are growing weeds. You think anybody's gonna buy something like that?"

"You're even stupider than I thought. It's a house! It don't matter if it's in bad shape—you can still get ten, maybe twenty thousand for it."

Dominic gave a snort. "You're crazy if you think anybody's gonna—"

"You're crazier if you think they won't. Butcher Fenway bought a house out there, in the new development that's a few miles from your grannie's place, and he paid upward of a hundred thousand for it."

"You're kidding."

"Nope," Broom said and downed the last of his drink.

Once the thought of the property being worth that much settled in Dominic's head, he began to see things in a different light. He knew for sure his grandma wanted him to have the farm.

All he had to do was come up with a story believable enough for her to buy into. She already knew about Celeste, so he couldn't say he'd been with Tracy. He'd have to come up with something new.

He and Broom sat there at the bar, drinking and plotting a dozen different scenarios to get around the issue. Finally, coming to the conclusion that Alice wasn't as concerned about Tracy as she was with Lucas, Dominic decided he had to create a plausible story to convince her Lucas wasn't actually his. After two beers and six bourbons, he'd worked through a tale Broom thought believable. Of course, by that time, Broom was nearly as drunk as Dominic.

When they staggered out of the bar laughing, they were both confident the plan would work.

Dominic knew his grandmother was a woman of habit; she found a measure of comfort in the everyday routine of doing things the same way each time. When she stacked cups in the cupboard, the handles were always turned to the right. When she did laundry, the first load was always the whites and the last load always the ink-colored work pants. She rose each morning before the cock crowed and in the evening went to bed early, said her prayers, and snapped off the bedside lamp at precisely ten o'clock. It had been that way since the day Dominic came to live with her.

He pushed through the front door and groped his way along the darkened hallway. Before he reached the staircase, the living room lamp clicked on.

"Dominic?" Her voice was crystal clear, not groggy or sounding of sleep. She'd been sitting there in the dark, waiting for him.

Startled by both the light and sound, Dominic stumbled and tried to collect his bearings.

"Is something wrong?" he asked. "It's late. What are you doing up?"

His thoughts were jumbled and poorly strung together, but he knew she would catch the smell of bourbon if he moved closer.

"I've been waiting for you," she said. "There's something we need to talk about."

"Now? Can't it wait until the morning?"

"You sleep all morning, so yes, it needs to be now."

There was no way out of it, at least not without hurt feelings.

"Okay," he said. "I need to use the bathroom, but I'll be right back."

Trying not to be obvious, Dominic ran his hand along the wall to steady himself as he walked past the living room toward the powder room. He was hopeful there'd be some toothpaste or cologne, anything to mask the smell of alcohol.

The small powder room held only the bare necessities; no toothpaste, mouthwash, or cologne. He rinsed his mouth with several handfuls of water, then splashed more on his face. In the medicine chest there was a tin of menthol cough drops; he took one and popped it in his mouth.

"Dominic?" she called. "You've been in there a long time; are you okay?"

"I'm fine," he answered. "I'll be right out."

He swished the cough drop around in his mouth, ran his tongue over his lips, then opened the door and stepped into the hall. He saw her walking toward him.

"I thought you wanted to talk," he said.

"I do, but I thought I'd fix some tea and we could sit in the kitchen."

"Oh. Okay." He turned and headed for the kitchen, walking ahead of her.

Keeping a fair bit of distance between them, Dominic passed by the chair he usually sat in and went to the far side of the table. He watched as she set the kettle on to boil, then, trying to hide the slur in his voice, said, "No tea for me, Grandma."

She turned and smiled. "Coffee, then? I'll make a pot."

He started to shake his head, but by then she'd begun to fill the pot with water.

She left the coffee on the stove and sat across from Dominic. For several moments, there was only the popping sound of the percolator; then she sighed.

"I hope you know how much I love you, Dominic. You're just like your granddaddy, and I loved him, too. He was a good husband and lived a happy life, but it might never have come about if it wasn't for your great-granddaddy. Daddy DeLuca's name was Dominic, same as yours. When you were born, I begged Dorothy to name you after him because he was the finest man I've ever known, and I was hoping you'd turn out the same . . ."

Her voice trailed off, and they sat there listening to the pot sizzle and then sputter to a stop.

Hoping to change the subject, Dominic said, "The coffee's done, Grandma."

"So it is." She stood, filled two cups, and carried them to the table, setting one in front of Dominic. She stirred a spoonful of sugar into her cup, then began.

"As much as I loved your granddaddy, I knew we'd never have gotten married if it weren't for Daddy DeLuca insisting Joe do the right thing; then Joe and I both would have missed out on a good life. I owe Daddy DeLuca a lot, and I'm going to do what I know he would want me to do."

"What's that?" Dominic asked.

"I'm going to make sure this farm is handed down to the next heir."

Dominic started to smile, but then he noticed she wasn't smiling.

Alice took a small sip of coffee, then continued. "I'm afraid you're a lot like your granddaddy, Dominic. You've got a fine family staring you in the face, but you're not willing to admit it. The Briggs girl would make you a good wife, but if you won't take responsibility for your son and do the right thing, then I'll have to do it for you."

"Wait a minute, Grandma . . ."

"This wasn't an easy decision, Dominic; I've given it a lot of thought and . . ." She hesitated a moment, glanced down at the narrow gold band she still wore, and grimaced. "I'm going to change my will and leave the farm to your son, because I think it's what your great-granddaddy would have wanted."

A sudden sense of desperation washed over Dominic. Nothing was going the way he thought it would. He lowered his face into his palms, sat hunched over the table, and began to sob.

After a night of drinking, crying came easy. He squeezed his eyes shut and waited for the tears to roll down his cheeks. Then, once he was certain she was watching, he brushed them back.

"It's not what you think," he finally said. "The reason Tracy and I broke up is because she was cheating on me with another guy. I'm not the daddy of that little boy. *He* is!"

Such news stunned Alice, and it was several seconds before she responded. "Why didn't you tell me this before?"

Although the tears had already dried, Dominic again brushed the back of his hand across his cheek. "I didn't want to admit she'd made a fool out of me."

Not knowing when to leave well enough alone, he continued, embellishing the story more and more as he went. He told of how he'd come home from a hard day at work and found another man in his bed and how he'd pleaded with Tracy to reconsider her actions.

"I know you think her son looks like me," he said, "but if you'd seen this other guy, you'd know right away that's who Lucas really looks like."

Alice listened but said nothing.

Once he was on a roll, Dominic went on to describe all that had happened. He even included a description of the would-be lover who, oddly enough, resembled himself down to the last detail. The only difference was the lover wore a gold ring and drove a Cadillac with leather upholstery.

22

Alice DeLuca

It's a painful thing to suspect a boy you've loved since the day he was born would look you in the eye and lie about something this important. I want to believe Dominic, but the sorry truth is I have my doubts.

Not at first, mind you. When I saw the tears rolling down his cheeks and he told about how Tracy Briggs had cheated on him, I thought my heart would break. But as he went on describing everything in such detail, I became suspicious.

The more he told, the more I doubted him. It simply made no sense. If Dominic walked in and found the woman he supposedly loved with another man, I can't for the life of me imagine he'd be calm enough to make note of what jewelry the man was wearing. It generally holds true that when a person is telling a lie, he's careful about the story, tying up the loose ends nice and tidy. A person telling the truth is so overwhelmed by heartbreak they don't notice those things.

I owe it to Daddy DeLuca to find out the truth. If that boy is Dominic's son, he should have what Daddy DeLuca intended him to have. And if, perchance, what Dominic said is true, then I'll have to set my doubts aside.

The problem is that I've never met Tracy Briggs, so I can't just walk up and ask if her boy is Dominic's son. And suppose I did, then what?

If she says yes, I'd be faced with the decision of believing her or my own grandson.

As far as I can see, there's only one way to get to the truth of the matter, and as much as it goes against my grain, I've got to do it. Tomorrow, I'm calling Charlie and telling him to bring over the card he has from that private investigator.

23

In Search of Answers

That night, Dominic went to bed satisfied with his performance, certain he'd convinced his grandma Lucas was not his child. Given the look of sadness that settled on her face, he was almost positive whatever thoughts she'd had about leaving the farm to Lucas were now forgotten. In the early hours of the morning, he heard the cock crow, but since there was no urgent need to check on things, he rolled over and went back to sleep.

Alice was awake long before she heard the cry of the rooster. It was early, too early to call, but when she couldn't wait any longer, she dialed Charlie Barnes's number. Charlie answered with a sleepy-sounding hello.

Without waiting for anything more, Alice said, "Remember that man you told me about? The investigator? The one you said could find out—"

"Alice, is that you? What time is it?"

"Five thirty, and of course it's me. I know it's early, but this is important."

"Are you all right?"

"Yes, Charlie, I'm fine, but I need your help."

She reminded him that a few weeks earlier, when she'd wondered if there might be more to the story than she suspected, he'd suggested a private investigator with a good reputation.

"I know I said I wasn't interested, but as it turns out, I am. Could you arrange a meeting with that gentleman?"

"Well, sure," Charlie said apprehensively, "but is this really what you want?"

"It's not what I want, but unfortunately, it's what I have to do."

At ten thirty that morning, while Dominic was still sound asleep, Alice climbed into Charlie's car, and they headed for Oakdale. The office of Tompkins Investigative Services was smack in the center of town. Charlie parked in front of the redbrick building.

"This is it," he said. "Floyd is on the third floor."

"You're coming with me, aren't you?"

Charlie gave an easy grin. "Only if you want me to."

"You know I do." Alice climbed out of the car and banged the door shut.

"Well, I thought it possible you might want privacy."

She turned and gave him a hard glare. "Charlie Barnes! You know good and well we have no secrets! If I can't trust you, then I can't trust anyone."

Alice continued to talk as she followed him into the elevator, but when they stepped out on the third floor, she stopped in the middle of a sentence.

"Oh, dear," she said solemnly. "I hope I don't regret this."

Charlie hooked his arm through hers. "There's no right or wrong here, Alice. Find out the truth, then do what your heart tells you to do."

She recalled having these same mixed feelings after Dominic's mama disappeared. At the time, she'd considered hiring an investigator to search for Dorothy but couldn't bring herself to do it. *Dorothy was her daughter. Family.* It seemed terribly wrong to track down your own daughter as if she were a common criminal.

Back then, Alice held on to the hope that Dorothy would one day return. All those years, she'd believed the bond of family was strong enough to overcome any opposing forces. Now she was no longer sure.

"I'm not going to make the same mistake again," she said and gave a sorrowful sigh as she pushed through the door.

Floyd Tompkins did not look anything like what Alice expected. He was skinny as a stick with a bald head and nonexistent eyebrows. He stood and motioned to the chairs in front of his desk.

"Have a seat."

The sight of him unnerved Alice. She'd expected someone taller, more capable of taking command of the situation, a man with broad shoulders and a healthy head of hair.

"I'm not all that certain I should even be here," she said apologetically. "It's possible I've made a mistake."

He sat and again motioned for her to sit. "Well, there's no consultation fee, so why don't we talk about your problem, then you can decide whether or not to move forward."

Alice gave an uncertain nod and started by saying it had been fifteen years since she'd received even a postcard from her daughter and eighteen years since she'd seen her. "That was the last time Dorothy was home for a visit. She came with her son, who was twelve at the time. After a few months, she told me she wanted to go see about a job. 'Let Dominic stay here with you, Mama,' she said. 'I'll be back to pick him up in a week or so.'" Alice hesitated for a moment, then pulled a hankie from her purse and blotted her eyes. "I think Dorothy already knew she wasn't ever coming back."

Even without eyebrows, Floyd Tompkins had an understanding face. When he sympathized with her and said he could understand how such a thing could tear at a mother's heart, Alice found herself starting to like him.

"I don't want you to waste your money," he said, "so you need to know finding someone who doesn't want to be found can be very time-intensive, and there's no guarantee—"

Alice leaned forward and cut in. "This isn't about Dorothy. I gave up looking for her years ago; it's her son I'm concerned about."

She explained how at first she'd believed Dominic was her only remaining heir, the one to whom she'd bequeath the farm, but recently she'd learned of a boy who may or may not be his son.

"Unfortunately Dorothy's boy is a lot like his granddaddy when it comes to owning up to his responsibility . . ." She let that thought hang in the air for a moment, then added, "If he won't do what's right, then I'll have to do it for him."

Floyd gave a solemn nod. "I hear you."

She told the story as she knew it, including Dominic's claim that Tracy Briggs had a lover who'd fathered the boy.

"I need to know the truth," she said, "regardless of how unpleasant it is."

They talked for nearly an hour with Floyd asking question after question and making note of her answers. Alice gave him what information she had, but at times it seemed pitifully little. She knew Dominic had worked in a bar, but she no longer remembered the name of it. She also knew Tracy and Dominic had lived together in Philadelphia but did not have the address of the building. She was pretty certain they'd never been married or divorced but was positive that Tracy and the boy were now living in Magnolia Grove. She had a picture of Dominic that had been taken over five years ago, but none of Tracy or the boy.

Floyd explained his fee was sixty dollars an hour, plus mileage and out-of-pocket expenses.

"There's some legwork involved here, so it will be two or three weeks before I can get back to you. Is that okay?"

"I suppose." Her answer was weighted with the sound of disappointment.

"And I'll need a ten-hour retainer."

Alice pulled a folded check from her purse and began writing with a shaky hand.

"How many hours do you think it will take to find out about the child?" she asked nervously.

Floyd heard the quiver in her voice, eyed the thin gold band on her finger, and saw the worn patches of leather on her purse. It seemed obvious she was a grandmother with a lot of love, but not a lot of money. He flipped through the pages of his scheduling calendar and saw he'd be working on a big-money divorce case most of the coming week. In the few scattered open spots, he penciled in DeLuca.

"Offhand I'd say it shouldn't take more than ten hours."

"Oh, that would be wonderful." Alice handed him the check. "Now if it's more, please let me know. I'm not a wealthy woman, but I don't want you to scrimp on trying to find out the truth."

He gave an understanding smile. "No worries about that," he said. "I'll get back to you as soon as I have something."

On the drive home, Alice sat looking out the windshield as if she saw something other than the road. There was a big black bug splatter, but other than that, there was only the blacktop road and endless stretches of peanut fields waiting for harvest.

"Anything you want to talk about?" Charlie asked.

She shook her head almost imperceptibly. "No, it's just that . . ."

He waited a long moment, then when she remained silent, asked, "Just what?"

She turned to him, her eyes dulled by sadness. "Just that you'd think a grandmother ought to know more about her own grandson." A sigh floated up from her chest. "Dominic has a hard shell around him, the same as Joe did. When a man's built a shell around his feelings, you get to see the outside, but never the inside."

"But you knew Joe loved you, didn't you, Alice?"

"I suppose," she said, then sat quietly for the remainder of the trip.

24

The Sweetest Season

After the awards dinner, Tracy and Gabriel began dating on a regular basis. They saw each other almost every Saturday night and Sunday afternoon. What had been obvious to Gabriel from the start came as a surprise to Tracy.

On the first Sunday of June, they picnicked at the lake and afterward sat watching Lucas toss bits of bread to the ducks. In the whole of her life, Tracy had never felt contentment greater than this. She could now say she was happy, truly happy.

Everything she'd ever wished for was right here in this moment. She looked up and let her eyes take in the beauty of Gabriel's face. As she gazed up at him, he bent and pressed his mouth to hers. The kiss was sweet and tender; it lingered for a moment, soft and warm on her lips, then was gone.

When he moved back, a sigh of contentment floated up from her chest, and she voiced the thought that came with it.

"Isn't it strange that we went all those years not realizing how right we were for each other?"

Gabriel laughed. "Not strange to me. Remember that first Thanksgiving Day when I had dinner at your mama's house?"

She nodded.

"That evening when we sat outside by the bonfire, I watched you holding Lucas in your lap and knew it would be easy to fall in love with you."

The memory of that day settled in Tracy's heart with a warm glow. She recalled how good it had felt when Gabriel draped an arm around her shoulder as they walked to the backyard, and how he'd later scooted his chair closer to hers. All along, she'd been telling herself she wasn't ready to love to anyone, but now it seemed as if Gabriel had proven her wrong.

She lowered her head onto his shoulder. "Why didn't you say something sooner? We could have been together all this time instead of letting it go by, wasted."

Gabriel wrapped his arm around her shoulders and tugged her closer.

"It wasn't wasted," he said. "We spent it getting to know one another." He reached across and lovingly traced his finger along the side of her cheek. "I had to wait until I thought you were no longer in love with Dominic."

Dominic. Tracy tried to shake loose the thought, but it remained stuck in her head, a ghost of the past that refused to move on.

She turned ever so slightly, and her eyes met his. "What about now?" she said.

He waited a moment, then smiled. "And now it's too late for me to do anything but trust that one day you'll love me as I do you."

Tracy leaned across and brought her mouth to his. She wanted to say, "I feel that way right now," but the thought of Dominic was still picking at her brain. It seemed that no matter how much she wanted the thought of him gone, it stayed.

The summer after Lucas's fifth birthday, they settled into a routine of having lunch together every Wednesday. Tracy suddenly found countless reasons for remaining at the school all afternoon. She helped out in the classrooms while Lucas joined in the activities of a play-and-learn group. On occasion she stayed even later, and in the evening the three of them had dinner together, sometimes out and sometimes at Gabriel's apartment. By the time she and Lucas returned to Magnolia Grove, the sky was dark and a sleepy-eyed Lucas was ready for bed. Twice, the time slipped away from them, and when the hour grew late, she and Lucas curled up in Gabriel's small guest room and spent the night in Barrington.

On Saturday evenings, Gabriel almost always drove to Magnolia Grove, and the two of them went out for the evening. Sometimes it was a movie, but more often, it was dinner at a restaurant with romantic lighting and booths where they sat side by side rather than across from one another. When they returned home, the house would be dark, with Lila and Lucas both sound asleep. That's when they sat on the front porch swing and pushed back and forth as they spoke of the future. Although he had not yet proposed, they both knew it would happen one day. For now, it was enough to talk about the abstract version of what was to be.

On just such a night in late June, after a storm had passed and the air was misted with the scent of night-blooming jasmine, they sat together and watched the last few droplets fall from the overhang.

"A five-year-old boy should have a yard to play in," Gabriel said, "and a dog. Look at how much Lucas loves Sox. That's proof enough he needs to have his own dog. A puppy that can grow up with him."

As he spoke, Tracy could envision them still sitting together on a porch swing when they were years older with silver streaks threading their hair, and the thought was as comforting as a warm robe.

He talked of how the school had grown and showed promise for even greater growth in the years to come. For a while, they continued to push back and forth; then he stopped the motion and turned to her.

"In July, the Barrington Chamber of Commerce is hosting a fund-raiser for the school, and they want me to do a presentation." He stopped for a moment, then added, "Since you know firsthand what we can do for deaf children, I thought maybe you'd like to do a testimonial."

"Me? But I'm not a speaker."

"I'm not looking for a speaker. I'm looking for someone who can share their story of how the school helps children with a hearing disability."

Tracy grinned. "Well, that's definitely something I know about."

That night, they sat talking until a slip of pink glowed on the horizon. Tracy told of the dark days before Lucas was diagnosed and how she'd prayed for him to say a single word. She recalled the day she'd first seen a glimmer of hope as she stood at the classroom door and watched a child born deaf asking questions and attaching names to the objects on flash cards. As she spoke, tears filled her eyes, but unlike the earlier years, these were tears of happiness.

25

Cause for Concern

Once she'd agreed to speak at the fund-raiser, Tracy feared she was going to be in over her head. She telephoned Sheldon Markowitz, the *Snip 'n Save* production assistant responsible for the final print layouts.

"I might be asking you to do a bit more work," she warned. "Maybe finish off and finesse some of the ad designs."

"No problem," he replied. "Just get everything to me a few days earlier."

Confident she now had a workable solution, Tracy began making notes and practicing her speech. At first, it seemed an easy enough task. She simply planned to tell her story as it had unfolded. Using one of the new composition books Meghan had left behind, she spent one whole morning making notes and yet another typing up a speech with exactly what she wanted to say. Then she spent that entire afternoon reading it aloud in front of the mirror.

On Thursday, Sheldon called and asked why he hadn't received any of the material for the upcoming issue.

Tracy glanced at the date on her computer and gasped.

"Oh, my gosh, I forgot about it! I'll get the drafts to you as soon as I finish my speech." She told him about speaking at the Hawke School fund-raiser. "I've written my speech out word for word, but it sounds so wishy-washy."

Sheldon laughed. "I've been working with you for over two years, Tracy, and I can't imagine you doing anything less than stellar."

"Thanks. It's nice to know I at least have your vote of confidence. Unfortunately, that's not going to help this speech . . ." Her voice drifted off, almost as if something else had caught her attention.

"Hold on," Sheldon said. "What makes you think the speech is no good?"

The question stumped Tracy, and several moments of silence passed before she answered. "I'm not sure. I've written down every single thing I need to say, but when I read it back, the words feel clunky in my mouth."

Sheldon laughed. "That's because you're reading from a piece of paper instead of speaking from your heart. Try using index cards with just one or two lines of prompts. That should keep you on track and leave room for being spontaneous."

"Index cards are a good idea."

"I've got to get back to work. When can I expect the ads?"

"Before noon tomorrow," she promised. Then they said their good-byes and hung up.

Tracy intended to get going and work through the evening, but with the idea of using card prompts now picking at the forefront of her mind, she was eager to try it. Before starting the ads, she pulled a packet of index cards from the desk and, in a tight, handwritten script, painstakingly narrowed the eleven pages of double-spaced text to twenty-eight cards. Then she felt compelled to check out the results.

Again standing in front of the mirror, she began speaking. Unfortunately, the handwritten words proved rather difficult to read, and the constant checking to make sure she hadn't missed anything was disconcerting. In the end, she realized this performance was only marginally better than the first. By then it was nearly eleven o'clock, and the words on the cards had turned to a blur of inked scribble-scrabble. She set the cards aside and sat at the computer to work on the ads.

In all, there were eleven new ads waiting to be done, but her eyelids were drooping before she'd finished the third one, an ad for Maggie's Shoe Palace. Leaving the ad with some lines of type stretched out and others squeezed into a too-small space, she powered down the computer.

I'll get up early in the morning and finish when I'm fresh, she thought as she headed upstairs and climbed into bed.

Lila was the one who dressed and fed Lucas in the morning, which was a good thing, because the next time Tracy opened her eyes, it was ten o'clock. With another eight ads to design and a noon deadline looming over her, Tracy bolted up, grabbed her cell phone, and texted Meghan.

Help! In a jam. Way behind on ads!

26

Sister Help

Meghan was checking the ears of a high-strung Pekingese when her phone beeped with a message from Tracy. She eyed it and sensed its urgency. Luckily she had only one appointment before three o'clock, and she was able to move it to later in the day.

It was not yet ten thirty when she pulled into Lila's driveway. As far as Meghan was concerned, her mother's house was still home, so she didn't bother knocking and hurried in. Stopping in the kitchen just long enough to kiss her mama's cheek and give Lucas a hug, she continued back to the *Snip 'n Save* office.

Tracy glanced up. "Thank goodness you're here!" She turned back to the computer and resized a line of type. "I'm way behind on the ads. Can you take over a few of these?"

A look of puzzlement swept across Meghan's face. "Sure," she said tentatively. "How come you're so far behind?"

"It's a long story," Tracy said without turning away from the screen. "If you do the two golf shop ads, the liquor store, and Fresh Farm Produce, I can handle the rest."

Meghan felt the tug of familiarity as she sat at the small desk that, years earlier, had been squeezed into the corner of the room. It was the same desk she'd occupied when her daddy was alive. She powered on the laptop, pulled up the *Snip 'n Save* site, and opened the first file. With almost no conversation between them, the sisters worked straight through lunch. Before one o'clock, the folder of ads was emailed to Sheldon.

"Whew!" Tracy rolled her shoulders and relaxed into the chair. "Thanks, Meghan. I couldn't have done it without you."

"How'd you get so far behind?" Meghan asked. "What happened?"

"I guess I've been preoccupied. Gabriel and I are working on something special, and it's taken more time than I expected."

"Gabriel?" Meghan gave a grin of satisfaction. "I had a feeling you two would be right for each other. So how's it going?"

Turning to face her sister, Tracy leaned back with a dreamy expression. "I like him. A lot. He makes me laugh and feel good about myself."

"Does he feel the same about you?"

She nodded. "I think he loves me."

"Did he come right out and say it?"

Tracy hesitated. Without mentioning that afternoon at the lake, she finally answered, "Yes and no."

Meghan raised an eyebrow. Issues such as this were precisely why she worried about her sister. "What is that supposed to mean?" she said. "He either did or didn't. Which was it?"

"Well, I guess he did. At least he started to . . ."

"And?"

"He said he wanted to wait until he was certain I was over Dominic."

At the mention of Dominic, Meghan felt a twinge of concern. "You told him Dominic was a thing of the past, right?"

Tracy turned back to the computer. "I'd rather not talk about it."

"What!" Meghan was out of her chair in a flash. She swung Tracy's chair around and stood glaring at her. "Are you crazy? Are you deliberately trying to ruin a relationship with a man who's perfect for you?"

Tracy's expression stiffened. "I'm not trying to ruin anything. I'm trying to be honest. Besides, none of this is even your business!"

"It's my business because I love you and want you to be happy. I stood by and said nothing when you ran off with Dominic the first time, but I am not going to stay silent again."

"You had nothing to say about it. I made my own choices."

"That might have been okay then, but now things are different. You've got Lucas to consider. I'm your sister. It's my responsibility to make sure you think long and hard about your choices."

"Not everything is your responsibility, Meghan. Sometimes you have to let other people make their own mistakes. I've made mine, and hopefully they're behind me. For now, I'm happy being with Gabriel."

"What do you mean *for now*?" Meghan slapped her hand against her forehead as if the truth had somehow dawned on her. "This *is* about Dominic! He's still in the picture, isn't he?"

"Of course he is. He always will be. You can't love someone, have a child with him, and then simply forget you ever had feelings for him when you're ready to move on. Don't forget, Dominic is Lucas's daddy."

Suddenly, all the concerns Meghan had held back became real and more threatening than ever. She groaned and rolled her eyes. Dominic's return would mean the end of everything—the end of Lucas attending the school, the end of Tracy and Gabriel, the end of Tracy managing the *Snip 'n Save*!

"Dominic's back in town, and you're seeing him again, aren't you?" Her eyes narrowed, and her words had the sound of an accusation rather than a question. "That's why you're late on the ads, isn't it?"

"Don't be ridiculous. He has nothing to do with it."

Meghan pushed forward. "Well, what then? What's so important that you neglected to send out the billing or get the ads finished in time?"

"The speech I'm doing at Lucas's school," Tracy replied flatly. "That's what."

"Speech?" The rigid furrows along Meghan's forehead softened. "You never said anything about a speech."

"I wanted to wait until it was really good before I told you." Tracy went on to explain that she was the main speaker at the fund-raiser.

Meghan reached out to pull her sister into a hug. "That's wonderful," she said. "I'm so very proud of you."

"Really?"

The relief of knowing it was something Tracy was doing for the school and not a reappearance of Dominic brought a smile to Meghan's face. "Yes." She sighed. "Really."

Tracy wriggled free and gave a grin. "If you've got time right now, I'd like to run through it and see what you think."

"I can spare an hour, but then I've got to get back. Tom's got a surgery scheduled, and he needs my help."

"An hour's good." Tracy grabbed the packet of cards. Talking to Meghan was easier than talking to a reflection, so this time her presentation went smoother.

She ran through the whole speech, then asked, "What do you think?"

"It's not bad," Meghan said, her expression thoughtful, "but it's not the real you. Why don't you ditch the cards and just tell the story the way you remember it?"

"With nothing? No cards? No script?"

Meghan nodded. "I think you'd come across as more believable."

Tracy looked pensive for a long moment, then said, "I guess it wouldn't hurt to try."

They had a quick sandwich together, and before Meghan left, Tracy asked if she'd come back later that night to listen to an off-the-cuff version of her speech.

"I don't mind coming back," she said, "but you're already behind on the *Snip 'n Save* billing, aren't you? So how can you find time to work on the speech?"

"I'll make time," Tracy replied.

That was precisely what worried Meghan.

27

Meghan Whitely

I don't want to make a big deal about it, because I know Tracy is nervous about speaking at the fund-raiser, but, honestly, I'm pretty ticked at her. If I hadn't dropped everything to come over and help out, some of the ads would have missed this week's edition. Daddy would turn over in his grave if he thought we were treating customers that way.

Tracy acts like it's a flexible job with time off whenever she wants. It's not. She knew that when she agreed to take over. I told her when an ad is booked for a certain week, it has to run that week. She can't bump it to the next week or let it slide until she gets around to it. We have an obligation to our customers. But unfortunately, she doesn't take that responsibility seriously enough.

If this was the first time she'd fallen behind, I'd understand, but it isn't. We've had this same argument twice before. I asked if she knew what would happen if a store had a special event going and then, boom, they find out there's no promotion to support it. She shrugged and didn't say anything. There was nothing to say. She knew as well as I did that would be a guaranteed disaster!

It's not that I mind helping out, but the truth is, she should be able to handle the amount of work there is, even with having Wednesday off to take Lucas over to the school. He only has class for a half day, but *she spends the whole day there. That would be fine if she didn't have work to do, but she does.*

When Tracy first took over, I worried that Dominic's return might cause her to forget her promise to run the Snip 'n Save. Now I'm starting to think I was worried about the wrong thing.

I feel bad about being mad at Tracy; she deserves to have a personal life the same as Mama and I do. Mama goes to dinner with her friend Bruce Pendergast every so often, but she doesn't just walk off if she's promised to babysit Lucas. Having a personal life doesn't mean blowing off your responsibilities.

The problem is I have no idea what to do about it. I spent eighteen months getting a veterinary assistant's license so I could work with Tom. It's what I want to do, and I don't want to give it up. But if Tracy walks out, I'll have no choice.

All I can do right now is hope that after the fund-raiser, she settles down and gets serious about running the Snip 'n Save. That would save us all a whole lot of heartache.

28

Ready, Set . . .

As the weekend of the fund-raiser grew near, Tracy became increasingly nervous about her presentation. So much depended on whether she was convincing. When she recalled Gabriel's speech at the awards dinner and remembered how the audience had cheered, she set her expectations even higher.

On Monday, she called Meghan and asked if she could possibly help out with the *Snip 'n Save* for the week.

"I'm really sorry about asking you to do this again," she said, "but I need time to practice my speech."

"You're still practicing?" Meghan asked in disbelief. "I've heard that speech a half dozen times in the last five days, and it sounds perfect."

"I still think it could be better." Tracy gave a weary-sounding sigh. "On Friday, I'm running through the presentation with Gabriel, and I was hoping it would be perfect by then."

"I thought the fund-raiser was Saturday night."

"It is. I'm staying over and spending the weekend in Barrington. After the dinner, it will be late and—"

"What about Lucas?"

"Mama's taking him for the weekend. After I do the speech, I'll probably be wiped out and way too tired to drive."

"But you'll be back at work on Monday, won't you?" A sound of concern was hanging on to the end of Meghan's question.

Tracy, having moved on to thinking about what she might wear to the event, said, "Yeah, sure."

"Oh. Okay." Meghan hesitated a moment, then said, "You're . . . you're just doing a speech like this one time, right?"

"With as worked up as it makes me, I would think so!"

On Monday afternoon, Meghan slid into the chair she'd used in the years following her daddy's death, but somehow it didn't feel quite the same. She leaned back and propped her feet up on the desk rail just as he had done and found it an oddly uncomfortable position. After wriggling from one side to the other, she snagged a throw pillow from the living room, stuck it behind her back, and logged on to the *Snip 'n Save* scheduling calendar.

At first, she thought maybe Tracy had simply forgotten to note the completed files, but when she opened the individual folders, she found twenty-eight ads waiting to be designed.

In the early days, after her daddy was gone and before Sheldon was hired, Meghan had handled the *Snip 'n Save* alone. Countless times she'd remained at the desk long after the sky had turned dark and most everyone in Magnolia Grove had gone to bed. Some nights, her eyelids felt as heavy as a sack of sand, but still she stayed there, designing ads, repositioning art, or selecting fonts that stood apart from the others. Back then, she'd felt a sense of reward in seeing it done right. Now the thought of tinkering with the ads when her family was at home waiting for her seemed almost painful. She closed her eyes and, for a brief moment, pictured the three of them sitting on the sofa—Sox curled up beside her, his head resting on her thigh, and Tom with his arm draped across her shoulders.

Meghan gave a rueful sigh, then opened the Daisy Dress Shop folder and started to work. She'd completed eight of the layouts when Tracy finally returned home.

"Where've you been?" she asked, not masking her irritation. "You knew you still had all these ads to get done; you should have at least stayed here to help out."

"Sorry. I had to get a dress for the fund-raiser." Without giving the apology time to settle in Meghan's head, Tracy pulled a pale-yellow dress from the box and held it up. "What do you think?"

Normally, Meghan would have gushed over the dress, elaborating on how it brought out the highlights in Tracy's hair, asking about shoes and the accessories she'd wear. Not this time.

"Nice," she said. With her lips stretched into a tight little line, she turned back to the screen. "This is the last ad I'm doing tonight. Hopefully tomorrow you can find time to help out so we can get the rest done."

"I can work for an hour or two, but I still have to practice my speech."

Meghan's expression turned hard as a rock, and her left eye began to twitch, but Tracy failed to notice.

29

The Event

On Friday afternoon, Tracy arrived in Barrington. After closing Gabriel's office door, she ran through the presentation she'd been working on for the past two weeks, and he listened. She told of how Lucas had gone through the surgery and spoke of his reaction the day the sound in his cochlear implant was first turned on. Although she remembered the torment of those moments as she'd watched and waited for even the tiniest indication he'd heard her voice, that thought was not part of her speech. At the end, Gabriel had only one comment.

"Don't worry about covering every phase of the process; just relax and let your feelings show through the way you did that night on your mama's front porch."

This was a curveball for Tracy. She'd practically memorized every word of what she planned to say, and none of it was about her. She felt a fluttering inside her chest and for a moment believed it to be the wings of words trying to break free.

All afternoon, as Gabriel checked and then double-checked arrangements for the fund-raiser, Tracy tried to remember what she'd said that night. Where was the magic in the words that had suddenly gone missing?

That evening, they went back to Gabriel's apartment and shared a pizza as he briefed her on some of the people who would be attending the following day.

"Be sure to talk to Nancy Throckmorton," he said. "She's one of our biggest supporters." He described Nancy as a lady in her eighties who had a sharply pointed nose and snow-white hair.

"But what if she doesn't like me?" Tracy asked nervously. "What if—"

Gabriel laughed and tugged her closer. "Be your own sweet self, and everyone will love you just as much as I do."

At ten thirty, Tracy mentioned she was tired and should turn in. Gabriel agreed. Since the awards dinner, this was the first time they'd been alone together in his apartment; every other time, Lucas had been there. Earlier in the week, she'd half expected it might turn into something romantic, but now those thoughts were nowhere to be found. He seemed to be focused on last-minute details, and she was searching for the magical lost words.

Gabriel kissed her lips softly; then she headed for the small guest room that had now become familiar. As tired as she was, sleep was difficult to come by, and for hours she tossed and turned, thinking back to that night on the porch and remembering only the warmth of Gabriel's thigh pressed close to hers and the feel of his arm curled around her shoulders. Whatever words she'd spoken that night were gone. Hopelessly and forever gone.

Saturday was spent at the school, talking with the caterer and going over the final seating arrangements. Once everything was in place, they returned to the apartment and dressed for the fund-raiser. When Tracy came from the room wearing the pale-yellow chiffon dress, he smiled.

"You look absolutely amazing," he said and kissed her cheek.

"I don't feel amazing," she replied. "I'm worried about this. That night on the porch, it was just you and me; sharing what I feel with you is completely different from talking to a room full of people."

"Don't worry, you'll be great." Gabriel took her hand in his. "I'll be sitting in the front. When you tell your story, look at me and pretend there's no one else in the room. Talk to me like you did that night."

Referring to it as "telling her story," as opposed to making a speech, eased her mind, but only slightly.

Before dinner, there was a cocktail hour, and with his arm looped through hers, Gabriel guided Tracy around the room, introducing her to the guests. She nodded and smiled, but even as she did so, she was trying to remember the magical words she'd somehow lost.

After what seemed an eternity, a chime sounded, and the guests turned toward the gymnasium. The athletic equipment had been cleared away and replaced with tables covered in white cloths and set with fine china brought in by the caterer. In the center of each table was a flower arrangement.

Gabriel and Tracy sat at the table closest to where a stage had been set up. Also at the table were the Throckmortons and the Blakes, two of the school's biggest benefactors. Nancy Throckmorton switched seats with her husband and sat next to Tracy.

"I understand you have a son who is hearing impaired," she said.

Tracy nodded. "We think Lucas may have been born deaf, but we didn't realize it until he was almost fifteen months old."

A sigh rattled up from Nancy's chest. "I had a twin brother born deaf, and like your Lucas, William's problem wasn't discovered until he was almost two."

Her pale-blue eyes grew misty as she spoke. "When I began to speak and William only made screeches or grunts, our papa thought something was wrong with William's mind." She gave a frail laugh. "That was over eighty years ago when there was little understanding of deafness."

As the waiters began to serve the salad, Nancy placed her hand atop Tracy's and gave an affectionate squeeze. "What you are doing is good, not only for the children who are deaf but also for the people who love them." She pulled her hand back. "It's a terrible thing to love someone and not be able to help them."

In the hour that followed, salad plates were carried off and entrees served, and afterward plates of cake came with china cups for tea or coffee. Slowly, the clatter of the room stilled, and Gabriel stepped to the microphone. He spoke about the school and how they were now able to take on more students because of the community's generous support. He shared the progress in teaching techniques and a new program of identifying words with similar sounds.

"Deafness isn't a problem that affects just the child," he said. "It affects the entire family." He segued into an introduction of Tracy and called her to the stage.

As Tracy walked to the stage, her knees were wobbly and her step uncertain. She moved to the center of the platform and looked out at the audience, every face turned toward her. Suddenly she feared she had nothing of merit to say, that all the hours of practice were for naught. An icy chill shivered along her spine, and she felt an itch at the back of her neck like a rash rising out of nowhere. When she moved to the microphone and looked down at it, the thought of what Nancy had said came to mind.

It's a terrible thing to see someone you love suffering while you stand helplessly by with no power to change it.

Tracy lifted her face, looked out into the room, focused her gaze on Nancy Throckmorton's tear-filled eyes, and found the magical words she'd been searching for.

She shared how, at first, she'd refused to admit there was a problem and how she'd feared Lucas would go through life unable to speak words that could be understood. She talked about how she'd prayed for him to say just one word.

"Back then, I would have settled for a single word," she said, "but because of what the Hawke School has done, my prayer has been answered a million times over."

When her presentation was finished and she stepped back from the microphone, the guests rose from their chairs with a round of thunderous applause. Moments after she returned to her seat, Nancy again took Tracy's hand in hers. She leaned in, kissed her cheek, and said, "The school is blessed to have you as a spokesperson, my dear."

That night, the pledges and donations were greater than ever before, and after an icy glare from his wife, Gregory Throckmorton doubled his contribution of the previous year.

It was nearly midnight when Tracy and Gabriel finally left the school. By then, the guests were long gone, the last goodbyes had been said, and the workmen were loading stacks of folding chairs into the caterer's truck. The heat of the day had dissipated, and the cool night air felt good against Tracy's shoulders.

"Let's walk home," she suggested.

Leaving the car in the parking lot behind the school, they walked the fourteen blocks to his apartment with Gabriel's arm around her waist and her head tilted toward his shoulder. As they crossed over Main Street, he leaned down and whispered in her ear.

"You look beautiful tonight."

She turned and smiled. The strange thing was she also felt beautiful.

When they arrived at the apartment, Gabriel pulled a bottle of champagne from the refrigerator and filled two crystal glasses.

"To the most beautiful woman I've ever known," he said and touched his flute to hers.

Tracy's heart swelled as that moment became part of her forever. She knew that even if she lived ten thousand years, she would always remember the happiness she felt right then. The tinkling sound of crystal rippled through the air as she lifted the glass to her lips.

For a long while, they sat on the sofa and talked about the evening, skipping past the sizable increase in contributions and focusing instead on the way she'd moved Nancy Throckmorton to tears.

"You have a gift," he said, "one that shouldn't be wasted sitting at a computer. Few people can open their hearts the way you did tonight."

"You make it easy for me to open my heart . . ." The remainder of her words drifted away. There was more to the thought, but she decided to wait, hoping he would be the one to ask.

When the clock chimed two, he stood and held his hand out for her.

"Tracy, please come to my room and be with me tonight."

She dipped her head ever so slightly, then looked up and smiled. He took her hand in his, and together they walked down the hall into the master bedroom.

That was the first time Gabriel made love to her. He kissed her mouth, then ran a trail of tender kisses along her neck as he pressed his hand to her back and brought her to him. He was slow and easy, touching her gently, whispering sweet words as he traced his fingertip along her collarbone and across the curve of her shoulder. There was none of the hungry wanting she'd known with Dominic; this was a different kind of lovemaking, one that promised tomorrow and a lifetime of happiness.

Afterward, they lay together, his arm curled around her, her head resting against the edge of his shoulder.

"Do you think you could be happy with me?" he asked.

She gave an almost musical laugh. "I already am," she said and snuggled deeper into his arms.

Placing his fingertips beneath her chin, he tilted her face to his, tenderly traced the curve of her cheek, then asked, "Forever?"

Tracy hesitated for a fraction of a second, thinking perhaps the specter of Dominic, who'd haunted her for years, would again raise its ugly head, but this time it didn't. It was gone. Completely gone.

"Yes," she whispered, "forever." She smiled and brought her mouth to his.

The clock struck five, and the first rays of light were feathering the sky when they finally fell asleep, their breaths evenly matched and their bodies pressed together so close that it would be impossible to find a point of separation.

30

Tracy Briggs

I am deliriously happy and can't help myself. Yes, I know Meghan is mad at me, and I'm sorry I disappointed her by letting the schedule get messed up. But let's be honest—an ad moving from one week to the next is not the end of the world. To me, helping Gabriel grow a school where kids like Lucas learn to talk is more important.

Last night, speaking at that fund-raiser, I felt like I was doing something worthwhile. I don't feel that way when I'm working at the Snip 'n Save. I like designing ads, but the truth is, it's nowhere near the same as helping kids have a better life.

Meghan always talks about how much Daddy loved the Snip 'n Save, but I don't ever remember him saying that. It could be she's the one who's got it all wrong. Maybe Daddy felt the same as me, that the Snip 'n Save is just a magazine full of ads, not a living, breathing thing.

I understand why Meghan wants to keep working with animals. It's the same as me loving my work at the school. Helping kids or animals have a better life makes you feel good about what you're doing.

Last night, I got to thinking that if she loves working with Tom and I'm happiest being here with Gabriel, maybe it's time for us to let go of the Snip 'n Save.

That's what I think, but knowing how Meghan feels, I'd never have the guts to suggest it. If I did, she'd probably go ballistic. She wants me to love the Snip 'n Save *like she does, but I don't. She believes loving the* Snip 'n Save *is the same as loving Daddy, but I disagree. I know Daddy would want us both to be happy doing whatever we love.*

I wish Meghan could be glad for how happy I am right now. Gabriel is the kind of man you dream of having fall in love with you. He's gentle and caring, and when he says he loves me, he means it—not just because it's a moment of passion, but for always.

It was never like this with Dominic, not even in the beginning. The first time we slept together, it was in the back seat of his car. He came from work, sweaty and smelling like beer. Instead of whispering in my ear about how he loved me, he was busy yanking my clothes off and saying how much he wanted me. Wanting someone is a lot different from loving them. It's a shame it took me all these years to figure that out.

Falling in love with the wrong man is like drinking beer and telling yourself it's champagne. I used to dream one day Dominic would come begging me to marry him; now I wouldn't have him if he were served on a silver platter.

After last night, I think Gabriel is going to ask me to marry him, and if he does, I will say yes right then and there. When you've got a prince at your door, it's downright stupid to keep worrying about the frog you left behind.

31

The Search

Floyd Tompkins was old school, a man reluctant to put too much of his trust in the results of an internet search, especially when it proved fruitless. When his initial search for Dominic DeLuca and/or Tracy Briggs turned up nothing of interest to him, he headed over to the Magnolia Grove County Clerk's office. After plowing through five years of marriage records, he still had nothing. On the off chance he'd overlooked some small detail, he returned to the office and googled their names again. This time Tracy Briggs came up in an article published in the *Barrington Post*.

She'd recently spoken at a fund-raiser for the Hawke School. Floyd pulled up the article and read it through. There were two excerpts from the presentation; the second one told how her son, Lucas, was born deaf.

Floyd printed out the article and the picture of Tracy standing with the Throckmortons and Gabriel Hawke, founder of the school. He now had the kid's name and a picture of the girl.

Two days later, he flew to Philadelphia. He'd thought of cutting back on the expenses by simply making a few phone calls, but Alice DeLuca had said not to scrimp on what it took to learn the truth. Floyd knew from experience that the truth was easier to discern when he was looking a person in the eye.

He now had a name, so he started with a search of birth records. He typed in "Lucas DeLuca" and found nothing. He then tried "Lucas Briggs" and came up with a hit. A boy born five years ago on June 10. This was the kid he was looking for. He pulled a copy of the birth certificate, looked it over, then gave a grunt of annoyance. The father's name was not listed, only the mother: Tracy Briggs.

Floyd thought of his own birth certificate. It listed both mother and father, even though his daddy had disappeared before Floyd was old enough to call out his name. Maybe Tracy Briggs suspected something like that was in the wind; maybe she left the space blank rather than give the boy a daddy who'd go missing in a matter of months. Although his job was simply to report the verifiable findings, he couldn't help feeling sympathetic toward Tracy, and less so toward Dominic.

Figuring there was a chance he might be wrong about Dominic DeLuca, he searched the marriage records for a year before and two years after Lucas's birth. There was nothing.

"Scumbag," he grumbled as he trudged over to the clerk's desk to pay for his printout of the birth certificate. Floyd folded the copy and slid it into the breast pocket of his jacket along with the picture of Tracy; then he stepped out onto the street and hailed a cab.

His next stop was 421 Adams Court, the address listed on Lucas's birth certificate. He scanned the names on the doorbells, then pushed the one that read "building manager."

The intercom crackled, and Jose Rodriguez answered with a gruff, "What?"

"I'm looking for information on a tenant," Floyd said. "Tracy Briggs, or possibly she went by DeLuca."

"Nobody here by that name."

"She lived here a while back. Two, maybe three years?"

"I been here a year and never heard of her."

"Is there somebody else I can—"

The intercom clicked off before Floyd could finish his question.

The building wasn't all that big; surely somebody would remember Tracy and Dominic. He tried the lobby door. Locked. Running his finger along the doorbell nametags, he noticed some that were yellowed. Those tenants had been here awhile and would most likely know. He was about to buzz Fred Molinari when he saw the elderly woman coming across the courtyard with two large grocery bags. He pulled the outside door open.

"Here, let me help you with those," he said and lifted the bags from the woman's arms.

Evelyn Ross smiled. "Well, aren't you just the sweetest thing."

Floyd followed her through the lobby door and rode up in the elevator with her. When they stopped on the fourth floor, he walked alongside Evelyn, carrying both bags.

"I don't think we've met," he said, making it sound almost as if he lived in the building. "Have you lived here long?"

"Nineteen years," she said as she opened the apartment door and held it back for him. "Georgia and I came just after the building was refurbished."

"Georgia?"

She nodded and pointed to the gray cat curled alongside the stove. "Georgia's like me, old but still feisty."

Although Floyd had no use for pets of any kind, he smiled, mumbled a few gushing words about the cat, then set the grocery bags on the table and moved on to asking questions.

"I'm looking for someone who used to live here. Tracy Briggs. Do you remember her?"

When Evelyn stood there looking puzzled, he pulled out the picture.

"This is Tracy," he said, holding his thumb over the date on the photo.

Evelyn took the eyeglasses hanging from a string around her neck, set them on her nose, and took another look at the picture. She looked up and smiled.

"Sure, I remember her. Sweet young thing; used to stop by when she had errands to run and ask if I wanted anything. She knew getting out in bad weather was hard on me, so she'd pick up whatever I needed and carry it back. I watched her baby a few times; he was a cute little devil. I believe his name was Luke."

"Lucas," Floyd said. "Was Tracy married, or did she live with anybody?"

"She lived with a fellow, but I don't think they were married."

Floyd pulled the picture of Dominic from his pocket. "Is this the guy?"

She frowned and gave a nod. "Unpleasant as they come."

Without needing encouragement, Evelyn went on to list a number of reasons for disliking Dominic.

"What puzzles me," she mused, "is why a lovely girl like Tracy would bother with the likes of him."

"Do you think it was because he was Lucas's daddy?" Floyd asked.

Evelyn shrugged. "He might have been the baby's father, but he sure wasn't a daddy. He wasn't even here the night that baby was born."

"Why? Where was he?"

"Supposedly working," Evelyn said and raised an eyebrow.

That afternoon, Floyd went from one apartment to another, asking questions. By the end of the day, he'd learned that to the best of anyone's knowledge, Tracy had been a devoted mother who worked during the early part of the day, then spent evenings at home alone. Dominic worked off and on, and the last anyone knew he'd been bartending at a place called Rosie's.

Michael Kudas, who lived directly across the hall from Tracy and Dominic, claimed it wasn't Tracy who'd had the affair but Dominic.

"The afternoon she came home and found him with that blonde from the fifth floor, you could hear the ruckus a mile away. A few minutes after they stopped yelling, she took the baby and stormed out. That was the last I saw of her."

"What did Dominic do?"

Kudas shrugged. "Stayed around a few months, then cleared out."

When he finished at the apartment building, Floyd stopped in at Rosie's and ordered a beer. As luck would have it, Rosie was behind the bar.

"How long have you worked here?" he asked.

She gave a husky laugh. "I don't work here. I own the joint."

"So you know Dominic DeLuca?"

Rosie rolled her eyes and gave a nod. "Unfortunately."

"Why 'unfortunately'?"

Rosie poured herself a beer, then leaned across the bar and told of how Dominic had quit with no notice, leaving her high and dry to find another bartender.

"He must've taken me for stupid with that cock-and-bull story about how he had to go home 'cause his grandma was dying."

Rosie had a number of other things to say about Dominic, none of them good. Floyd listened for a while, then downed his beer and left. It was almost eight when he returned to the airport and hopped aboard a flight headed for Atlanta.

It had been a somewhat discouraging day. After talking to a dozen people, he had a dozen different opinions and not a single shred of evidence proving Dominic was or wasn't Lucas's father.

On the drive home from the airport, he decided to check out the Hawke School the following day. If Lucas was attending the school, maybe they had a record of his father's name.

The next morning, Floyd drove to Barrington, and, as fate would have it, that Wednesday Lucas was attending classes.

Floyd spotted Tracy on her way in from the parking lot and recognized her from the newspaper photo. He quickly moved into her pathway and said, "Aren't you Tracy Briggs?" When she nodded, he fell into step alongside her.

"I have a granddaughter who has a hearing problem," he said, "and after I saw that newspaper article about how the school helped your son, I thought maybe I could ask you a couple of questions."

"I'd be happy to talk with you," she said, "but Lucas is on his way to class. If you don't mind waiting a few minutes, I'll drop him off and come back."

"I don't mind at all," Floyd said and parked himself on the lobby bench.

When Tracy returned, she sat beside him and answered question after question, explaining how she hadn't at first realized Lucas had a hearing problem, and because of that, his deafness had gone undetected for fifteen months.

"What about his daddy?" Floyd asked. "Didn't he notice?"

Tracy made it obvious she had no desire to talk about Dominic. "Lucas's daddy is not in the picture," she replied, then she moved on to telling of the cochlear implant surgery.

They spoke for almost an hour, and when there was nothing more to be said, Floyd thanked her and stood.

"If you want, I can take you back to meet Gabriel Hawke. He can tell you more about the school. He's the founder."

"Not now," Floyd replied. "I'll come back when I've got my granddaughter with me."

As he pulled out of the parking lot, Floyd realized he was no closer to knowing whether or not Dominic was the father, but he'd learned that Tracy was indeed a very good mother.

32

The Report

On Thursday, Floyd spent the morning preparing a report for Alice DeLuca. He felt none too good about it, seeing as how he'd spent twenty-two hours combing through records and talking to everyone who was willing to talk and still had nothing. At least nothing that would answer Alice's question.

He recapped the document findings and stated that while the time frame of Lucas's birth coincided with the period when her grandson and Tracy Briggs were living together, no paternal name was listed on the birth certificate. After he'd detailed the comments of the apartment neighbors, he went back to the previous paragraph and added another sentence saying it was possible that the absence of a father's name on the birth certificate may have been nothing more than an oversight.

Floyd prided himself on his ability to judge people effectively. After a two-minute conversation, he could say if a man was straight up or leaning to the shady side. It was part of being an investigator—anticipating a person's actions and knowing what to watch for—but this case stymied him. That gut feeling, the one that was almost always right, was telling him the boy was Dominic's son, but he couldn't come up with a shred of evidence to prove it.

He wanted to state Tracy Briggs appeared to be a concerned and loving mother, not the kind of woman who'd be living with one man and having an affair with another, but again that was his gut talking. It was fine to follow his gut instinct when he was working a case, but the final report had to be based on proven facts.

He concluded with a paragraph telling how Lucas was born deaf and currently attended the Hawke School for Deaf Children. Moments before he folded the report and slid it into an envelope, he added a single line telling of his conversation with Tracy.

"Outward appearances would indicate the child's mother is a responsible person who is devoted to the boy's well-being."

That night, Floyd tossed and turned, unable to sleep because the investigation was still on his mind. It was a relatively small case, one he'd spent a number of unbillable hours working. Plus, there were expenses he'd paid for out of his own pocket. He'd done all he could do and knew it would be best to simply set it aside, consider it over, and move on. But he couldn't.

He recalled the worn leather handles of Alice DeLuca's purse and the odd way she reminded him of his own mama.

It wasn't his job to have an opinion. His job was to uncover the facts and report his findings to the client. He had a reputation for being accurate, not speculative, and yet . . .

When morning finally came, he was up earlier than usual. He shaved, dressed, and went to the diner for breakfast. After two cups of coffee and a plate of scrambled eggs that sat there and grew cold, he pulled out his cell phone and called Alice DeLuca.

It was not yet seven o'clock, but she answered on the first ring.

"I hope I didn't wake you," he said.

"Not at all; I'm an early riser."

"I wanted to let you know I've sent a final report, and it will likely be in today's mail. The thing is," he said, "a report tells the findings but not my observations, so if you'd like to hear those—"

"Well, of course I would," Alice answered.

"Please understand, my intention is not to speak poorly about anyone," he said, "but since you're the lad's grandma and paying to know the truth, I feel you're entitled to my opinion."

"I appreciate that," she replied.

"Granted, there's no hard evidence proving Lucas is Dominic's child, but I have reason to believe he is. I know your grandson insists otherwise, so the only way for you to get proof positive would be with a DNA test."

Alice gasped. "DNA test? Like on those crime shows?"

"Yes."

"Dominic may have some less-than-honorable tendencies, but he's certainly not a criminal."

"I wasn't implying . . ." He hesitated a moment, then softened the thought by saying, "It's really nothing more than a paternity test. Nowadays, it's a fairly simple thing."

"I wouldn't feel right about it."

"It's the only way to prove paternity."

"No, it's not," Alice replied indignantly. "Why, given a mother's instinct, I should be able to tell whether or not he's my grandson's boy."

"But I thought you said—"

Alice cut him off. "It's not as I would wish it to be, but since there seems to be no other choice, I'll do what I have to do."

"And what exactly is that?" Floyd asked.

"Meet with Tracy Briggs." There was a momentary pause, then she added, "It will be uncomfortable perhaps, but if I can find a reason to call on her, she might let me see the boy. Once I can look into his face, I believe I'll know whether or not he's Dominic's child."

Floyd remembered his own mama's ability to tell when a person was lying and smiled. "I think you might be right," he said. "In fact, I'm certain of it."

He ended the call and asked the waitress for a fresh plate of eggs.

"It seems these have grown cold," he said.

For the remainder of the morning, Alice sat at the living room window, watching for the mailman. It was nearly eleven when she finally heard his truck rumbling down the road. By the time he reached her mailbox, she was standing there.

Normally, she would have stayed and chatted and passed the time of day, but not today. She thanked him, then took the mail and hurried back inside.

There were three pieces of mail, but her hands immediately went to the thick envelope with "Tompkins Investigative Services" printed in the upper left-hand corner. It was the report she'd been waiting for. She slit the envelope open and sat at the kitchen table to read.

It was pretty much a recap of what Floyd had told her, but she went through the items one by one. Nine residents of the building in Philadelphia figured Tracy to be a good mother. The neighbor across the hall knew for a fact Dominic had been caught with a blonde from the fifth floor but had no knowledge of Tracy ever having an affair. When she read how Lucas had been born deaf and now attended a special school, tears came to her eyes and blurred her vision.

After she'd read each page three times, she refolded the report, slid it back into the envelope, and tucked it away in the kitchen drawer where she kept spare keys and important papers.

She knew without a doubt what she had to do.

33

Alice DeLuca

You never want to believe the worst of your own child or grandchild, but there comes a time when the truth is staring you in the face and the only thing you can do is see it for what it is. I believe now is that time.

I only wish Joe would have allowed me to be firmer with Dorothy. Maybe things would have turned out differently. He had an excuse for every irresponsible thing she did. Either it was growing pains or learning to spread her wings or not the way they did things anymore. He didn't see that each time she got away with something, she became a bit more irresponsible and devil-may-care. She didn't just wake up one morning and decide to shuck off the responsibility of her child. It took years and years of not having to answer for her actions that led her to it.

It's too late for me to do anything about Dorothy, and maybe it's too late to do anything about Dominic, but it's not too late for that little boy. If he is Dominic's son, I've got to set things straight.

This cycle of irresponsibility has to stop somewhere.

No one ever said being a parent is easy. It's the hardest job in the world. There are no days off or vacation time; there's no such thing as being too busy or too sick. From the time the nurse lays that little baby in your arms until the day they bury you, that child is your responsibility.

Daddy DeLuca understood that, but Joe never did. And unfortunately, Dominic is more like Joe than I care to admit.

This afternoon, I'm going to go see Miss Tracy Briggs, and I don't plan to beat about the bush, either. I'll come right out and ask if her little boy is Dominic's son.

It's a yes-or-no question. If it's no, then it's no, and that's the end of it. If it's yes, then I'll have some heavy thinking to do. I've never met this girl, but if she's as good a person as Mr. Floyd Tompkins seems to believe, she'll be willing to hear an old woman out.

I'd like to pretend I'm not nervous about doing this, but the truth is I'm scared to death.

34

The Visit

Alice waited until Dominic left for work, then changed into the blue dress she wore for church. She pinned the matching hat in place, checked her reflection in the mirror, and then removed the hat. It somehow seemed too formal, intimidating perhaps.

She wanted this to be a friendly conversation, one in which both parties would feel free to speak their minds.

True, driving was a bit of a problem, but Alice was certain she could manage. After all, she'd driven that car for a number of years and knew everything there was to know about it. So what if it had sat idle for a while? Driving was driving, and it was not something a person forgot.

She'd considered asking Charlie to come along and handle the driving, but if Tracy Briggs slammed the door in her face, the embarrassment would be too overwhelming. No, this was something she had to do herself.

She tucked a spare hankie into her purse, nervously lifted the ring of keys from the peg where they'd hung for as long as she could remember, and started for the garage.

Once inside the car, she sat there for a full two minutes remembering the step-by-step process. Since she'd been ill, she was getting more forgetful, but driving was almost like walking. It was something you did without having to think about it.

She turned the key in the ignition, and the engine sputtered but didn't catch. She switched it off. There were other times when the car had refused to start, and she remembered having to pump a pedal a few times.

Is it the gas or the clutch?

Uncertain, she did both and tried again. This time the engine caught but clicked off seconds later. She slid her seat as far forward as it would go, pumped the pedals again, then tried for a third time. When the engine grumbled and came to life, a sense of relief washed over her, and she smiled. *I can do this.* She checked the rearview mirror a third time, inched back until she was clear of the garage, then pulled out onto the road.

The telephone book had a single listing for Briggs. Since G. Briggs was the only one in Magnolia Grove, she'd copied the address in large block letters, the kind she could see without her reading glasses. Starting out, she'd felt rather confident, but once she turned onto the main road that ran through town, her palms grew sweaty and she felt her heart thumping against her chest.

Talking to no one but herself, she said, "Nothing to be nervous about. I'll flat-out ask if the boy is Dominic's son, and if she says no, I'll turn right around and come home."

A small voice inside her head argued, *But what if she says yes?*

Following a route she hadn't driven for seven, maybe eight years, she made a left onto Lakeside and a mile later turned onto Baker Street. Going at the speed of a turtle, she drove along the street, checking the house numbers until she came to the Cape Cod with a brick walkway and freshly painted black shutters. She pulled to the curb and sat, taking it in. With impatiens overflowing the flower beds and a weathered swing hanging from the roof of the front porch, the house had a welcoming look. Hopefully that was the case.

Alice summoned her last ounce of courage, tucked her purse beneath her arm, opened the car door, and started toward the house. Her finger trembled as she pushed the doorbell and listened to it *bing-bong*.

A woman with streaks of silver in her hair answered. She looked a bit like the photograph in the newspaper but older. Too old for Dominic.

Alice tried to smile, but her face felt frozen. "Tracy Briggs?"

The woman laughed. "Heavens, no, I'm Tracy's mom. Did you want to talk with Tracy?"

Alice nodded and this time managed a feeble smile. "If it's no trouble."

"No trouble at all." Lila pulled the door back. "Come in, make yourself comfortable." She turned toward the back of the house and hollered, "Tracy! You've got a visitor."

Alice sat on the sofa. She placed her purse square in the middle of her lap, then decided such a position seemed rigid and too unyielding. She moved it to the floor alongside her feet. Her head was ducked down when Tracy entered the room.

"Hi, I'm Tracy. You wanted to see me?"

Alice's head jerked up, and she looked at Tracy. She looked younger than the picture. With her hair in a ponytail and jeans cuffed around her ankles, she could have passed for a schoolgirl.

Although she had planned to come right out and ask what she had to ask, Alice now felt the need to buy time, to talk to the girl and get to know her before she had a chance to say no. She introduced herself only as Alice and then, without leaving room for questions, moved ahead.

"There was an article in the *Barrington Post*, and I was so impressed by what you said that I wanted to meet you."

Tracy gave a lighthearted laugh. "I just spoke about what the school has done for my son. The one you should be impressed with is Gabriel Hawke. He's the founder of the school."

She went on to say that the school had helped thousands of children with the most severe hearing problems.

"I only got involved because of Lucas; he was born deaf."

"Yes, the article mentioned that. How terribly sad."

"It *was* sad. Actually, it was pretty traumatic. I didn't realize Lucas couldn't hear until he was fifteen months old." Tracy's voice turned solemn. "Just remembering the ordeal we went through gives me the shivers. It was the scariest time of my life."

Her face softened. "I would have never made it through all of that if it weren't for my sister, Meghan. She's the one who discovered Lucas couldn't hear." Tracy gave a lopsided grin. "Well, Meghan and Sox together. Sox is her dog."

"Oh my." Alice chuckled. "A dog?"

Tracy nodded. "Yes. Meghan noticed that when the dog was behind Lucas and barked, there was no response, but when he could see the dog barking, he'd react like it was the best thing ever. Right away, she suspected Lucas had a hearing problem."

The conversation went back and forth as Tracy told about the months of testing and then waiting to see if the cochlear implant would be successful.

"You said you were interested in the school," Tracy said. "Do you have a deaf child in your family?"

"There's a possibility . . ." Alice hesitated, thinking she would use that moment to say she was Dominic's grandmother and that Lucas was quite possibly her great-grandson, but she was interrupted when the boy came running into the room.

"Mama, mama!" He opened his small hand and held out the broken shell of a robin's egg. "Burr baby!" he said proudly.

"Yes, it's the shell of a baby bird," Tracy replied, carefully pronouncing every syllable. "But, Lucas, don't you see we have company?"

He glanced at Alice, then gave a sheepish nod.

"Don't you think you should say hello to Miss Alice?"

He gave another shy nod and backed in closer to Tracy.

"Hello, Miss Awice."

Alice's heart melted. One look at the boy's face told her everything she needed to know. She thought back on Daddy DeLuca's soft brown eyes and smile; this boy was the spitting image of the father-in-law she'd loved. There would be no more wondering, no more guessing; Lucas was indeed her great-grandson. If she could bottle a single moment of her life and hold on to it forever, it would be this one.

"Hello to you too, Lucas," she said. "Your mama has been telling me that you go to a special school where you learn all kinds of wonderful things."

He took a single step forward and held out his open palm with the piece of blue eggshell. "Baby burr."

"It's the shell, but where's the baby bird?"

Lucas thought for a moment, then raised his index finger and pointed upward. "Burr in sky!"

Alice clapped her hands with delight. "That's absolutely right! Your mama is very lucky to have such a smart little boy."

"Do you have a wittle boy?"

Alice laughed. "I'm much too old to have a little boy. Years ago, when I was younger than your mama is now, I had a little girl. Her name was Dorothy."

"Does Dowothy go to school?"

"She did, but now she's all grown up with a boy of her own."

"What's his name?"

Alice lifted her eyes and looked at Tracy. "Dominic."

In less than a heartbeat, Tracy's expression grew icy cold. Keeping her voice level, she turned to Lucas.

"I think Grandma has some cookies in the kitchen. Tell her I said to give you cookies and milk."

Without a moment's hesitation Lucas dashed off, hollering, "Gwandma, Gwandma!"

As soon as he was out of earshot, Tracy looked across the room with a frosty glare. "Why are you here?"

Alice could no longer look Tracy in the eye. She lowered her face, looked down at her lap, and mumbled, "I'm sorry. I didn't mean for it to be this way. I was going to ask right off, but then—"

"Ask what?"

Alice raised her chin and in the humblest voice imaginable replied, "If Lucas is Dominic's child."

"You know he is; otherwise you wouldn't be here."

"You're wrong."

"Wrong? Wrong about what?"

With her eyes again turned to her lap, Alice nervously fingered the gold band she wore.

"I'm ashamed to say this, ashamed my grandson would do this to both you and me. God knows I would have rejoiced at the thought of a great-grandson, but Dominic told me he wasn't Lucas's father."

"He's a liar!" Tracy snapped. "He lies about everything. But this is the lowest he's ever—"

"I agree."

Tracy's eyes widened. "You agree?"

Alice gave a sorrowful nod. "Dominic takes after his granddaddy, which isn't necessarily a good thing."

She told Tracy the whole story, starting with how Dorothy had left Dominic in her care, then vanished into nothingness, and circled back to how much respect she had for Daddy DeLuca.

"I'd always hoped Dominic would take after Daddy DeLuca, who was his namesake, but he didn't."

Tracy's expression softened as she listened to Alice tell of heartache and dashed hopes.

"I'm sorry about everything you've gone through," she said, "but I don't see what Lucas or I can do."

"I'm an old woman riddled with cancer. I've got a few months left, maybe less. The only thing I want is to go to my grave knowing the last of Daddy DeLuca's line is being cared for properly."

The start of a smile tugged at Tracy's mouth. "I think that's pretty obvious."

Allowing herself to relax a bit, Alice nodded. "Yes, it is." She hesitated, then said, "If it isn't asking too much, I'd like to visit with Lucas a time or two."

Noting the apprehensive look settling on Tracy's face, she added, "And with you, also."

"I don't know if that's such a good idea. Lucas and I have a different life now, and Dominic's not a part of it."

"I'm not asking for Dominic to come," Alice pleaded. "Just me."

The look of apprehension was still there but softening at the edges.

"Lucas wouldn't have to know I'm his grandma or anything like that. We could just all have lunch together or maybe meet at the park."

Giving in a bit, Tracy said, "You have to promise that Dominic wouldn't be around. I don't want him anywhere near Lucas. He gave up that right when . . ."

She shook off the bitter memories and let the rest of the thought drift away.

Alice caught the implication. She gave a mournful sigh and said, "It must have been something terrible."

"It was," Tracy said, then one word led to another, and before the clock chimed again, she'd told Alice the whole story of why she'd left Philadelphia and how Dominic then cut her and Lucas from his health plan.

"He knew I needed to take Lucas to the doctor, but he didn't care. Getting even with me was more important than taking care of our son."

When she finished telling the story, Tracy seemed to sit taller in the chair, her back straighter, her shoulders less rounded. It was as if the weight she'd been carrying around all these years had suddenly been lifted. She looked across and saw Alice's sorrowful expression.

"I'm sorry. I shouldn't have told you about all that; I mean, you *are* Dominic's grandma."

"Don't be sorry. It's better I know. As I said, Dominic takes after his granddaddy. Joe might've done something like that, but Daddy DeLuca never would have. I only wish Lucas could have known Daddy DeLuca; at least he would have had one relative to be proud of."

Alice fumbled in her purse for a moment, then pulled out an old photograph and passed it to Tracy. "That's Daddy DeLuca when he was a young man. If you want, you can keep that picture and maybe someday give it to Lucas."

Tracy looked at the photo and smiled. "He's got wide-set eyes like Lucas."

Alice nodded. "Joe and Dominic both have those hooded eyes, the kind that make you think—"

"They're up to no good," Tracy cut in and laughed.

After they'd talked for almost an hour, Tracy invited Alice to join her and Lila for a cup of coffee and cake.

"Right now?" Alice asked eagerly.

Tracy nodded. "Mama makes the best carrot cake you've ever tasted."

As they headed for the kitchen, Alice walked with a bit of bounce in her step, the cane dangling loose in her hand.

35

Tracy Briggs

Without a doubt, this has been the weirdest day ever. The whole time Dominic and I were together, he never once mentioned that his grandma was living here in Magnolia Grove. All he ever talked about was how his mama dropped him off and then disappeared. Sure, that's a terrible thing to have happen, but living with a woman like Alice couldn't have been so awful. The truth is Dominic had a way of taking something good and making it seem bad. That's obvious when you think about how he acted with Lucas.

I understand people can fall in and out of love, but your child is your child, and you don't stop loving them just because you stopped loving your partner. I almost said "wife," because at the time I felt like we were husband and wife. At first, even Dominic acted like that's how it was. He used to say the only reason we weren't married was because relationships went from true love to boring responsibility once a couple tied the knot. He kept mentioning Brad and Angelina to prove his point.

Of course, we all know how they turned out.

Now that I think about it, maybe it's a good thing we didn't get married. I'm glad Dominic's out of my life and Lucas's. He's not good for either of us.

When Alice DeLuca walked in, I thought she was just a sweet old lady looking for a cause to help out. A lot of older people do that. They volunteer to sit at the reception desk, answer phones, or stuff envelopes. Alice is sweet as all get out, but when I saw how frail she was, I wasn't sure how much volunteering she could do.

Then she said she was Dominic's grandma, and it knocked me for a loop. My first thought was to tell her she needed to leave, but I'm glad I didn't. She's got a good heart, and I guess she can't help what Dominic did any more than I could.

The truth is I started liking her after she told me about Daddy DeLuca, and when she gave me that picture for Lucas, my heart kind of melted. I could tell the picture meant a lot to her, and the fact that she was willing to give it up let me know she was nothing like Dominic.

I like the idea that Lucas has a relative with a kind heart, even if he is three generations back. If Lucas grows up to be a mix of my daddy and Daddy DeLuca, I'll be pretty proud.

She's coming back to visit with Lucas again, and I think I'll tell him that she's a grandma on his daddy's side. He's probably too little to understand family relationships, but I think he'll enjoy having another grandma, even if it's only for a little while.

36

The Best of Times

Some people say summertime in Georgia is way too hot. They claim if you step out onto the sidewalk in the noonday sun, your shoes will melt and your brain will sizzle like a fried egg.

The summer that followed Alice's meeting with Tracy was different. It was as if all good fates had come together to make it the best summer ever. As July turned into August, the mornings started off cool and temperatures topped out in the low eighties. At night you could throw open your windows and sleep comfortably without air conditioning. The townspeople of Magnolia Grove went about their business happily nodding to one another and expressing a hope that this weather would hold through September, which, with its deluge of rainstorms, tended to be the worst month of the year.

Alice came to visit throughout the summer. On her second visit, Tracy explained the relationship to Lucas.

"Alice is your daddy's grandma, so that makes her your grandma, too," she said. "Aren't you a lucky little boy to have two grandmas?"

Looking a bit confused, Lucas peered over at Alice and gave a shy smile.

Tracy pushed him forward with an encouraging nudge. "If you want to, you can give your new grandma a hug."

He turned and looked up. "Weally?"

Tracy nodded. "Yes, really."

Lucas made his way across the room with trepidation, his eyes turned to the floor until he stood directly in front of Alice, then he looked up.

"Awe you weally my gwandma?"

The wrinkles on Alice's face seemed to disappear as she broke into a smile. "I'd like to be, if you'll have me."

He nodded. "Okay, I have you." He cautiously hugged her waist, then ran back to Tracy. "Mama!" he said excitedly. "Miss Awice is weally my gwandma!"

Before Alice left that afternoon, he'd taken to calling her "Grammy," which was what Tracy suggested.

Although Lucas couldn't remember a daddy, he was nonetheless happy to have a second grandma fussing over him.

Alice came at least once a week, and she often brought small gifts: a toy truck, a book, or board games such as Zingo and Ladybug where she would sit for hours playing with Lucas.

After a few weeks, Alice was like a member of the family. Lila welcomed her visits and set aside whatever she was doing to join in the spirited conversations. On those afternoons, Tracy forgot about the *Snip 'n Save* work waiting to be done and joined in as the women gathered at the table with a freshly baked cake and a pot of coffee.

There was always something to talk about. Alice told tales that had been handed down for decades, and Lila talked of when the girls were babies. There were stories Tracy could have told, stories of things that had happened in Philadelphia or of the long drive back to Georgia in the dark of night, but she kept those things in the past and spoke only of how Lucas was growing and learning.

Dominic's name was seldom mentioned, and even on those few occasions, it was in the context of something else. One afternoon when his name came up, Alice mentioned that he was back in town.

"He's living with me," she said, "and working at the Texaco station over near the highway."

"Oh?" Tracy took a moment before carving off a piece of fudge ripple cake and handing it to Alice. "Well, I hope he's better behaved than he was when he was living with me."

Alice gave a regretful-looking half smile. "He's not," she said and forked off a piece of cake.

That was the end of the discussion. Tracy seemingly had no interest in seeing or hearing from Dominic. Although Alice wished it were different, she accepted the way it was and never told Dominic that she'd met Tracy and was growing ever closer to Lucas.

She did mention it to Charlie one morning when they were having breakfast together. She scooped a spoonful of sugar into her cup and said, "If Dominic saw what a lovely child Lucas is, I believe he'd be more willing to step up to his responsibilities."

Charlie looked across the table, wide-eyed. "You're not planning to say something to him, are you?"

"Well, not unless I discussed it with Tracy first."

"That's not a good idea," Charlie warned. "Dominic knowing you're friends with her might open up a whole new can of worms."

"I don't see why."

"You can't trust what he'll do. If he gets riled up and goes over there, carrying on like a crazy man, Tracy might not want you coming back."

With that thought in mind, Alice decided to leave things as they were.

Happy to be free of the arguments, Dominic didn't question the long afternoons she was gone from the house. When he crawled out of bed, he always found a casserole dish ready for the microwave or a sandwich wrapped in tinfoil on the kitchen table. As far as he was concerned, that was just fine.

37

Cherished Moments

In early August, the pain in Alice's back grew worse. One morning, as they sat at the kitchen table having coffee, she reminded Charlie she had an appointment with Dr. Willoughby later that week.

"I know," he said, "I've got it marked on my calendar."

She fumbled with her spoon for a moment, then asked, "You think maybe this time you could come in with me, instead of staying in the waiting room?"

Charlie suddenly lost interest in the muffin he was about to bite into and looked up. "Is there something you're not telling me?"

She shook her head. "Not really, but it gives me a great deal of comfort to have you beside me."

Alice suspected that this visit would bring bad news. She'd felt it in the way her limbs had grown heavy and breathing more labored. Her back ached from morning to night, and, when the spasms came, it felt as though her body were being torn apart. Twice when Lucas wanted to toss the ball back and forth, she'd had to stop. Even though she was sitting on the sofa, lifting her arm was more than she could bear.

Charlie reached across the table and covered her hand with his. "Of course I will," he replied. "We'll make it a nice day. After the doctor, we'll have lunch at the Copper Kettle, and then I'll drive you over to the Briggses' house so you can visit with Lucas for a while."

The bond between Alice and Charlie was such that she knew without asking he'd understood, and he'd responded just as he always did—by giving her more than she'd asked for.

Alice smiled. "I'm lucky to have a friend like you, Charlie. I don't know what I'd do without you."

He laughed, then turned his head and coughed. Alice had seen him cough that way before. It happened when an emotional thought got stuck in his throat and words refused to come.

Dr. Willoughby studied the X-ray, his expression solemn and drawn. "The mass is considerably larger," he said. "Are you experiencing increased pain in your back?"

She nodded.

He came around to where she was sitting and felt along her rib cage, his touch light as a feather. "What about here?"

She winced and gave another nod.

"Not good." Dr. Willoughby's jowly face wrinkled itself into a map of discouragement. "You're stage four, Alice, metastatic. The tumor has become aggressive, and, with this accelerated rate of growth, I'd say the most you've got is two, maybe three months."

"Three months?" Charlie gasped. "Isn't there something you can do?"

"Three months at the outside, Charlie," Dr. Willoughby said. "It's likely to be less." He looked between them, sorrow in his eyes. "At this point, there is nothing we can do to slow the growth." He looked over at Alice. "The thing we've got to be concerned with is keeping you comfortable and pain-free. I can increase the dosage on your meds, but if that doesn't do it"—he gave a hopeless-looking shrug—"then we'll have to look at using morphine."

"No morphine," Alice replied, "not yet."

"It's important for us to keep you pain-free."

"With so little time, it's more important that I spend every possible moment cogent and with my great-grandson."

When they left the doctor's office, Charlie walked at the same slow pace as Alice. Although his arm was snug around her waist, he had the look of a man who'd been run over by a truck.

"I thought we'd have more time," he said. "You told me the cancer was back, but you never mentioned—"

"I didn't want to worry you," she cut in.

"Worry me? Hell's fire, Alice, I never stop worrying about you! I want to be there with you at your house, see you're comfortable and taken care of. I don't need to sleep in your bed, but let me come and live there so I can—"

She touched her hand to his arm and shook her head. "You know that's not possible. Seeing you there all the time would upset Dominic. He's already worried enough."

"Not all that worried," Charlie said. "Instead of being home to look after you, he's out carousing every night."

"He's young," Alice reasoned. "We sometimes forget what it's like to be young and want to do things, go places, and take life by the horns."

Charlie gave a huff of irritation. "I know what it's like to care about someone, be concerned for their well-being, and want to watch over them." He took her hand in his and gave it a gentle squeeze. "I could move the recliner into your bedroom and sleep there. I don't see how that could upset anybody."

"You sleeping in my room." Alice chuckled. "Now what kind of an example would that set for Dominic if I up and did what I've chastised him for doing?"

"It's not the same thing at all," Charlie argued, but Alice shook her head and turned away.

Charlie planned to wait in the car, listening to the radio, but once Lila heard he was out there, she called him to join them. They gathered around the table, and Lila brought out a buttery pound cake.

"I've been saving this for just such an occasion," she said.

Charlie laughed. "I don't see my being here as much of an occasion."

"That's where you're wrong," Lila argued. "Having guests at the table is definitely an occasion to be celebrated." She scooped a ball of ice cream, set it atop a slice of butter cake, and passed it to Charlie. "For food to be pleasurable, it needs to be shared with friends. There's very little joy in sitting down to a solitary meal."

Alice gave a weary smile and bobbed her head in agreement.

After they'd been talking for a few minutes, they happened upon the subject of Meghan and the *Snip 'n Save*.

"Oh, Alice, you have got to meet Tracy's sister," Lila said and grabbed the phone. Before anyone could protest, she'd dialed the veterinary office and asked Meghan to take an hour off and come by for coffee.

"Right now?"

"Yes, now. I'm serving that butter cake you love."

"I wish I could, but I've got appointments all afternoon."

"Alice DeLuca is here with her friend," Lila said. "I thought it would be nice if you could meet them."

"I'd love to, Mama. I just can't do it today. Why don't you plan something for Sunday, then Tom and I can both be there."

A broad smile swept across Lila's face, and she turned to Alice. "Are you and Charlie available for Sunday dinner?"

Alice glanced over at Charlie. "Are we?"

He nodded. "As long as you're sure you feel up to it."

"Sunday would be fine," Alice replied.

"Then Sunday it is," Lila said happily.

That afternoon, Alice never even tasted the butter cake. She broke off a piece and pushed it from one side of her plate to the other while everyone else ate. Once the plates were emptied, she caught Charlie's eye and gave a nod indicating it was time to go.

He stood quickly and hurried around to help her out of the chair.

When they left the Briggses' house, Alice clung to Charlie's arm as she turned and gave one last wave goodbye.

On the drive home, he reached across the seat and covered her hand with his. "Was coming over here to visit the boy too much for you?" he asked. "If you're not up to Sunday dinner, I'll call and say we can't make it."

She turned to him, a tear cresting in her eye. "I'd never do that. No matter how bad the pain is, it's still less than the heartache of wasting one of the few precious days I have left."

Charlie's jaw stiffened, and he leaned into the steering wheel, coughing as if he again had something stuck in his throat.

38

Sunday Dinner

That Sunday, when they all gathered at the table, Lila was smiling.

"Food and family," she said. "This is the best of life."

Everyone at the table agreed. Only Tracy noticed the sorrowful way Alice twisted the gold band on her finger.

Tracy lifted her glass and said, "I'd like to propose a toast to the newest members of our family, Grammy Alice and Uncle Charlie."

Alice smiled, and her eyes grew watery. "You can't imagine how much it means to have you consider me part of your family. I can't even begin to thank you."

"Me too," Charlie said, but with less sentimentality attached to the words. He reached across, gave Alice's knee an affectionate squeeze, and then asked Lila to pass the mashed potatoes. Moments later the conversations started, with shared thoughts and comments crisscrossing the table.

Tom spoke of how the veterinary clinic had nearly doubled its client base and was rapidly outgrowing the building.

"We're either going to have to build an addition or find another spot, and it's all because of Meghan," he said. "Her way with animals is an absolute gift. Walt Kerrigan's bulldog will bite a man's hand off, but he's like a lamb with her."

Meghan laughed. "If you keep talking like that, I'll have to ask for a raise."

"I think both of these girls have a gift," Gabriel said. "Tracy's like that with the kids at the school. Last week, when one of the counselors called in sick, she stepped in and took over the class without even thinking about it."

"It's not a gift," Tracy replied laughingly. "It's all the years of sitting in on Lucas's classes and spending time at the school. If you listen long enough, you're bound to pick up things. When I was teaching that class, Bobby Feldman . . ."

Once she started talking, Tracy went on for a good length of time without noticing the look of agitation on her sister's face.

Finally Meghan asked, "What about the *Snip 'n Save*? Doesn't that keep you rather busy?"

When Tracy caught the sarcastic tone of Meghan's question, it rubbed her the wrong way. "Of course it does," she replied curtly, "but I'm managing."

"Barely managing or managing fine? You let the ads pile up before and—"

"They aren't *piled up*! Some haven't been done yet, but—"

"How many is some?" Meghan challenged.

Lila quickly jumped in. "Enough about work," she said. "I'm thinking that after dinner we could play a game of charades. Who's up for it?"

Alice chuckled. "In all my years, I don't know that I've ever played a game of charades."

"Well, then, I guess it's long overdue," Lila said and began suggesting teams.

Once the table was cleared, they settled in the living room, and the game got underway. Alice said she'd be the timekeeper, seeing as how it was difficult for her to continually sit and stand. They played with Tracy, Gabriel, and Charlie on one team and Lila, Meghan, and Tom on the other. When Charlie had to act out the movie *One Flew Over the Cuckoo's Nest*, Alice nearly split her sides laughing.

That was the first of five such dinners they had that summer.

Before the month was out, Tracy noticed how Alice had begun to lean heavier on her cane and held tight to Charlie's arm as she rose from the chair or walked across the room. By the time August gave way to September, Alice's visits became less frequent. Some days she'd call and say she wasn't going to be able to make it over. When she did come, there was no more tossing the ball to Lucas; instead she'd suggest they play a board game where she could sit in the padded chair and move only her wrist and fingers. Twice she was unable to do even that. She simply sat in the chair and listened as Lucas told of what he'd done in school.

39

Top of the World

In mid-September, when the evenings took on a chill and people began to hang harvest wreaths on their front doors, Gabriel took Tracy to lunch at the café. They were crossing over on the corner of Hamilton Street when she spotted a colorful sign in the front window of the dry cleaner and came to a dead stop.

"Oh, look! The fair will be in Barrington this weekend!" She eyed the poster with its jugglers and acrobats and, in the background, a Ferris wheel that towered above everything else, then turned to Gabriel. "Have you ever been to the county fair?"

He hesitated for a moment, then shook his head. "Afraid not."

"You'd love it! The year I graduated high school, Daddy took Meghan, Mama, and me, and we all talked about what a good time we had for months afterward."

Gabriel eyed the poster for a moment, then asked, "Would you like to go this weekend?"

"I'd love to." She turned to him, her eyes alight and a broad smile stretched across her face. "And I think Lucas would be thrilled to pieces."

"Then it's a date. We'll make a weekend of it. The fair on Saturday and maybe a visit to the pumpkin farm on Sunday."

Throughout lunch and for the remainder of the afternoon, the fair was all Tracy thought about. Later that night, as she climbed into bed and clicked off the lamp, she pictured the day as it had been all those years ago: the music along the midway, the games of chance, the cotton candy, and, most of all, the Ferris wheel—a small carriage high atop everything else, her mama sitting next to her, Meghan and her daddy just across.

"This is the top of the world," her daddy had said. "From here you can look out and see the future that lies ahead."

That night Meghan had sworn she'd seen the lights of the *Richmond Times-Dispatch* twinkling in the distance and had known for sure she was going to be a journalist. Mama had said she didn't need to look outside because she could see the whole of her future right there in the carriage. But Tracy had wanted to see, so she'd leaned toward the open window just as a gust of wind blew by. A speck of cinder had landed in her eye, and she'd seen nothing but the blur of watery tears. By the time she'd blinked the speck away, the carriage was back at the bottom of the wheel.

This time it will be different, she promised herself as she drifted off to sleep.

——— ❧❧❧ ———

That Saturday morning, Tracy woke to the sound of raindrops pinging against the bedroom window. She opened one eye, saw the water cascading off the roof, and groaned.

"Of all days . . . ," she grumbled.

Hopeful it would soon stop, she washed her face, dressed, and then joined Lila and Lucas for breakfast. As she sat there nursing a second cup of coffee, the rain continued. By eleven, she was almost certain the fair would be a washout. She dialed Gabriel's number.

"I think we'd better scrap plans for the fair," she said. "It's pouring."

"The weatherman said it's supposed to stop this afternoon."

"I doubt—"

"Why don't you come anyway," he suggested. "Leave Lucas at home with your mama, and we'll have a date night. If it doesn't stop raining, we'll go somewhere special for dinner."

Tracy had been looking forward to the fair all week, but there wasn't much anyone could do about the weather, and a date night was a good alternative. "Hold on," she said. "Let me check if Mama's okay with watching Lucas."

Seconds later she was back. "Mama's good with it," she said, "so I'll finish up a few things I have to do for the *Snip 'n Save* and drive over later this afternoon."

After emailing Sheldon the three ads that were already past due, Tracy showered and started to pack. The gabardine slacks she'd planned to wear to the fair were hanging on the door. She packed them, then at the last minute, turned back and folded a black dress into the bag.

At three o'clock when she left the house, it was still raining. The traffic was slow, and with a fender bender on Grant Street, the drive to Barrington turned out to be twice as long as usual. When she pulled up in front of the apartment building, Gabriel was standing in the doorway with his big black umbrella. As she eased her mama's Ford into the parking spot, he hurried out.

"I didn't want you to get wet." Holding the umbrella overhead, he bent to kiss her before she was out of the car.

"Too bad about the weather," she said. "I was really looking forward to the fair."

He gave a nod of agreement. "So was I. The forecast still says it's going to clear, but I went ahead and made dinner reservations at Le'Abeille."

Tracy stood and gave him a crooked grin. "Good thing I brought a dress." She retrieved her bag from the back seat. "I've heard great things about that restaurant, but isn't it kind of far to drive in all this rain?"

"It's a forty-five-minute drive, but I think you'll enjoy the place. It's beautiful, and the food is supposed to be spectacular."

"Sounds wonderful. This could turn out to be a great weekend after all."

Gabriel slung her bag over his shoulder, then kissed her nose. "That's what I'm hoping."

Huddled together under the umbrella, they made a dash for the building.

The reservation was for six o'clock, so Tracy changed into her dress and freshened her makeup. Then they were off.

Rumored to be as good as Atlanta's Le Bilboquet, the restaurant was everything Tracy expected and more. The tables, dressed in white cloths, were decorated with candle globes, gold-trimmed china, and sparkling crystal. There was the sound of a violin, and muffled conversation.

Tracy gave a whispered sigh. "Beautiful."

Hand in hand, they followed the maître d' back to a table tucked into a romantic alcove; the maître d' then stopped, slid the burgundy velvet chair back from the table, looked at Tracy, and said, "Madame."

As Tracy sat, Gabriel shook hands with him and said, "Thank you, Henri. We were hoping to take in the fair tonight, so if the rain stops, please let me know."

"Most certainly, monsieur."

As soon as Henri was beyond hearing distance, Tracy said, "You know him?"

Gabriel gave a sheepish grin and shrugged. "I knew you were really disappointed about the fair, so I tried to pick someplace special. I drove over this afternoon to check it out, and Henri let me reserve this table."

The thought of Gabriel going to such trouble to plan a date night made it all the more special. Tracy planted a kiss on the tip of her finger, then reached across and transferred it to his cheek. "Thank you," she said in a breathy whisper.

Moments later, a bottle of pinot noir was delivered to the table, and they toasted. As they sat and talked, she told the story of how at the top of the Ferris wheel she'd gotten a cinder in her eye and had never seen her "forever." "I doubt Daddy's tale was true anyway," she said and laughed. "Meghan swore she saw the *Richmond Times-Dispatch*, but she didn't become a journalist after all."

Gabriel smiled. "Since we didn't know each other then, I'm sort of glad you didn't see your future, because it might not have included me."

He stretched his arm across the table and took her hand in his. As they talked about first one thing and then another, the waiters came and went like silent shadows. They were there when you needed them, invisible when you didn't. They refilled the wine glasses, delivered a platter of Chateaubriand, and disappeared.

Partway through the meal, Henri came by and said the rain had stopped.

As they left the restaurant, Tracy felt a chill in the air. A slight breeze had come up and puddles were scattered about, but the streets were mostly dry.

Gabriel wrapped his arm around her shoulders, then glanced at his watch. "If you're not too cold, it's early and the fairground is only a ten-minute drive; we can still go if you'd like."

A grin brightened Tracy's face. "Absolutely!"

When they arrived at the fairground, Gabriel parked the car, and they headed for the south-side entrance. As they neared the ticket booth, she heard the calliope music from the carousel. It was not a tune she could identify but one that she somehow remembered.

"I love this," she said with a shiver of excitement. "I only wish Lucas were here."

"Next year," Gabriel promised as he wrapped his arm around her waist. "Next year we'll come again and bring Lucas with us."

"That would be nice," she said and snuggled a bit closer.

They walked up one aisle and down the other, listening to the happy sound of country music coming from the bandstand, sniffing the sweetness of roasted corn and caramel apples, catching bits of laughter from riders on the Tilt-A-Whirl and shrill screams from the House of Horrors.

At the Gypsy Fortune Teller machine, Tracy dropped four quarters into the coin slot, then placed her hand on the palm reader. The machine whirred as the gypsy's head bobbed up and down and her eyes blinked. When she came to a stop, a card popped out of the machine. Tracy picked it up and read.

"There is trouble ahead, but you will soon be in a place of happiness."

A look of apprehension tugged at her face. *Trouble ahead?* She studied the card for a moment, then, concerned that such a warning might justify a second glance later on, she tucked it in her pocket and walked off arm in arm with Gabriel.

As they passed by the milk-bottle-game booth with its rows of stuffed toys on display, the carnie behind the counter tossed a baseball to Gabriel.

"Try your luck," he called out. "Five balls, five bucks. Clearing the deck gets winner's choice."

Gabriel eyed the pyramid of bottles. "Looks pretty easy. And Lucas might like one of those teddy bears."

Tracy grinned. "I'm sure he would."

Pulling a five-dollar bill from his pocket, Gabriel stepped to the counter and took aim. Twice there was a wind-up and a pitch, and after the second ball, two bottles toppled over. On the fifth ball, the bottle on the right side wobbled but remained upright.

"Try again!" the carnie hollered. "Can't let that pretty missus go home without a prize."

Gabriel laughed and plunked down another five-dollar bill. With the second ball, he cleared all but that same right-side bottle. Again it wobbled but didn't topple. The third and fourth ball breezed by and did nothing. The fifth ball hit the remaining bottle dead on, and down it went.

Tracy clapped, then squeezed Gabriel's arm as she excitedly pointed to the floppy brown dog. "Lucas would love that!"

Strolling past the stretched-out row of game booths, they started down the midway. There at the end was the giant Ferris wheel, outlined in what seemed to be a million twinkling lights and towering over everything.

Tracy looked up. "It's just as I remembered!" she exclaimed with delight.

A handful of people waited at the entrance as the wheel slowly moved from one carriage to the next, stopping at the platform long enough for the car to empty out and new riders to climb in. Once the people were seated, the door clicked shut, and the next carriage moved up to the platform.

Gabriel steered Tracy into the line, then said, "Wait here; I'll get the tickets." He disappeared behind the throng of people coming off the ride. For a moment, she saw him talking to the operator, then lost sight of him again.

The wheel moved to the next carriage, and the group in front of her stepped onto the platform. Fearing he wouldn't make it back in time, Tracy was about to step out of the line when he returned. Moments later, they climbed into a carriage and sat side by side. Instead of stopping for the carriage behind them, the wheel kept moving.

As they rose higher and higher, a galaxy of stars surrounded them, and moments before the sky exploded into bursts of sparkling light, Tracy leaned toward the window, hoping to see what she'd missed all those years ago.

Gabriel touched his hand to her shoulder and said, "I think you can see the future clearer if you look this way."

Tracy turned and saw the blue velvet box in his hand. He thumbed it open and in the center was a sparkling diamond ring.

"I'd like to be your 'forever,'" he said, and offered out the ring. "I love you more than anything else in the world, Tracy. If you'll marry me, I swear I'll spend the rest of my life trying to make you happy."

A sigh floated up from her heart and her eyes sparkled brighter than all the stars above and the lights below as she answered. "You don't have to try, you've already made me happier than I ever imagined possible."

When he slid the ring on her finger, they were at the topmost point of the Ferris wheel, and the carriage was rocking gently in the breeze. As he folded her into his arms and covered her mouth with his, the sky exploded into sparkling bursts of light.

"Oh, Gabriel," she gasped. "This is magical! I've never seen anything so beautiful!"

He smiled. "I'm looking at something far more beautiful right now," he said, then kissed her again.

——— ❧❧ ———

Later on, after they'd left the Ferris wheel and started for the parking lot, Tracy pulled the gypsy's card from her pocket and tossed it into a garbage can.

"Trouble ahead?" she said laughingly. "No way!"

40

Lessons of Love

A week later, Alice and Charlie came for Sunday dinner. Charlie held tight to Alice's arm; he eased her into the club chair, then brought a straight chair from the dining room, placed it beside her, and sat by her, his hand holding hers. Opposite them, Tracy and Gabriel were together on the sofa.

Before Tracy spoke, Alice knew—maybe not knew but certainly suspected—it would happen. She'd seen the way they looked at one another. Although it would not be what she'd wished for, it would be as it should be. Life had taught her that a forced love is not always a true love. The only true love is the one your heart leads you to. She glanced down at the calloused hand cradling hers, then smiled and settled back into the chair.

Tracy made the announcement a short while later. Gabriel sat beside her, his arm draped across her shoulders and leaning in so close they seemed inseparable. "Gabriel and I are getting married," she said, then stopped and looked at Alice. "I know you're Dominic's grandma, but all the same, I hope you can find it in your heart to be happy for us."

"Of course I can." Alice gave the brightest smile she could muster, then said, "Now come on over here and let me give you a hug."

When Tracy knelt beside the chair, Alice stroked her cheek. "You chose wisely," she said. "A man like Gabriel will be the rock you and Lucas can build your lives on."

Although the pain in her back was more powerful than the blow of an ax striking a centuries-old oak, Alice leaned forward and kissed Tracy's cheek.

Later on, after the dinner dishes were cleared away, Lila served the frosted cake she'd made to celebrate the engagement. Although Tracy said they hadn't yet begun making plans, there was talk of a winter wedding.

"Best cake I've ever tasted," Charlie said.

Alice nodded her agreement even though she'd eaten only a few tiny bites. She pushed the remainder onto Charlie's plate.

In time, the conversation moved on to other things. Tracy spoke of how Miss Margaret had given Lucas a gold star for sharing his book with another child.

Lucas beamed. "Miss Magwhet said I am a good fwiend."

"It's so much fun watching the kids play together," Tracy said. "That's one of the reasons I love helping out at the school."

Meghan let the comment slide by without saying anything.

Alice gave a sigh and a fragile smile. "I envy you. I'd give anything to see Lucas in one of his classes."

"Why don't you come and visit the school?" Gabriel suggested. "You can sit in on Lucas's class, and I'll give you the grand tour."

"That sounds wonderful, but I doubt I could handle so much walking."

"You won't have to; we've got a wheelchair. Once you get out of the car, you can just sit back and enjoy the ride."

The look on Alice's face indicated she was thinking it over. "How far . . ."

Before she could finish the thought, Charlie gave her hand a squeeze. "I'll take you no matter how far it is."

She smiled at Charlie, then turned to Gabriel with a broad grin. "Well, then, I guess it's settled. We'd love to take you up on your kind offer."

Lucas jumped down from his chair and circled the table. Standing next to Alice's chair, he hugged her waist. "Gwammy, you can see Miss Magwhet."

Alice smiled like it was Christmas. "Indeed I can, Lucas, and see her I shall."

The following week, Alice and Charlie visited the school. True to his word, Gabriel met them at the car with a wheelchair, then led them across the parking lot and up the ramp.

"Tracy's helping out in one of the classrooms," he said, "but she'll join us for lunch."

When they arrived at Margaret Pringle's room, the class had just begun. Gabriel pushed the door open, and Charlie rolled the wheelchair into the room.

"Gwammy!" Lucas shouted and bolted from his seat.

"I'll be back when class is over." Gabriel squeezed Alice's shoulder, then disappeared out the door.

Few things rattled Margaret Pringle, and having visitors in the classroom was not on the list.

"Lucas, would you like to introduce your grandparents to the class?" she asked.

Lucas nodded happily, then proceeded to introduce first "Miss Magwhet," then the others in the class. He was spot-on with the pronunciation of the names with the exception of Rebecca Riley who became "Webecca Wiley."

"I think you had a little trouble with Rebecca's name," Margaret said. "Try again."

"Webecca."

"Do you remember what sound the lion makes?"

Lucas scrunched his face and bared his teeth. "Grrrrrr!"

"Right. Now use the last part of that growl to say Rebecca's name."

Lucas hesitated a moment, then gleefully said, "Grrrbecca."

Margaret gave a nod. "Much better."

For the remainder of the class, Charlie stood beside Alice and watched as the children worked at identifying sounds. They did the hum of a bee, the shushing sound of a call for quiet, the tick, tick, tick of a clock, and the mew of a kitten. First they practiced the sound, then called out words that used that sound. It seemed to Alice that Lucas bumped his chest out and tried harder because he knew she was watching, and that made her all the prouder.

The lesson was almost over when Gabriel slipped quietly back into the classroom and stood alongside them.

"Enjoying yourself?" he whispered.

Alice looked up with a smile. "Very much so."

She didn't mention how she'd taken stock of every child in the class or how she'd noticed the way Margaret never hurried the children but gave them time to find their tongues. In the short while she'd been there, Alice hadn't just noticed everything but committed it all to memory.

She had a month, maybe less, but for as long as she was here, she'd remember how the room was not at all like a regular classroom. It was cozier, friendlier in an odd sort of way. She'd remember the colorful books stacked high and the playthings scattered about. Tomorrow and the next day and the day after she'd think back on how three little girls squeezed together in the big overstuffed chair; not a classroom chair, but the kind you'd find in a comfortable living room. Most of all, Alice would remember the sound of the children with their less-than-perfect voices singing nursery rhymes. She was certain that sound would remain in her heart even after she'd left this earth.

Once the class was dismissed, Lucas hurried off to meet Tracy, but they stayed behind and chatted with Margaret for a few minutes. When Margaret spoke of what a wonderful student Lucas was, Alice beamed with pride.

"He takes after his great-granddaddy," she said, not mentioning the two generations that came between.

Just then, Gabriel saw Alice's back stiffen and her hand clench the arm of the chair. She was obviously in pain.

"It's time for us to get going," he said and eased the wheelchair into the hall. "I was planning to show you around the building, but if you're not feeling up to it . . ."

"I doubt I'll ever have the chance to come back," Alice said, "so I'd like to see everything this time."

"You're sure?" Gabriel asked.

She nodded, and they started down the hallway. Instead of taking them from one classroom to the next, Gabriel kept to the hallway, explaining the use of each room but stopping in only a few. At the end of the long hallway, he slowed in front of the sound studio.

"We'll just peek through the glass here," he said. "Our sound technician is working with a family, and I don't want to disturb them."

He went on to explain, "This is where the children with cochlear implants have their sound turned on for the first time. It's usually about a month after their surgery."

"Oh my." Alice sighed. "I can imagine that's quite an experience."

"It is. Once they realize they're hearing their mother's voice, their happiness is almost uncontainable. Most of these children have been living in a world of silence, so the first time they hear a noise, they don't know what to think. Some of them scream, some laugh, and some cry. And when the child is a bit older, it can take days, or even weeks, for them to become comfortable with the concept of hearing."

"Did Lucas . . ." Alice let the remaining words trail off. She knew Gabriel understood her question when he nodded.

"Lucas was puzzled at first and tried to tug the receiver off. After a few minutes, he seemed to realize it was Tracy's voice, then he turned to her and pulled her mouth open to see if he could find where the words were coming from."

Alice held her hand to her mouth and gave a soft chuckle.

"He was almost sixteen months old at the time. Meghan had taught him a little bit about the feel and vibrations of speech, and we believe that's what prompted his reaction. Although we can't say for sure, we think it was the first time he ever heard Tracy's voice."

Alice allowed that thought to settle and then gave a sympathetic sigh. "How sad. Do the doctors know what caused his deafness?"

"They know the cause but not the reason. No one can explain why something like this affects one child and not another. Most babies are tested at birth, and if the baby is deaf, they know it before he leaves the hospital. In Lucas's case there was no evidence of deafness at that point."

"Then what happened?" Charlie asked.

"It could be they missed finding it, or it could have happened in the first few months of his life."

A sharp pain fluttered through Alice's chest, and she couldn't help wondering if, in some unknown or untold way, Dominic was responsible.

"In those first few months, would there have been a way to prevent this from happening?" she asked.

Gabriel shook his head. "It's doubtful."

They moved on, but as she rolled by the big window, Alice took one last look at the couple in the room. The woman held the toddler in her lap, and the concerned father offered out a toy for distraction.

Tracy went through that alone.

———— ❧❧ ————

Once the tour was over, they headed for the conference room to meet Tracy and Lucas.

"Supwise!" Lucas hollered. "Lunch pawty!"

The conference table was set with a bouquet of flowers, colorful place mats, and trays of sandwiches and pastries.

Alice's eyes widened, and her mouth curled into a smile. "Good gracious, I wasn't expecting all this."

Gabriel wheeled her chair over to the table. "We thought having lunch here would be easier than going to the café."

Alice gave a nod of appreciation and said nothing of the pain that was constant. Sitting, standing, walking, even rolling over in bed, it was always there, stabbing her in the back like a sharp butcher knife. Day by day, things were becoming more difficult. It was happening just as the doctor warned it would.

As she picked at the food, she looked at the faces around the table. Charlie, a man who'd been her friend forever and in an odd way more of a partner than Joe. And Lucas, sweet adorable Lucas, with his bright smile and trusting heart. She could imagine him growing into a fine young man, a man Daddy DeLuca would be proud of. How sad that she would not be here to see it.

A dull ache throbbed in Alice's left hip, and she leaned heavily on the arm of the chair, trying not to make it obvious. As soon as everyone finished eating, she looked over at Charlie and gave a nod. He stood and came around to Alice's side.

"It's time for us to be heading back," he said. "All this excitement has tuckered us old folks out."

Alice gave an appreciative smile. Even though she'd taken just small sips of her sweet tea and forced down a few bites of a ham sandwich, Alice said it was the finest lunch she'd ever experienced. Which in many ways was true.

———— ❧⟡❧ ————

Alice was silent for most of the drive back to Magnolia Grove, but when they turned onto Lakeside Drive, she looked at Charlie and said, "I've made my decision."

Having seen her wincing and trying to push through the pain, Charlie said, "About the morphine?"

She shook her head. "About the farm. I've been thinking this over for a good long time, and while there's no easy choice, I'm going to do what I think Daddy DeLuca would do if he were here to make the decision."

Charlie stretched his arm across the seat, took her hand in his, and gave it an affectionate squeeze. "I'm guessing you'll want me to take you to see the lawyer, then."

"Yes," she said. "Tomorrow."

41

Alice DeLuca

Today the pain was worse than ever, and it forced me to come to grips with the reality of how little time I have left. When Dr. Willoughby first told me the cancer was back, he said six months, and in an odd way, that seemed to be enough. Now I'm looking at weeks, maybe days, and I'm feeling a sense of panic.

I thought it would be a simple thing to get my affairs in order, but life is so much more complicated than we realize. It's not one long stretch of time that starts on the day you're born and ends on the day you die; it's a collection of meaningful moments with spots of happiness and sorrow in between.

Looking back, I know some of the most meaningful moments flew by with me not taking enough time to truly appreciate them. The day I first held Dorothy to my breast, I was so worried about doing it right I couldn't let myself relax and enjoy the moment. The same is true of the day I married Joe. It was what I wanted, yet I stood there wondering if he would ever love me as I did him. It seems that the truly memorable moments, the ones that shape your life, are often a mix of pleasure and pain. That held true even on the day I met Lucas. I fell in love with the child right from the start, but loving him also meant knowing Dominic had lied to me.

There are other moments, ones most people would consider too small to qualify, but I can look back on those and know there was nothing but pure joy in them. Charlie holding my hand in his, Daddy DeLuca hugging me tight to his chest, Lila baking her special lemon cake because she knew it was my favorite. Those are the special, every-day moments the Lord Himself hands down to you.

The sad part is, I've sometimes wasted too many of those moments trying to convince myself that what I wanted to believe was the truth. Now that I'm here at the eleventh hour, I can look back and see more clearly: Joe never did have Daddy DeLuca's goodness in his heart, and neither does Dominic. Lucas does, though; I'm almost certain of it. I realized that the first time I saw him.

Hopefully it's not too late for me to make things right. Now that I know what I need to do, I pray the Good Lord will give me enough time to take care of it before He calls me home.

42

The Appointment

Alice heard the rooster crow but remained in bed. The pain in her back was excruciating, and her legs felt as if they were weighted with something too heavy to move. Between the slats in the blinds, she could see the first rays of dawn creeping into the sky. She watched until the sun cleared the horizon, then she pushed through her pain and climbed out of bed.

Instead of pulling on a bathrobe and heading downstairs for a cup of coffee as she usually did, she dressed; it would save a trip back up the stairs. Although the forecaster had promised a day in the eighties, she chose wool slacks and a sweater. As a young woman she'd worn sundresses and cotton frocks well into November, but now she was always cold. Even when the Georgia sun blazed so hot that men pulled out handkerchiefs and mopped their brows, she felt a chill on the back of her neck or goose bumps rising up on her arms.

Today was the day she would do what she had to do, the thing she'd been putting off for all these weeks. Once downstairs, she poured a cup of coffee and sat at the table. Dr. Willoughby warned she had to force herself to eat, but today she couldn't stand even the thought of plain toast.

Maybe later, after this is done and over with.

When the cup was empty, she poured another half cup, then wrapped her hands around the mug to warm them. She glanced at the clock. Fifteen minutes. The office didn't open until nine o'clock. If she called earlier, the machine would answer, and she dreaded talking to the machine.

To be on the safe side, she waited until 9:02, then dialed the number for the office of McGinley & Hudson. Years ago, Sandra always answered the phone. She'd take a moment to ask how Alice was doing. Now there was a new girl, one who answered in a sharp, hurried voice and wasted no time on chitchat.

"This is Alice DeLuca. I'd like to meet with Mr. McGinley today."

"Hold on, and I'll check if he's available."

In the background, Alice heard a muffled conversation; then the girl came back and said the only availability he had was at eleven.

"That's fine," Alice replied.

Her next phone call was to Charlie. "I have an eleven o'clock appointment."

"Okay," he said. "I'll pick you up at ten thirty."

There was a moment of silence. Then Alice said, "Come earlier if you can. We'll have a cup of coffee together."

"Is Dominic there?"

"Sleeping. It was another late night, so he won't be up before noon."

"I'll be there in fifteen minutes." He'd been expecting her call, and, like Alice, he was already dressed.

Earlier, she'd reheated yesterday's coffee; it was good enough for her but not for Charlie. She poured the last of it down the drain, set a fresh pot on to brew, and filled a wicker basket with corn muffins she'd brought home from the market.

Once the table was set, she stood by the front window, watching for Charlie's car. On the off chance that Dominic might wake up, it would be better if Charlie didn't ring the bell. When she saw his car coming down the drive, she stepped onto the porch and waited. He greeted her with a kiss on the cheek, then followed her back to the kitchen.

They sat for a while, talking softly and taking small sips of coffee. Charlie helped himself to a muffin and spread butter on it. After he'd taken the first bite, he grinned.

"These are good but not the same as yours."

Alice gave a sad smile. "I haven't baked for weeks. Maybe tomorrow, if I'm feeling better . . ."

She knew tomorrow would be no better, but it wasn't a thought she was willing to voice. It was happening, and there was little she could do about it. Dr. Willoughby had suggested morphine to dull the pain, but so far she'd resisted it. The drug made her groggy, and she lost track of time. Time was the one thing she couldn't afford to lose—not a single day, not even a minute.

43

McGinley & Hudson

When they arrived at the lawyer's, Alice followed Matthew McGinley back to his office, and Charlie sat in the waiting room. He took a *Bloomberg Businessweek* from the table and leafed through the pages; not that he was interested in the pipeline coming in from Canada or a recycling method for used tires. He was too worried about Alice to focus on any of those things. He'd noticed the way she winced when she moved from one spot to another, and he'd seen her skin growing more yellow with each passing day.

Alice sat across from Matthew McGinley and explained what she wanted to do. He nodded and made notes, just as his father had done years earlier.

"I can set it up," he said, "but are you sure about your decision?"

Alice gave a sorrowful nod. "I've thought about it long and hard, and it isn't an easy choice, but I think it's what Daddy DeLuca would have wanted."

When she stood to leave, Alice felt her heart banging against her chest and her knees threatening to give way. Charlie had been keeping his eye on the door, so when he saw her come out, he tossed the magazine aside and hurried over.

"Are you okay?" he asked.

She nodded. "Just tired."

That afternoon, instead of going back to the farm, Charlie bought a carry-out order of sandwiches and colas, then drove to the lake. With the sun warm on their shoulders, they rolled the windows down and sat in the car watching the ducks on the pond. Once Alice had calmed herself, Charlie handed her a sandwich, and she ate almost half of it.

She didn't miss her handbag until she had need of a pain pill. That's when she realized she'd left it sitting alongside the chair in Matthew McGinley's office.

It was almost one when Pamela Rose, Mr. McGinley's secretary, spotted the purse sitting on the floor. She recognized it as belonging to Alice DeLuca. Scooping it up, she carried it back to her own desk, then called the farm.

Nursing a worse-than-usual hangover, Dominic was sitting at the kitchen table when the phone rang. Figuring it to be another telemarketer, he sat there and let it ring five times without answering. It stopped, then started up again a minute later. This time he answered on the third ring.

"Is this the DeLuca household?" Pamela asked.

"Yeah."

"Oh, good, for a minute I thought I had the wrong number in the file. May I please speak with Alice?"

"She's not here."

"Oh." There was a moment of hesitation, then Pamela said, "Can you please give her a message? Tell her she left her purse in Mr. McGinley's office but not to worry, I have it."

Brushing the cobwebs from his brain, Dominic asked, "She left what where?"

"Her purse. She left it in Mr. McGinley's office." When there was only silence on the other end, she added, "Of McGinley and Hudson."

More silence.

"Okay, then, let me give you my phone number, and she can just call me."

"Hold on. I gotta get something to write this down." Searching for a pencil, Dominic pulled open the kitchen drawer where Alice kept an assortment of papers and junk. He rummaged through until he found a ballpoint pen, then wrote Pamela's number on an envelope he took from the drawer.

It wasn't until after he hung up that he noticed the envelope's return address.

"Tompkins Investigative Services? What's she doing with . . ." He pulled the report from the envelope.

For the next half hour, he sat there, reading and rereading the report. It was not good. It as much as said that although his name was not on the birth certificate, it was probable that Dominic was Lucas's father.

"Shit," he grumbled. He folded the report, slid it back into the envelope, and returned it to the drawer.

Was it possible she'd done what she threatened—changed her will and left the farm to Lucas?

Stomping back and forth across the kitchen floor, he railed against such a thought, arguing aloud that Lucas was just a kid who didn't deserve what rightly belonged to him. After several minutes, he came to the conclusion that he needed to find out exactly what she was up to. He looked at the envelope again and dialed the number he'd written.

"McGinley and Hudson."

"Say that again. Who's this?"

"It's the law office of McGinley and Hudson. Do you know who—"

Dominic slammed the receiver down, now certain she'd done precisely what she'd threatened.

He was counting on that money; it was as good as in his pocket. Now he had to contend with this. Well, if she changed the will once, she could change it back. All he had to do was figure out a way to prove he deserved it.

Right now his head was fuzzy. He needed a drink. He could think a lot better if he had a drink; a pick-me-up just to get him going. Yanking the kitchen cupboards open, he pushed aside containers of oatmeal, bread crumbs, and canned peaches, looking for whiskey. Didn't older people keep a bottle around for medicinal purposes?

After several minutes of searching, he gave up and dialed Broom's number. Broom had a half-ass job working at the junkyard. He made next to nothing, but he knew how to skim off the top, and he could come and go as he wanted.

"Meet me for a drink," Dominic said.

"Don't you gotta work today?"

"Screw work. I gotta take care of something more important."

Broom hemmed and hawed, then finally said he'd be at Murphy's in twenty minutes.

"Bring your thinking cap," Dominic said, then hung up.

44

The Plan

By the time Broom got to Murphy's, Dominic had already polished off two bourbons. With his chin dropped down onto his chest, he stared at the empty glass and moaned, "I got unbelievable problems."

Broom ordered a beer, then asked, "You wanna talk about it?"

Dominic nodded, then told about the private investigator's report and how he feared his grandma was going to do what she'd threatened. He waved to the bartender and ordered another drink.

"The kid is five years old," he said with a groan. "What the hell is a five-year-old gonna do with a farm?"

Broom sucked down a swig of beer and sat there for a moment before answering. "Maybe his mama's gonna sell it and let the kid use the money for college. My sister got a divorce settlement, and she—"

Dominic turned with a look of disgust. "Shut your idiot face. I was just thinking out loud. You think I really give a rat's ass about what he can or can't do with the money?"

"Well, you said—"

"Shit, Broom, you ain't even got half a brain. The point is that the money from selling that farm is supposed to belong to me, not the kid. I gotta come up with an idea to make her change her mind back."

They sat there for a long time, commiserating over the turn of events and unable to come up with a way to get around the situation.

Broom picked at the stubble of his beard. "As far as I can see, you're screwed unless you make your grandma believe you're more deserving of the place."

"No shit, Einstein. How am I supposed to do that?"

"Maybe say you and Tracy are getting back together. Tell her you're doing it because of the kid."

Dominic rolled his eyes. "You think she's gonna believe it after the story I fed her last time?"

"She might if she saw you and Tracy together."

"Forget it. Me and Tracy are done."

"Yeah, well, then I guess you and the money from the farm are done, too."

They sat there for another five minutes with Dominic nervously drumming his fingers against the bar and Broom staring down at the half-empty beer glass.

"Does Tracy know about this?" Broom finally asked.

"Know about what?"

"That your grandma is gonna give the farm to her kid?"

Dominic shrugged. "I don't think so."

Broom gave a wide grin that showed where his eyetooth was missing. "That's good, 'cause then she ain't gonna be suspicious. Just tell Tracy you're going crazy without her, and you wanna get back together. Say you're concerned about the kid not having a father."

"What are you, insane? I don't wanna get back with her, and I sure as hell don't want the responsibility of that kid."

"Dummy, this ain't for real. Pretend long enough to convince your grandma. Then, when you get the farm, break it off."

Dominic thought back to years earlier, how Tracy had left everything behind and gone off to Philadelphia with him. If she'd loved him that much then, there was a possibility she still might.

"If I can get her to believe me, that could work . . ."

They bounced the idea around for a while, and, after almost two hours of passing it back and forth, decided the best approach would be to convince Tracy he'd changed, was interested in Lucas's future, and wanted to get married. If she bought that, then he'd invite them to dinner at the house and let Alice see for herself. He figured that would be enough to convince her that he should be the one to inherit the farm.

The following morning, Dominic was up early. He showered, shaved, and came down to breakfast before nine thirty.

Alice smiled. "Well, now, this is a pleasant surprise."

He bent and kissed her cheek. "Yeah, Grandma, I'm sorry about sleeping late so often; I guess this gas station job is harder than I thought it would be."

He poured himself a cup of coffee and sat at the table. "I probably ought to give up working there. You know, maybe fix up Grandpa's tractor and plant something in the south field next summer."

Alice looked across with a raised eyebrow. "Plant what?" she asked.

Dominic shrugged. "Peanuts or maybe tobacco."

He waited for her to pick up on the conversation so he could follow her lead, but she just sat there looking down at a half cup of coffee.

"I've been doing a lot of thinking lately." He hesitated for a few moments, then added, "Especially about times I've been less than truthful."

Maybe if Dominic wasn't so much like Joe, such a statement would have been believable, but given the circumstances, Alice had her doubts.

"Less than truthful about what?"

"Lucas being my son." He buried his face in his palms and shook his head sorrowfully. "I'm not proud of how I acted, but I'm trying to fix it."

Just then a sharp pain snapped across Alice's back.

"Likely as not, it's too late," she said wearily, then got up from the table, limped into the living room, and lowered herself into the recliner. The thought that even now, even with the end already in sight, Dominic still chose to lie to her was like a great stone dropped down on her chest. Alice pushed back in the chair and closed her eyes to hold back the tears.

45

Alice DeLuca

The pain is something fierce. I try to move past it, but sometimes doing that is almost impossible. Dr. Willoughby has given me pills, but they don't help much anymore. It might be time for the morphine, even though it makes your brain so cloudy you give up on living.

I need to keep my wits about me, at least until I finalize the last few details of what I'm about to do. Agatha Parsons, a woman who sang in the choir at church, was a widow like me. She died the summer before last and left a terrible mess behind. Her children and grandchildren squabbled over every stick of furniture in the house, and they actually got into a fistfight when it came to dividing up the little bit of jewelry she had. That happened because she didn't have a will and didn't leave so much as a note saying what her wishes were. Agatha was sick for nearly a year before she passed, and I keep wondering if in all that time she didn't think to mention what she wanted her sister, Matilda, to have or if she intended her wedding band to be given to her oldest daughter.

I've spent a long time thinking it over, and now that I've made up my mind, I plan to make sure things happen as they're supposed to. Tomorrow I go back to sign the final copy of my will, and afterward, I'm writing letters for Mr. McGinley to hand out when he reads it.

When I listened to Dominic this morning, I wanted to believe he was telling the truth, but I know better. I can't say if it was a flat-out lie or just wishful thinking on his part, but this I can say: Gabriel Hawke is the man Tracy Briggs is marrying, and there's nothing Dominic can say or do to change that.

46

Two Days Later

It took time for Dominic to work up the courage to confront Tracy. Twice he drove by the Briggses' house, trying to get a glimpse of her as he passed. The first time, he'd seen nothing but a tricycle left out on the front porch. The second time, Lila was in the side yard tossing a ball back and forth with Lucas.

The sight of the boy running and playing wasn't what Dominic expected, but then he wasn't certain what he'd expected. It had been nearly four years, but in his mind, Lucas had remained a toddler.

He slowed to a crawl, then circled the block and parked on the opposite side of the street, two houses back. As he sat watching, the sour taste of regret churned in his stomach, then rose in his throat. He reminded himself that he hadn't walked away, Tracy had. But still he wondered if he could have done something more to patch things up. They'd been good together. Maybe if he'd tried harder, she would have come back to Philly. As he sat remembering the loneliness of his room above the bar and comparing it to the sound of his son's laughter, Dominic began to want what he'd lost. Getting Tracy back was no longer just a means to an end, it was something he *wanted*. He waited for twenty minutes, hoping she would come out, but she didn't. When

Lila took Lucas inside, he stayed another five minutes, then pulled away from the curb and drove off.

On the third day, as he drove by, Dominic saw Lucas pedaling his tricycle along the sidewalk. Bent over, busily plucking dead blooms from the flower bed, Lila had her back to the boy. Dominic parked the car on the far side of the street, crossed over, and stood in front of Lucas.

"Hi, Lucas. Remember me?"

Lucas looked up and said nothing.

"I'm your daddy." Dominic squatted beside the tricycle. "Don't you remember when we lived in that nice apartment, you and Mama and me? It's been a while, but I've been thinking—"

Lila lifted her head, spotted Dominic, and tore down the block. "Get away from him!"

"He's my son; you've got no right to—"

"Tracy!" Lila screamed, her voice loud enough to be heard two blocks over.

Street noise was seldom heard in the back of the house where the *Snip 'n Save* office was, but panic makes a scream shriller and more terrifying. The moment Tracy heard it, she bolted up from the computer and came flying through the front door like a woman on fire. By then, Lucas had begun to wail.

"Get away from him!" she screamed. Without a moment of hesitation, she scooped Lucas up and held him in her arms.

"It's okay, sweetie; there's nothing to be afraid of." When Lucas's wailing turned to a soft sniffle, she turned to Dominic, her eyes narrowed and expression unyielding. "What are you doing here?"

"I wanted to see my son."

"After four years? Bullshit!" She handed Lucas to Lila. "Mama, will you take Lucas inside? I can handle this."

Nothing more was said until Lila and Lucas disappeared inside the house. Once they were gone, Dominic spoke.

"I'm sorry for the things I've done. I've been a fool, and I know it." He reached for her hand, and she smacked it away. "Don't be like that, baby; I said I was sorry."

"Sorry? Sorry for what, Dominic? Sorry that for four years you didn't even call to ask about your son? Sorry you canceled his health insurance when he needed it? What exactly are you sorry about, Dominic?"

"I'm sorry for all of it," he replied. "It was a bad time for me."

The resentment Tracy had harbored for all those years came forth in a burst of anger. She shoved Dominic, then took another step forward, leaning in nose to nose.

"A bad time for *you*? Asshole! You don't even know what a bad time is! Being afraid your son will never lead a normal life, that's a bad time! Running out of booze is not!"

Again Dominic reached for her, and she whacked his hand away.

"Get out of here," she snapped. "Lucas and I are doing fine without you. We don't want you in our lives." She whirled on her heel and started off.

Dominic followed, reaching out and grabbing her by the arm. "Wait! I've got something to say, and you're gonna listen!"

When she stopped and turned back, his voice softened. "I love you, Tracy. I've always loved you. I know I've acted like an ass, but all that's done. I've changed. I realize now what it means to be a family, and that's what I want for us. You, me, and Lucas, we're a family, and we should be together."

"We're not a family. We never were."

Dominic's voice turned pleading. "Yes, we were. I was too blind to see it back then, but now I do. We'll get married, give Lucas the kind of home he deserves . . ."

Tracy shook her head. "It's too late, Dominic."

"Just give me a chance to prove myself," he said. "I know you've gotta remember all the good times we had. You loved me before, and if you let yourself—"

"Dominic, I'm engaged."

A look of shock swept across his face. "To who?"

"It doesn't matter. What does matter is that I need you to leave us alone."

"No," he said angrily. "Lucas is my kid, and I want to see him!"

"Why?"

It was a simple question, but one he hadn't expected. He grabbed on to the first thought that came to him.

"Because I'm his daddy, and a kid ought to know his daddy!"

Tracy shook her head in disgust. "After four years you suddenly feel this overwhelming parental need? Sorry, Dom, I'm not buying it."

"Hey, this isn't all my fault! You're the one who walked out on me, remember? Maybe if you'd stuck around—"

"Oh, you mean like stuck around long enough to catch you screwing the babysitter a second time?"

Dominic hardened his chin, gritted his teeth, and spoke as if his jaw were wired shut. "You just can't give it up, can you, Tracy? I said I was sorry. What more do you want?"

"The only thing I want is for you to leave us alone."

"No! Lucas needs to know he's got people on his daddy's side. My grandma's sick, maybe dying. Let me take Lucas for a while so she can get to know him before it's too late."

Tracy stood there for a moment, allowing the shock of his request to register. "You're not taking Lucas anywhere," she finally said, then turned and started toward the walkway.

Again he ran after her; this time he yanked her shoulder and spun her around.

"Don't walk off on me like that! I want to take my kid to see his grandma; is that asking too much?"

She shook loose of his grip. "Yes, it is. He doesn't even know you, Dominic. To him, you're a stranger. If you want to visit him here at our house I might be willing to think about it, but there's not a snowball's chance in hell I'd let him leave here with you!"

He grabbed Tracy's shoulders and shook her. "Listen up! I'm Lucas's daddy, and I've got rights! My grandma's a good person, and I say we give her a chance to get to know the kid."

Tracy banged her fists against Dominic's shoulders, broke free, and double-timed it up the stairs and onto the front porch. She stopped for a second and turned.

"Lucas already knows your grandma. She's been visiting him for the past two months."

Not leaving him time to respond, she stepped inside and slammed the door.

Dominic just stood there, dumbfounded.

47

Dominic DeLuca

I feel like a truck just ran over me. Of all the people in this world, I never thought Grandma would be the one to stab me in the back. The only reason I can think of is that Tracy fed her a sorry-ass story about how I'm such a miserable daddy and she's a saint.

That's probably why Grandma came up with the idea of giving Lucas the farm instead of handing it down to me. No doubt Tracy's been buttering her up, figuring if Lucas gets the farm, she'll be the one in charge of it. To her, it's money in the bank. She'll sell the place and pocket the cash. I know that's what I'd do.

I can't help feeling betrayed. I thought if anybody was on my side it would be Grandma. I never figured she'd turn against me like Mama.

I could really use that money, but I'm not willing to sell my soul to get it. After Grandma goes, I'm leaving Magnolia Grove and never looking back. Tracy can keep the damn farm and grow peanuts till they're coming out of her ears. I don't want to know about it or hear about it.

It won't be easy, but I'm gonna try to remember Grandma the way she was before Tracy poisoned her mind.

48

The Darkest Night

After the shock Tracy had given him, Dominic desperately needed a drink. He didn't bother to call Broom but went straight to Murphy's, plopped down on a stool, and ordered a double. It was midafternoon, and the only other person in Murphy's was Kenny, the bartender.

"Kind of early in the day for a double, isn't it?"

Dominic gave him a mind-your-own-business look and didn't bother answering. He'd already downed two doubles when Broom came walking in shortly after five. He sidled onto the stool next to Dominic and ordered a beer.

"Ain't you working at the gas station tonight?"

Dominic shook his head. "Called in sick."

"Okay."

"You're not gonna ask me why?"

Broom shrugged. "Nope. I figured you'd tell me whether I ask or not."

"Tracy's engaged to some other guy, and that's not even the worst of it."

He hiccuped, then told about how Alice had been going over there to visit the kid for months.

"And there's not a damn thing I can do about it. The farm was supposed to be my inheritance, and Tracy stole it right out from under my nose."

It was after eleven when Dominic finally stumbled out of the bar, and by then he was listing like a sailboat in a windstorm. For the past two weeks, he'd been driving Alice's car, and the fact that he made it home without wrapping it around a lamppost was somewhat of a miracle. Turning into the driveway, he inched along the dirt road, and when he finally got within ten feet of the garage, he killed the engine and sat there.

All evening he'd been thinking about this moment. At first he'd planned to say nothing and let Alice go to her grave without ever knowing how he felt. Then he remembered his mama.

He'd said nothing when she left. When she'd promised to come back for him, he'd just nodded and said okay. Maybe if he'd screamed, yelled, and insisted on going with her, things would have been different. Maybe after a while they would have grown used to doing things together. If he'd gone with her, he might be living in California right now, maybe working in a movie studio or parking cars at some fancy restaurant on Rodeo Drive.

Dominic folded his arms across the steering wheel and dropped his forehead onto them. He'd made a thousand wrong decisions in his life; maybe saying nothing again would be one of them.

It was well after two when he climbed out of the car and dragged himself into the house. Every night since his return to Magnolia Grove, Alice had left the lamp burning for him, but tonight it was pitch black in the hallway.

Tracy probably called and told her what happened. So, what, now Grandma's punishing me? Is she showing me I'm no longer welcome in what should be my own house?

He fumbled his way down the hall to the staircase. The missing lamp prickled him like quills sticking in his back. Before he reached the top landing, he decided this time he wasn't going to stand by and say nothing. This time he was going to say he deserved the farm. He'd lived here all those years, and he had a right to stay. Lucas was a dumb kid with no use for anything but a tricycle.

The moon was high in the sky, and it cast a pale shadow across the upstairs landing, enough that he could see his way down to her room. He pushed open the door and snapped on the light. The bed was empty, the coverlet smooth and unwrinkled, a throw pillow placed in the center just the way it always was.

"Grandma?"

He turned and retraced his steps back down the stairs, thinking maybe he'd passed her by. She must have been sitting in the recliner, waiting for him to come in so that she could have another *talk* with him.

He clicked the switch at the foot of the stairs, and light flooded the hallway. Walking through to the living room, he could already see she wasn't in the recliner. He snapped on the table lamp and continued into the kitchen. Before ten minutes had passed every light in the house was burning, and he'd walked through every room searching for her. He'd even searched the attic, although he knew the stairs were too rickety and she almost never went up there.

It made no sense. She was nowhere in the house. He stood in the center of the living room, looking mystified. He had her car, so she couldn't have gone anywhere, and if she had, she would have left a note.

He tried to think who might know where she'd gone, and his first thought was Tracy. She'd gotten close with Alice, so maybe . . .

Her cell phone number was still in his contact list. He pulled it up and pressed "Call." It rang three times, then a message came on saying she was unavailable. He recognized her voice asking the caller to leave a number and she'd get back to them.

He jabbed "End" without bothering to leave a message.

Who else?

Remembering Alice kept a worn-out address book in the kitchen drawer, he headed there, pulled the drawer open, and rummaged through the contents. Beneath the clippings of recipes, birthday cards yellowed with age, and the envelope from Tompkins Investigation Services, he found the book. It was older perhaps than he was, with loose pages held together by a thick rubber band.

He leafed through the pages, but no name popped out at him. Several names were crossed out with a date written alongside of them. As he started through the pages a second time, he noticed the name and number written on the inside front cover: "Charlie Barnes, 769-5439."

That name stood out. He remembered how Charlie used to come around after Joe's death. He'd stay for hours on end, drinking coffee at the kitchen table. Dominic hadn't seen him lately, but there was a chance . . .

He dialed the number. Charlie answered on the eighth ring. "Do you know where Grandma is?"

"What's that?" Charlie's voice sounded groggy.

"This is Dominic DeLuca. I just got home, and my grandma isn't here. Do you know where she is?"

There was a moment of silence; then Charlie said, "I'm sorry, Dominic. I called the gas station, and Ed said you were out sick. When I tried you at the house, there was no answer. I didn't have your cell phone number and didn't know where else—"

"Okay, okay. So where's Grandma?"

"Today was a very difficult day for your grandma. The pain got so bad that she couldn't stand it, and I took her to the hospital."

"She got that bad in one day?"

"It wasn't one day. She's been going downhill for the past month; surely you've noticed it."

Dominic lowered himself into Granddaddy's chair. "I guess we haven't seen a whole lot of each other since I've been home." His voice was solemn, regretful almost.

"Don't worry. Dr. Willoughby has her on a morphine drip, so she's resting comfortably for now."

"What hospital?" Dominic asked.

"Mercy General." Charlie rattled off the address and Alice's room number, then assured Dominic she was being well cared for.

When Dominic hung up, he sat there feeling overwhelmed. He'd thought there was more time. He knew she was sick, but she'd seemed okay, like maybe the cancer was something to worry about in the future. Not right now.

Not once had she told him she was in pain. True, she barely picked at her food and spent long hours sitting in the recliner, but he'd attributed that to growing older.

Suddenly a feeling of loneliness settled inside of him. It was greater than any he'd ever known, greater even than after his mama had disappeared down that long dirt road. Even back in Philadelphia he'd felt Alice was there for him. He knew when he wanted to return, he'd find her waiting with open arms. Even when they'd had their *talks*, he never felt separated from her; scolded maybe, but never abandoned.

Leaving the house ablaze in light, he walked out the door and got into his car. Mercy General was normally a twenty-minute drive, but he made it in ten.

There were only a handful of cars in the lot, so he parked close to the front entrance and pushed through the glass doors. Inside, the lobby looked deserted. A uniformed guard standing near the elevator spotted Dominic and walked over.

"Can I help you?"

"I'm here to visit my grandma."

The gravity of the situation made Dominic more coherent, but it was easy enough to catch the slurring in his speech and the liquor on his breath.

The guard glanced across at the clock above the door. "It's four o'clock in the morning. Visiting hours don't start until ten; come back then."

"Well, I'm here now, and I'm going to see—"

The guard turned his head and spoke into the walkie-talkie on his shoulder. "Jack, I think we've got a problem."

When Dominic started to go around, the burly guard stepped in front of him again. "I said visiting hours don't start until ten."

By the time Jack arrived, Dominic was nose to nose with the guard.

"Hold on here," Jack said and eased them back from one another. He motioned to the sofas on the far side of the room and told Dominic, "Let's talk."

Dominic followed him over, and they sat opposite one another.

"I'm not looking to make trouble," Dominic said. "I'm just asking to see my grandma."

Jack nodded, then asked his grandma's name. "Let me check with the nurses. If she's awake, I'll walk you up and you can have five minutes, but if she's sleeping, you've got to agree to come back tomorrow and not disturb her, okay?"

Dominic gave a reluctant nod.

Jack went to the phone on the main counter and buzzed the nurses' station on Three West. He gave Alice's name and asked for her status.

Dominic couldn't hear their conversation, but he could see Jack bobbing his head in response to whatever was being said. Several minutes later, Jack returned to the sofa and dropped down beside Dominic.

"Your grandma's been sedated, and she's sound asleep. According to the nurse, she was in quite a bit of pain earlier, so I think the kindest thing you can do is let her get the rest she needs."

Dominic sat silent. Jack could see his resolve waning.

"You don't want to see your grandma in pain, do you?"

"Of course not."

"Then let her rest. She's had a rough day."

"Can I see her tomorrow?"

"Absolutely."

Dominic sat there for a few minutes; then he walked back to his car and drove home.

That night, he left every light burning and didn't go to bed. Sometime around dawn he fell asleep on the sofa.

49

The Next Day

Alice saw herself walking beside Joe. Not as they'd been in the later years, but as they'd been at the beginning. Her long hair fell loosely across her bare shoulders; the white sundress was bright against the summer bronze of her skin. A breeze ruffled her skirt, and overhead, the Founder's Day banner flapped against the building. Joe wrapped his arm around her waist and hugged her close. He whispered something in her ear, and she laughed.

Beyond the crowd, she saw someone standing in front of the town hall building with his straw hat tipped back and a briar pipe in his hand.

"I want you to meet my dad," Joe said and tugged her across the street.

Alice tried to say she already knew him, but the music coming from the bandstand was too loud.

When they broke through the crowd, Daddy DeLuca was standing right in front of her, his dark hair pushed to one side and his mouth curled ever so slightly.

He looked down, and his smile broadened. "I've been waiting for you."

Thinking those words were meant for him, Joe answered, "We were over by the bandstand, listening to the music." Then he introduced her to his father, acting as if they'd never met before.

They talked for a while; as they turned to leave, she looked back, and Daddy DeLuca mouthed the words *Do the right thing*.

Alice woke with a start, at first not knowing where she was and then remembering the trip to the hospital. The room was dark with a narrow shaft of light coming from the hallway. In the distance there were muffled voices and the whirring of a machine. She listened, but the sounds were foreign to her ear.

She could still picture Daddy DeLuca telling her to do the right thing, but she couldn't recall whether or not she'd done it. There had been so much to do, and the past few days seemed fuzzy.

In the darkness of the room with no way to know the time, she wondered how long she'd been here. She was trying to remember if a second day and night had passed since she'd come here when a razor-sharp pain ricocheted along her spine. She reached for the pain pump hanging on the side of her bed and pressed the button. Moments later the pain was gone, and she was again asleep.

Tracy was at Mercy General before visiting hours began. She'd spent a sleepless night looking at shadows on the ceiling and thinking about Alice DeLuca. In the few short months they'd known one another, she'd grown fond of Lucas's great-grandmother, and now the thought of losing her was painful.

Alice was asleep when she entered the room, so Tracy sat in the chair beside her bed. After a few minutes she lifted the frail hand into her own and held it. Alice looked peaceful, not narrow-lipped and wincing as she'd been the last time she came to visit Lucas.

Before long, a nurse entered the room, a round woman with a cheerful voice.

"Good morning, Alice," she sang out and then went about the tasks of checking the chart and feeling for Alice's pulse.

"She's asleep, isn't she?" Tracy asked.

The nurse nodded. "It's a deep sleep because of the morphine."

"Do you know when she'll wake up?"

The nurse gave a polite smile and almost imperceptible shrug. "There's no way of knowing. She's pretty heavily sedated and that keeps her comfortable, which at this point is all we can do."

"There's nothing . . . ?"

The nurse shook her head. "Her spine is almost disintegrated; how she stood the pain this long is a miracle."

A heavy sigh came from Tracy as she sat silently and watched the nurse move about the room, updating the chart, resetting the machine that counted Alice's heartbeats, and changing the IV bag that hung from a pole alongside the bed.

When those tasks were finished, the nurse turned to Tracy. "Are you her daughter?"

Tracy shook her head sadly. "Just a friend."

The nurse crossed over to where Tracy was sitting and gave her shoulder an understanding squeeze. "I know how difficult this is. Hopefully it helps to know she's not in pain."

"It does," Tracy replied, "but there were things I wanted to tell her and haven't had the chance."

"Tell her now. Many doctors believe that even when patients are comatose, they hear people speaking to them."

The nurse told a story of a young woman who actually brought her husband out of a coma by reminding him of how much their family depended upon him. Then she squeezed Tracy's shoulder again.

Once the nurse was gone, Tracy took Alice's hand in hers. It was as light as a baby bird, little more than a skeletal frame covered over with parchment paper. She bent and kissed the gnarled fingers.

"I wish we could have gotten to know you sooner, Alice. You came into our lives so unexpectedly, but in the short time we've had together, Lucas and I have both come to love you. You're a wonderful grandma to him, and you've been a true friend to me. We're going to miss . . ." She stopped and brushed back a tear, her voice now thick and quivery. "I never had the chance to say it . . ." She hesitated a moment, listening to her words and then changing them. "Actually, that's not true, I did have the chance, but I didn't take it, because I always thought we'd have more time. I wanted us to have more time. The little bit we've spent with you has been far too short, but I hope you know you've given Lucas memories that will last a lifetime, and when he's old enough to understand, I'll tell him how very much you loved him. I promise you, Alice, you'll be a part of his life forever."

After she'd said the things she needed to say, she went on to talk of small everyday things. Bits about Lucas and Meghan and how Lila was baking a coconut pineapple cake stacked five layers high. She talked of how she'd fallen behind on the *Snip 'n Save* ads again and needed to catch up, and she spoke of how the nights had turned chilly enough for an extra blanket on the bed.

After two hours of one-sided conversation, Tracy stood and gently laid Alice's hand back on the bed.

"I'll be back tomorrow," she said. "Until then, get some rest, and maybe you'll be feeling better."

As she walked down the long corridor to the elevators, her eyes welled up, and the tears began to roll down her cheeks.

Had Tracy left a minute later or Dominic arrived a minute earlier, they would have met at the elevator, but as it was, they passed by without seeing one another.

50

Dominic's Visit

Dominic intended to be at the hospital early, but he'd fallen asleep on the sofa and didn't wake until the glare of the noonday sun crested the peak of the roof and hit the front window.

Still feeling the effects of last night's liquor, it took a full minute for him to come to the realization of where he was and to remember what had happened. He wearily pushed himself upright and sat there until he felt steady enough to stand.

Last night he'd had a thousand things he wanted to get off his chest, thoughts about the unfairness of life and how he deserved more than he got, but now those things seemed irrelevant. Now there was only a need to tell his grandma that she'd been the only real mother he'd ever known, and he'd keep right on loving her no matter what she did with the damn farm. It was something that couldn't wait; he had to pull himself together and get to the hospital right away.

He stumbled into the kitchen looking for something to ease the ache in his head. After sliding open several drawers and finding nothing but an assortment of pot holders, dish towels, and cutlery, he tried the top cupboard and came up with a bottle of Tylenol. He shook two tablets into the palm of his hand, then swallowed them down with a glass of water. His hand was shaky and his legs still wobbly. He couldn't let his grandma see him this way.

Torn between dashing off to the hospital as he'd intended or first ridding himself of what was an obvious hangover, he considered his grandma's disdain of drunkenness and decided on the latter.

Coffee and a bite to eat, that'll fix me up.

The coffeepot was sitting beside the sink. Dominic poured the little bit left from yesterday into a mug and slid it into the microwave. Taking a biscuit from the refrigerator, he sat at the table and started to eat. After only two bites he pushed it aside.

The stale coffee and cold biscuit were tasteless reminders of Alice. When she was here, the biscuits were fluffy and warm from the oven, the coffee rich with an aroma that called him to come to breakfast; yet he had ignored that. He had kept to himself and stayed in his room, angry about a dozen different things, all of which had been brought on by his own behavior.

Dominic left the half-full mug sitting on the table and hurried upstairs to shower. He glanced into the bathroom mirror and almost immediately regretted doing so. He looked like hell, his eyes red-rimmed and bloodshot, the stubble of a beard shadowing his face.

Screw it, he thought and stepped into the shower.

When Dominic arrived at the hospital, the lobby was crowded with people coming and going. On the right side of the room was a stanchion sign that read Obtain Visitor Pass Here. Alongside the sign a silver-haired woman sat behind a desk. He stopped, got a pass, then hurried back to the elevators.

Dominic expected his grandma to be sitting up in bed, a bit pale perhaps, but none the worse for wear. Instead, she was lying in a prone position with her eyes closed. In a voice that was loud enough to wake her, he said, "Hi, Grandma. I came to see how you're feeling."

There was no response, but he figured she was resting her eyes the way she did in the recliner and continued talking.

"I want you to know I found the report from the investigator, and I'm not mad about it. Disappointed, maybe, but not mad. I wish you could have loved me for who I am instead of going behind my back and hiring an investigator . . ."

He paced at the foot of her bed and kept talking. After several minutes of explaining how he hadn't come home expecting to get anything, that he'd come just because she'd asked him to, he stopped, turned to her, and said, "Grandma, aren't you gonna say anything?"

She didn't answer.

"Grandma?"

He stood alongside the bed and gently shook her shoulder. When she still didn't respond, he went running down the hall in search of a nurse.

Mamie Sayre was on duty that afternoon. He spotted her walking down the hall, ran after her, and grabbed her by the arm.

"You've gotta come quick. Something's wrong with Grandma!"

Mamie swiveled her head and looked at the unfamiliar face. "Grandma who?"

"DeLuca," Dominic replied and turned back toward the room.

Mamie followed him down the hall. "I checked on Miss Alice fifteen minutes ago, and she seemed to be doing okay."

Once they got to the room, Dominic stepped aside and made way for Mamie. Talking to Alice as if she was sitting up, wide-awake, Mamie began a check of one thing and another.

"Miss Alice," she said, "your grandson done scared me to death, saying something was wrong, but here you are resting nice and comfortable . . ."

After she'd flicked a finger at the IV bag to make sure it was dripping properly, she came around to the other side of the bed, saying, "I think you might be a tad more comfy if I raise your head a bit . . ."

She pressed a button, adjusted the bed, then turned to Dominic, who was leaning back against the wall with his mouth hanging open.

"Son, you've got no cause for worry. Miss Alice is doing just fine."

She motioned for Dominic to follow her out of the room. As soon as they stepped into the hallway, he said, "What kind of a nurse are you? My grandma is lying there like a dead person, and you're talking to her like you're expecting her to answer!"

"Calm down," Mamie said and touched Dominic's shoulder. "I understand how you're feeling. This is a hard thing to be going through."

He shook her hand loose. "Don't give me that crap. Just do something to help my grandma!"

"Your grandma's not in any pain. We're keeping her comfortable, and that's all we can do."

"What do you mean, that's all you can do? I need to talk to my grandma. Get a doctor to come wake her up."

Mamie looked at him with a raised eyebrow. "There's nothing a doctor can do. Your grandma might regain consciousness on her own, and she might not." She stepped closer and reached out, but Dominic pulled back. "Son, you do realize your grandma is terminal, don't you?"

Dominic's breath caught, and his stomach churned. The stale coffee he'd had belched into his throat, and for a moment, he was certain he was going to throw up. When he could speak again, he mumbled, "Of course, but . . . I thought she had more time . . ."

"Not anymore, I'm afraid. She's end-stage."

"Shit!" He smacked his hand against the wall. "Why? Why now? Last time, she had chemo and got better. Why not now?"

"Different time, different cancer."

This time, Dominic didn't answer. He just stood there with his chin dropped down on his chest and a wretched look wrinkling his face.

Mamie moved closer and clamped her hand onto his arm. "Son, we're doing everything we can to make sure your grandma is comfortable and well cared for." Seeing his reddened eyes and stooped shoulders, she added, "The best thing you can do is go home and get some sleep. There are gonna be tough days ahead, and I think your grandma would rest easier if she knew you were strong enough to handle whatever comes your way."

Without a word, Dominic turned and went back into Alice's room. He stood there for several minutes, looking at her and watching the neon-green zigzag line bouncing across the monitor. Every rise and fall of the line was the measurement of a heartbeat, and he cringed at the thought of how few she might have left.

After a while the room seemed to grow smaller and the air thin. Cold beads of sweat popped up on his brow, and a feeling of nausea rose from his stomach.

"I gotta go, Grandma." He bent, gave her cheek a kiss, and then hurried from the room.

51

Two Days Later

For the next two days, Alice lingered on the edge of consciousness. The morphine drip gave her the necessary pain relief, but it also brought long hours of what the doctors classified as deep sleep.

Dominic called the hospital twice a day, asking about his grandma, and each time the nurse responded with the same answer.

"Right now she's unresponsive, but perhaps later on or tomorrow morning . . ."

"Okay, then," Dominic replied, "I'll wait until she's awake to come for a visit."

Mamie tried to explain that Alice's moments of lucidity were few and far between, but by then, Dominic had already hung up the phone.

Tracy came in the morning and stayed for two, and sometimes three, hours. She dropped Lucas off at the Hawke School, then drove back to the hospital and stayed until it was time to pick him up.

Tracy began speaking to Alice in much the same way Mamie did, as if she were awake and hearing every word. That first morning, she came in waving a piece of construction paper. "Good morning, Alice," she said and crossed over to the cork bulletin board. "Lucas made a get-well drawing for you. I'm going to pin it up over here so you can take a look when you're feeling up to it."

She turned and saw Alice's eyes flicker open. Although her head never moved, for a fleeting moment it seemed as though her eyes shifted to the far side of the room where the bulletin board was.

"Alice, you're awake!" Tracy hurried over to the bulletin board, grabbed the drawing, and carried it back to the bed.

By then, Alice's eyes were again closed.

Mamie came in a short while later, continuing to talk to Alice as if she were wide-awake and sitting upright. "You're looking mighty fine today, Miss Alice," she said. "Mighty fine, indeed."

"Alice really was awake a few minutes ago," Tracy said. "She opened her eyes to see the get-well card Lucas made for her."

"I don't doubt it for one little minute," Mamie replied. "She must have a powerful lot of love for that boy."

"She does." Tracy nodded as she blinked back a tear.

Charlie came early in the afternoon and remained at Alice's bedside until the corridor lights were dimmed and the nurse insisted it was past time for visitors to leave.

He pulled the straight-backed chair alongside Alice's bed and held her hand in his. For hours on end, he talked, reminding her about the good times they'd had together and the storms they'd weathered.

And, on that first day while Alice's eyes still flickered open from time to time, he said the things she'd not allowed him to say before.

"You know how much I love you," he whispered. "I think you've known it all along, Alice. How could you not? There were times when I'd sit across the table from you, sipping a cup of coffee, and all the while imagining how sweet it would be if the two of us were married. Why, I'd have married you in a heartbeat if Joe hadn't gotten there first. A thousand times I started to say something—but you wouldn't hear of it."

The words grew wobbly in Charlie's throat, and a single tear rolled down his cheek. He brushed it away with the back of his hand and gave a heavy sigh.

"We wasted a lot of years, Alice. Years we should've spent sleeping in the same bed and waking up together. You were loyal to Joe, even though he wasn't deserving of it." The sound of regret was there, threaded through his thoughts, clinging to all the words that, for too long, had gone unspoken.

That second night, the nurse never came to remind him of the hour or shoo him from the room. Long after the lights were dimmed and the sound of footsteps gone from the hallway, he remained by her side.

In the wee hours of the morning, Alice's eyelids fluttered open, and, ever so softly, she brushed the tip of her index finger across Charlie's thumb.

He stood, leaned over the bed, and gently kissed her cheek. "You're awake, aren't you?"

Her finger moved again.

With his face inches from hers, he whispered, "I love you, Alice. I've always loved you. I'm never going to stop loving you."

The corners of her mouth lifted in an almost imperceptible movement. A smile. One so small, Charlie could have easily missed it, but he didn't. It was the sign he'd waited for all those years, her way of telling him she felt as he did.

Moments later, her eyes closed, and her breathing became labored. Charlie stood beside the bed, her hand cradled in his. He'd said a part of what he had to say, but there was so much more. Years and years of stored-up feelings and missed opportunities. As the minutes ticked by, Alice's heart slowed, and the green line on the monitor stretched out longer and longer between the spikes that counted heartbeats. For the past few days, it had beeped in a steady cadence; now it came in erratic spurts. Three fast beeps, a long monotonous hum, then a smaller pulse. A flurry of footsteps came from the hall, and the room was suddenly filled with people—a doctor, two nurses, an aide who did nothing but move him aside.

"You may want to step out into the hall for a few minutes," she said.

Charlie didn't. He had been there for Alice all those years, and he was determined to stay until she no longer had need of him. He moved to the foot of the bed and stood with his hand on the sheet covering her feet.

Before the sun crossed the horizon, she was gone.

52

Saying Goodbye

The day Alice died, Dominic drank himself into a stupor. It began the night before when he'd felt a sense of the inevitable hovering over him like a black storm cloud. He'd left Murphy's early and driven past the hospital, but when he turned onto Bellingham Street, he'd lost his courage. He wanted to see her, but not as she was. To see her in such a state was the same as seeing her dead, and he couldn't deal with that. On the way home, he stopped at the liquor store, bought a bottle of bourbon, and carried it back to the house.

When the call came, it felt like the last nail in his coffin. He'd stood there with his stomach heaving and his hands trembling as he listened to Dr. Willoughby tell how she'd gone peacefully and not suffered. Moments after he hung up the telephone, he threw up in the kitchen sink.

Afterward, he poured three shots into a juice glass, carried it into the living room, then sat on the sofa and cried. "I miss you, Grandma," he sobbed. "Sure, I'm hurt that you went behind my back and started visiting Lucas, but I ain't mad at you. I accept you got your reasons, but if you'd given me half a chance, we could've talked it out. I'm blood, Grandma. You said it yourself, I'm blood. So why? Why'd you, of all people, turn your back on me, too?"

When the juice glass was empty, he went back to the kitchen and refilled it. All afternoon, he raged about the unfairness of life and swore that given more time, he would have straightened out the mess he'd made.

The bottle was more than half empty when the doorbell rang.

"Go away!" he yelled.

The bell chimed again and then again. Dominic ignored it and downed a long swallow of bourbon.

A short while later, a key clicked in the lock, and the door swung open. Charlie walked in with a McDonald's bag. He set it on the coffee table and dropped down on the sofa.

For almost five minutes, they sat side by side, neither of them speaking.

Charlie leaned back, rested his head against the cushion, and looked up at the ceiling. His legs were stretched out, his body as limp as that of a man who'd gone without sleep for a week.

Dominic remained hunched over with his right hand curled into the fist he kept smacking against his left palm, the bourbon bottle now at his feet. Twice he gave an exasperated huff, hoping the uninvited guest would leave.

When it became apparent Charlie wasn't going anywhere, Dominic asked, "What are you doing here, Charlie?"

"Your grandma said I was to look in on you, and that's what I'm doing."

"I don't need anyone to look in on me. Just get out of here and leave me alone."

"Alice said you'd say that. She knew you'd take it hard and told me I needed to be there for you."

Dominic bent over and lowered his face into his palms. "Look, Charlie, I can deal with this myself. I don't need you hanging around to tell me Grandma was a good person."

"Alice *was* a good person. She was the kind of woman who found good in everybody."

Dropping his hands into his lap, Dominic raised his head and turned. "Almost everybody."

"No, everybody. Even you."

"I doubt that."

"Yeah, I found it pretty hard to believe, too, but it's what she said."

Again there was silence.

"What exactly did she say?" Dominic finally asked.

"That you were born with the goodness of the great-grandpa you were named for, but it had been stifled by circumstance. 'Give him time,' she used to say, 'and he'll live up to his name.'"

Dominic shrugged and said nothing.

Alice had known this moment was coming, and she'd prepared for it. The afternoon Charlie took her to the lawyer's office, she'd handed him an envelope.

"I'm going to need you to take care of my final arrangements," she'd said.

At the time, Charlie had asked if maybe she wouldn't want Dominic to do it, but she shook her head.

"He's going to have more to deal with than he can handle."

The envelope contained a paid-in-full receipt from the Spenser Funeral Parlor and instructions indicating there was to be a single day of viewing with burial the next morning. In death, she would lie next to Joe, the man she'd married some fifty years ago.

In Dominic's eyes, his grandmother was a simple woman, someone who crocheted doilies, drank tea, and attended church socials. He never imagined her friends would not only fill the funeral home parlor but also spill out onto the parking lot. One by one, they came to him with teary eyes and tales of how she'd been there in their hour of need, or of how she'd babysat their children or brought casseroles when they were sick.

People he couldn't even place put their arms around him and hugged him close, whispering, "If you need anything, anything at all . . ."

The viewing was to be from seven o'clock until nine, but before the first hour ended, Ignatius Spenser whispered to his wife that she was to keep the doors open until the last person had the chance to come through to pay their respects.

Beverly Carter wasn't from Magnolia Grove; she was from Brewster, which was seventy miles to the north. Although she'd spoken to Alice only once, she'd read about the funeral and driven over. It was 8:40 when she pulled into the funeral home driveway, but with having to circle the lot three times in search of a space, it was five of nine when she finally got in line. From the moment she stepped out of the car in a red skirt short enough to cause a scandal, you knew she was different from the other mourners.

With her heels click-clacking across the parking lot, she took her place in line. As luck would have it, the woman in front of her was wearing a hat that made it difficult to see past. Concerned she might not make it inside before the doors closed, Beverly inched up alongside the woman, stood on her tiptoes, and craned her neck, trying to get a better look. Just then the crowd moved forward, and Beverly fell sideways into Emma Huggins.

Emma pushed her off and frowned. "Whatever are you doing?"

"Sorry," Beverly said. "I was just trying to see if the DeLuca grandson is here."

"Of course he is," Emma huffed indignantly. "He's the only family Alice had!"

Beverly smiled. "Oh, good. I was worried."

"Good? That he's the only—"

"Of course that's not good!" Beverly jumped in. "I meant good that he was able to be here for the services."

Emma gave a muffled harrumph and turned away as the line moved forward.

It was almost ten when Beverly finally got to speak to Dominic. She stepped forward and said, "Sorry for your loss," then leaned in and whispered, "Call me," as she pushed her business card into his hand.

He glanced at the card, then slid it into his pocket.

———— ❦ ————

The funeral unnerved Dominic. For the past week, it had been one piece of bad news after another. First it was that thing with the private investigator. Then he discovered Grandma, the one person he thought he could trust, was cozying up to Tracy; then he'd learned Tracy was engaged to some other guy. The backbreaker came the day before the funeral. He'd called the gas station to say he wouldn't be coming to work for a week or two, and Ed Farley had fired him. Told him not to bother coming in ever again.

"Don't expect a reference, either," Farley said. "Because with your grandma gone, I don't owe you anything. If someone calls here asking about you, I'll tell them the truth that you're a liar and a thief!"

For three nights preceding the funeral, Dominic had been unable to sleep, and he hadn't eaten anything more than a McDonald's hamburger and a few fries. The refrigerator was full of casseroles, cakes, and fruit platters, but he couldn't bear the thought of sitting at that table alone.

Yeah, he'd eaten alone hundreds of times back in Philly, but it wasn't funeral food. It was pizza or Chinese takeout, food that didn't have a bundle of grief attached to it. To make matters worse, Charlie, who was sitting in the front pew right next to Dominic, sniffled and dabbed a handkerchief to his eyes the whole time Pastor James was speaking.

After what seemed an eternity, the service ended, but when Dominic stood and turned to go, he spotted Tracy and Lucas with a guy who had to be the fiancé. He lifted Lucas into his arms; then as they left the church, he wrapped his arm around Tracy's waist.

The sight of the three of them snuggled up together was like a slap in the face. Dominic imagined them going from the church to a restaurant where they'd celebrate Lucas inheriting his great-grandma's farm.

Once that picture settled in Dominic's mind, he couldn't rid himself of it.

Later, as he stood at the graveside, he searched the crowd, looking for Tracy, but she wasn't there. Neither was the fiancé. A bunch of other mourners were circled around the gaping hole in the ground. They cared about his grandma but not about him. Dominic was alone, more alone than he'd ever been in his life. He'd hoped perhaps somehow, some way, his mama would get word of Alice's death and be standing there at the graveside to comfort him. She wasn't. The sorry truth was that nobody gave a crap about him. He had no one and nothing to look forward to, except a bunch of leftover casseroles.

Pastor James bowed his head and read from Ecclesiastes. "All go to one place; all are of the dust, and all return to dust again."

As Dominic stood there listening, he thought back on the previous night and remembered how Tracy had not been among those who'd come to share his grief. She was not one of those who'd whispered, "If you need anything . . ." She was somewhere else, with someone else.

When Pastor James said the final "amen," Dominic was lost in thought.

Charlie stepped forward and laid a single rose on Alice's casket, then stepped back and nudged Dominic to do the same.

Afterward, as they walked away, Charlie asked, "Would you like to come over to my place for a bite to eat? A few of Alice's close friends will be there."

Dominic shook his head and walked on. By then, he'd already decided that before a week was out, he'd be gone from Magnolia Grove. There was nothing here for him, not even the money he'd hoped to get for the farm.

53

A Changed Outlook

Dominic was glad he would soon be leaving the smell of sorrow, dirt, and flowers behind. He was sick of strangers asking if he needed anything; the only thing he needed was another bottle of bourbon to get him through the next few days. Then he'd be gone.

He climbed into his grandma's Chrysler and drove to the liquor store. When he pulled his wallet from his pocket, Beverly Carter's card fell out. He read it again. Beverly S. Carter, Sales Agent, Community Real Estate. She wasn't one of Alice's Magnolia Grove friends; she was from Brewster.

What would a real estate agent from Brewster want to talk to me about?

After he'd paid for the bottle and carried it back to the car, he pulled out his cell phone and dialed Beverly's number.

She answered on the first ring. Dominic was going to ask what she wanted to talk to him about, but he didn't have a chance. As soon as he mentioned his name, her voice turned honeysuckle sweet.

"I am so very happy you called," she cooed. "I was hoping I could get to you before the others did."

"What others?"

"Why, the other real estate agents, of course. I can assure you that even if you do talk to someone else, no one will get you a better deal than what I can offer."

"A better deal on what?"

"You're teasing me, aren't you? Surely you know that farmland of your granny's is worth a pretty penny."

Dominic was too stunned to speak.

"Come on now, don't play hard to get. I've got a developer who's already offered three hundred, but if I push I know I can get him up to three-fifty."

With his mind racing, Dominic remained silent.

Beverly gave a feathery sigh. "Well, if you're determined to play hardball, there's a possibility I could push him to four hundred thousand. But I'm only going to do that if you're willing to give me an exclusive listing agreement."

Dominic couldn't believe what he'd heard. *Four hundred thousand?*

This was a whole new ball game. He wasn't going to stand around and let Tracy get her hands on something worth four hundred thousand dollars when it rightfully belonged to him. He needed time to figure things out, get a lawyer, and get squared away before anyone else could find out what the place was really worth. "I need time to think about it," he said. "You know, with the funeral being today and me grieving my grandma as I am . . ."

"I understand," Beverly said in that same honeysuckled voice. "All I'm asking is for you not to talk to another agent until I can firm up an offer, okay?"

Dominic promised that before he entertained any other offers, he'd call.

He pressed "End," then sat in the car laughing aloud. Four hundred thousand was more money than he'd earn in a lifetime of working in bars. With that much money, he wouldn't need to worry about having a job. He could go wherever he pleased and live like a king. He envisioned the balance in his checkbook with all those beautiful zeros squeezed together on a single line.

He was thinking about what kind of car he'd like when he remembered the very real possibility that his grandma had left the farm to the kid. She'd been going over there for visits; Tracy admitted it. What else had gone on?

Had there been a discussion of how much the place was actually worth? Had Tracy lifted her hand and sworn she'd take care of the farm just as Daddy DeLuca had done? The new fiancé—was he part of the scheme?

The more Dominic thought about it, the angrier he got. On the drive home, he decided there was no way in hell he would let the kid have the farm now that he knew it was worth that kind of money.

Charlie said Alice saw the good in everybody, even him. Did she see enough goodness to believe he deserved to inherit the farm? Maybe she thought if she left it to him, he'd settle down and take such a responsibility seriously. But then again, maybe not.

The bottom line was that he didn't know what his grandma's final decision had been, and he couldn't afford to chance it. There had to be a way to make certain he got what was rightfully his. All he had to do was find it.

———— ◦⊱~⊰◦ ————

That night, Dominic sat on the sofa drinking bourbon long into the night. A thousand different images ran through his mind. At times he could see himself a wealthy man; other times he imagined himself a beggar standing on the street corner as Tracy and her boyfriend drove by in their fancy new car. Images such as that caused a fiery rage to burn inside him.

In the wee hours of the morning, he decided he would find a lawyer, one who could guarantee he'd get what was coming to him.

When he woke, tired and bleary-eyed, Dominic brewed himself a pot of strong coffee, then sat at the kitchen table flipping through the yellow pages. He started with Gordon, Smith, and Keller, the law firm housed in the same building as the Magnolia Grove Bank.

"There's a lot of money at stake, and I've got to know if your firm is the best for me," he told the receptionist.

The girl claimed since he was a new client, the earliest she could fit him in would be in three weeks.

"I can't wait that long," Dominic said. "This is an emergency!"

All but ignoring his plea, she insisted three weeks was the absolute best she could do.

He hung up and moved on. Algonquin Law said they charged a consultation fee but could set an appointment for next week.

After he'd tried every law firm in Magnolia Grove other than McGinley & Hudson, he moved on to calling those in the surrounding towns.

Hiram Selby, a lawyer located over in Aldridge, was the eighth call. Hiram answered the phone himself, and when Dominic pleaded a pressing matter that couldn't wait, Hiram said to come in that afternoon and there'd be no charge for a consultation.

Hoping to make a good impression, Dominic rinsed his mouth with Listerine and dressed in the sport jacket and slacks he'd worn to his grandmother's funeral. The drive to Aldridge should have been thirty minutes, but he got caught behind a school bus that stopped on every corner. Three times he tried to pass it, but on a two-lane road with cars coming and going both ways, it was impossible. He inched along, cursing what seemed to be a never-ending stream of bad luck.

His appointment was for three thirty, but it was almost four when he arrived, and by then, beads of perspiration had risen on his forehead.

It didn't help that the address he'd been given was a squat wood-frame house with a shingle hanging from a post alongside the walkway. He'd expected a brick building, something like the Algonquin Law building in Magnolia Grove.

"More bad luck," he grumbled as he hurried up the walkway.

The man who answered the door was the size of a boy. The only thing that marked him as a man was the bushy black mustache.

"I'm here to see Hiram Selby," Dominic said.

"I'm Hiram, but you can call me Hi."

The man pushed the door back, and Dominic followed him through a long hallway leading to a tiny one-room office. As he settled into the chair in front of a desk piled high with papers, a feeling of uneasiness settled in Dominic's stomach.

"Are you a real lawyer?" he asked.

Hiram frowned. "You trying to be a wise guy?"

"No, but this isn't what I expected. Where's your office? And what about a secretary?"

"This *is* my office. I work independently." Given the way Dominic's face was scrunched into a knot, Hi stood. "Maybe you should just leave and find yourself another lawyer."

Knowing there was no other lawyer, at least not one who had an open appointment schedule and offered free consultations, Dominic shook his head. "No, I'm okay with you being an independent."

Hiram scribbled notes as Dominic told of how he suspected that his grandmother had changed her will, leaving the farm to Lucas, and that he also suspected but could not prove that Tracy was the instigator of such an action.

"But this boy is actually your son, right?"

Dominic gave a one-shouldered shrug. "Yes and no." He went on to say that he was Lucas's father, but Tracy had left his name off the birth certificate for no reason other than spite.

"We weren't married, and she was ticked off about it."

A look of concern began tugging at Hiram's face. When Dominic finished telling the tale from his point of view, he leaned back in the chair.

"That's it. What do you think?"

Hiram shook his head doubtfully. "From what I've heard, it looks like the only hope you've got is that your grandmother didn't change her will. If she did, you can try to challenge it, but it's unlikely you'll get a reversal. All this Tracy has to do is prove the boy is a blood relative of your grandmother, and your case is out the window."

Dominic shifted forward and glared across the desk. "I don't need you to tell me what I can't do; I need you to show me how to get around it."

Hiram looked down at his notes and again shook his head. "Without something more to go on—"

"Four hundred thousand. That's what the place is worth. Maybe even more. Find a way for me to keep the farm, and I'll give you a piece of the action."

Hiram laughed. "That's for sure. I take thirty percent on contingency cases."

"Thirty percent!"

"Yeah, thirty percent. But I only take cases that are a slam dunk. This one feels iffy."

"What do you mean, 'iffy'?" Dominic's voice sounded higher and on the verge of panic. "I'm counting on you!"

Hiram still had that look of doubt. "Any chance you could get guardianship of the boy?"

"You mean bring him home to live with me? Tracy would never go for that."

"Guardianship isn't the same as custody. Custody means the child lives with you; guardianship means you have legal say over him and whatever assets he has."

Dominic smiled. "Genius! Friggin' genius! We're gonna win this!"

"Hold on a minute. I haven't said I'll take the case. Something like this is time-consuming and definitely not a sure thing. For me to take a case like this, I'd want more."

"How much more?"

"Fifty percent."

"Are you kidding me? That's half of what I'd get!"

Hiram nodded. "Yes, it is, but if I don't take the case, all you've got is one hundred percent of nothing."

After a bit of bickering, Dominic agreed to the terms, and they started working on a strategy. Hiram suggested they throw in joint custody, because it gave the plea greater authenticity.

54

Dominic DeLuca

Hiram is a crook, I know that. But he's a smart crook. The idea of filing for guardianship was nothing short of genius. It won't matter whether Grandma left the farm to Lucas or me, because either way, I'll have control of it.

The first thing I'll do is sell the place and clear out of here. I keep thinking there's a good life out there just waiting for me to come and claim it, and that's exactly what I plan to do.

It kills me to give Hiram half of what I get. He's good, but he isn't worth that much. I figure I'll wait and see what happens. If it turns out Grandma left the farm to me, then I'll tell Hiram he gets nothing. If I already have the place, then why should I pay him for getting it?

Okay, he'd probably raise holy hell and threaten to sue me, but by then I'd be long gone, so who cares?

It sounds crazy, but seeing Tracy with that guy bothered me. I didn't think it would, but it did. I guess, deep down, I always figured we'd get back together, but now that she's hooked up with somebody else, it probably won't happen.

I do miss her . . . sometimes. We were good together; she got me. Once I get the money for the farm, I think I'll get myself a snazzy new car and show up on her doorstep with a bunch of roses or something.

Then we'll see how long this new guy lasts, especially after Tracy finds out I'm the one who'll have guardianship of Lucas.

Once you've got a relationship like Tracy and I had, it doesn't just disappear. It's still there, but you gotta do something to bring it back to life. For guys, just saying we're good with each other is enough, but women want more. I always thought Tracy was an exception, but she's not, so I'll do whatever I gotta do.

55

The Battle Begins

Alice's funeral left Tracy feeling down. Although Alice had visited just once a week, knowing that she'd never come again caused a hole to open up in Tracy's heart. After they left the church, she couldn't face the thought of working, so she, Gabriel, and Lucas spent the afternoon at the lake. As they sat there reminiscing about the good fortune of having known Alice, Tracy promised herself that the next day she would get back to work and catch up on the *Snip 'n Save* ads.

The next day came, but inspiration did not come along with it. She went into her office and sat behind the computer, but simply couldn't get started. It seemed of little importance whether the font size for the Barn Yard Stables was twenty-four or twenty-eight points. After a while, she powered down the computer and took Lucas into the backyard, where they played catch for most of the afternoon.

After two days of not working, she woke on the third morning with a new determination. Before lunch, she had finished three ads and started a fourth.

"I only have time for a quick sandwich," she told Lila. "Then it's back to work."

Lucas looked across the table, his mouth pulled into a pout. "You pwomised we'd go to the pawk."

Tracy smacked her hand to her forehead. "Oh, my gosh, I did."
She gave a sideways glance at Lila. "Mama, do you think you could—"

Lila grinned. "Of course! I'll take my darling boy to the park."

Tracy gulped down the last few bites of her sandwich and hurried
back into the office. A short while later she heard the front door slam
and knew they were gone.

She polished off the ad for Fine's Wines and moved on to Susan's
Boutique. She was positioning the illustration of a cameo brooch when
the doorbell rang. As she hurried through the living room, she saw a
sheriff's department car parked at the curb, and her heart stopped.

She flung open the door. "What's wrong?"

"Are you Tracy Briggs?" the officer asked.

"Yes," she replied nervously. "Dear God, don't tell me something—"

He handed her an envelope, politely said, "Have a nice day," then
turned and walked back down the walkway.

Feeling totally confused, Tracy stood there for a moment, then
glanced down at the envelope. It was addressed to her, but the return
address was the Magnolia Grove Courthouse.

Thinking there had to have been some mistake, she tore open the
envelope and unfolded the packet of papers. On the first page in large
bold type it read:

DeLuca vs Briggs

Petition for Guardianship/Legal Custody of Minor

Lucas Briggs DeLuca

For several minutes, Tracy was too stunned to do anything but
stand there leafing through the papers.

The document charged that she had willfully and with malicious
intent not included the biological father's name on the child's birth

certificate, then kidnapped the baby and moved him out of state. It went on to say this was done without permission of the plaintiff, the child's biological father, and it was thereby believed that the defendant, the child's biological mother, should not be trusted to make sound decisions as to the minor's welfare and financial circumstances. It stated that in an effort to right this wrong, the plaintiff had voluntarily relocated to Georgia in the hope of establishing a relationship with his son, but was summarily denied visitation. The third page went on to say the plaintiff was now seeking joint custody and legal guardianship to stabilize the situation and assure there would not be a recurrence of the incident.

By the time Tracy returned to the kitchen, her heart was pounding so furiously she thought it would burst out of her body. She dropped the document on the table, then dialed Meghan's cell phone. It rang several times, then went to voice mail.

"Call me back right away," Tracy said. "It's important!"

Moments after she hung up, the phone rang.

"I was with a patient," Meghan said. "What's wrong?"

"I need you to take over the *Snip 'n Save* for a while so I can—"

"I knew it!" Meghan snapped. "You promised you'd run the magazine, and now because you've got something better to do, you're looking to dump it back—"

Already on the verge of tears, Tracy cut in. "It's not something better. Dominic is suing me for custody of Lucas, and I've got to fight it."

"What?!"

"Yeah. He's saying he wants joint custody and guardianship."

"That's ridiculous! He hasn't cared enough to come and see Lucas for the past four years. Why would he want joint custody all of a sudden?"

Tracy brushed back the tears rolling down her face. "I don't know. All I know is that he's got a lawyer, and he's taking this to court."

"Well, then, we'll get a lawyer and fight him in court," Meghan said. "No sane judge or jury would give Dominic custody of Lucas once they find out how he's acted!"

"He claims I kidnapped Lucas."

"He can *claim* all he wants, but it won't get him anywhere. I'm calling Prescott Anderson right now, so sit tight."

Tracy heard a click; Meghan was gone.

She folded her arms on the kitchen table, then dropped her head and began to cry thundering sobs that racked her body like a tidal wave crashing ashore. When the phone rang ten minutes later, she gasped a near breathless hello.

"Tracy Briggs? This is Prescott Anderson of Algonquin Law. I just spoke with your sister, Meghan, and she asked that I represent you in this custody case with your ex-husband."

"We were never married," Tracy said tearfully.

Prescott gave a lighthearted chuckle. "All the better."

He asked if Tracy could stop by his office later that afternoon and bring the documents she'd received.

By the time Tracy pulled herself together and got to the Algonquin Law building, it was almost five. The receptionist ushered her back to Prescott's office, and they settled across the desk from one another. Tracy handed him the envelope, and he went through the papers one by one.

As he read, he asked questions, and little by little, Tracy told him the whole story, going back to when she and Dominic had first moved to Philadelphia.

"I really did think he'd marry me," she said, "but one month turned into two and then three. When Lucas came along, I thought, married or not, we could still be a family."

"Well, under normal circumstances, that would work, but once there's a problem in the relationship, then legally you have limited rights."

"Yeah, too bad I had to find out the hard way."

She sat with her hands in her lap, nervously fingering her engagement ring as she told of how she'd found Dominic in bed with the babysitter and Lucas scampering about the apartment by himself.

"Mr. Anderson, do you have children?"

He nodded. "Two girls; the youngest is Lucas's age."

"Then you understand. You have to watch a toddler every minute; all it takes is turning your head and they can fall out a window or pull a table on top of themselves."

He gave a thoughtful nod. "The terrible twos."

"Lucas was only fourteen months old, and there he was running around the apartment with a wet diaper and no one watching him. That's when I made up my mind to come home where I've got family to help me."

"After you left, did Dominic know where you'd gone?"

"Yes. He called my mama's house so many times, and he kept yelling and screaming that I stole his car."

"Did you?"

"I didn't exactly steal it. I kind of borrowed it to bring Lucas home to Georgia. And in any case, I shipped it back to him five days later."

"Did you pay for the transport?"

Tracy laughed bitterly. "I'll say. Hauling that wreck back to Philadelphia cost more than the car was worth, but at least it got him off my back."

"After you left, did he ever try to visit Lucas? Ask to take him for the weekend? Anything like that?"

She shook her head. "Never."

"What about cards or gifts? Did he remember Lucas's birthday and send presents?"

"No."

"In this claim, Mr. DeLuca says that you willfully and maliciously left his name off the child's birth certificate. Is that true?"

Tracy dipped her head with a guilty-looking nod. "I'm afraid so. We had an argument the day I went into labor, and Dominic stormed out. I thought knowing that my labor was starting, he'd come back as soon as he cooled down. He didn't. I went to the hospital alone. When I gave the nurse the baby's name, I said Lucas Briggs because I felt if Dominic couldn't make time to be there for his son's birth, he didn't deserve to have any part of him." She hesitated a moment, then added, "I thought once I got over being so angry with Dominic, I'd go back and add his name, but I never did."

"That just might work in our favor," Prescott said, then moved on to another question. After nearly two hours of going back and forth on every issue, he said he thought she had nothing to worry about.

"This feels like a nuisance lawsuit. Based on what you've told me, I don't think he wants your son. My bet is he's using this to get a bargaining point on something else."

"From me? I don't have anything he'd want."

"Money, maybe? Community property?"

"The only thing I have is my job at the *Snip 'n Save* and Lucas. I'm sure he's not after my job, so it has to be Lucas."

Prescott shook his head. "My intuition is telling me that's not it. He's after something; we just don't know what it is yet."

"So what do we do?"

"We wait. He can't possibly win this case, so sooner or later, he'll make a play for whatever it is he really wants, and when he does, we'll be ready."

56

True Calling

It was almost eight o'clock when Tracy arrived home, and much to her surprise, Meghan's car was in the driveway. She went into the kitchen and greeted Lila. As soon as they started speaking, Meghan came from the *Snip 'n Save* office and hurried into the kitchen. "So what happened?"

Before Tracy had a chance to talk, Lila shoved a plateful of food at her. "I won't have you getting sick on me, so sit down and eat your dinner, then you can tell us all about the meeting."

Tracy sat, peeled back the plastic wrap from her plate, and began eating. Earlier that afternoon, her stomach had been so queasy she thought she'd never again want to even see food, but oddly enough, she was now hungry. Meghan dropped into the chair across from Tracy, and Lila sat where she always sat: the chair closest to the counter, a spot where she could reach out and grab a forgotten utensil or missing saltshaker.

"Thanks for setting this up," Tracy said, looking at Meghan. "Prescott Anderson was great. Very understanding and kind. I have no idea how much he charges or how I'm going to pay him, but I'll worry about that later."

"He's doing it pro bono."

Since her mouth was full of meatloaf, Tracy shot Meghan a startled glance.

"He's not charging you anything. When he first started at Algonquin, Dad used to run free filler ads for him all the time, so he said he owes us."

Tracy swallowed her food and smiled. She told Meghan and Lila about the meeting and how Prescott had the feeling it was a nuisance lawsuit.

"What's that?" Lila asked.

"It's when a person sues you for one thing, but what they're really trying to do is back you into a corner so they can get something else."

"That doesn't make any sense at all. What would Dominic want from you?"

"That's exactly what I told Mr. Anderson. He said we'd have to wait and see."

"So what happens now?" Meghan asked.

"Nothing. Mr. Anderson said it will be a few days before he knows what judge the case has been assigned to."

That evening, Tracy and Meghan worked together in the *Snip 'n Save* office, first scouring through receipts to find the invoice for shipping Dominic's car to Philadelphia, and then catching up on the backlog of ads. As she worked her way through the ad folder, Meghan's mouth tightened into a thin narrow line. When she realized the file for Lucy's Nail Salon was dated almost a month ago, she could no longer hold her tongue.

"I understand you've been upset about losing Alice and everything that's happening with Dominic, but some of these ads are over three weeks old! You promised me that you'd—"

"I know, I know. I'm sorry. I've been meaning to catch up, but . . ." Tracy let the words trail off because, in truth, there was no excuse, at least not one that readily came to mind.

"But what?" Meghan said sharply.

Without turning to face her sister, Tracy shrugged. "There was a lot going on with the school."

"The school isn't your job. This is!"

Perhaps because the day had been so very difficult, or possibly because she had no other excuse, Tracy turned and glared at Meghan.

"It's my job, but it's not my life! I'm not like you, Meghan. I'm not in love with the *Snip 'n Save*, and if you'd be really honest with yourself about it, you'd admit you're not, either!"

"What's that supposed to mean? I'm here helping you, aren't I?"

"Yes, but not because you love the *Snip 'n Save*. You don't really want to be doing this. Not just tonight but other days, too—days when you're at the clinic working with the animals. You'd rather be there doing something you love, and I can understand that. I'd rather be at the school working with children."

A weighted silence fell between the two sisters, and it was a long while before Meghan spoke. When she did, her voice was softer and less riddled with anger.

"You're right. I would rather be working at the clinic. But Daddy loved this business, and we owe him—"

Tracy cut in. "What makes you so sure he loved it?"

"It was his baby. He took it when it was just a few pages and built it into what it is today. He always said—"

"What he said was that he loved working from home and being with his family. That's not the same as loving the magazine."

Meghan sat there, letting the silence grow heavier and heavier.

"That's not the way I remember it," she finally said and turned back to the computer.

For a long while, she worked, trying to finish the ad for Lucy's Nail Salon, but nothing was right. The headline was clunky, the photograph seemingly out of focus. She blamed the blurriness on low resolution, but if she'd looked at herself in the mirror, she might have seen it was because of the tears welling in her eyes.

That night, sleep was almost impossible for Meghan to come by. She lay awake, feeling the warmth of Sox at her feet and Tom beside her. It was true; this was where her heart was.

She loved working with Tom, feeling his hand brush against hers as they passed an instrument from one to the other. She loved the rambunctiousness of young puppies that came for shots and the gratitude in the eyes of animals that came to be cured of their illness or injury.

She did love these things more, but that didn't mean she was willing to turn her back on what her daddy had held dear. If Tracy wanted to walk away, then so be it. If it came to that, Meghan would leave the clinic and go back to running the *Snip 'n Save*. She'd do it because it was what her daddy would have wanted.

Over and over again, she reminded herself how much the magazine meant to him, but try as she might, she couldn't recall a single time he'd actually said it. It was easy to find the memory of him sitting behind the computer, bent forward, squinting at the screen. She could see the crinkles at the corner of his eyes and recall how when she'd walked into the office, he'd set aside whatever he was working on and stood to give her a hug. She could even remember how at the end of the day he'd pull the office door closed, smile, and say, "Well, now, that's done!"

Was he smiling because he loved his work? Or was it because the workday was over?

In a single heartbeat, she could find an endless strand of memories, like the times he'd held her hand as together they searched for Clancy, her dog, the one that disappeared from the backyard. She could find even more of the evenings when they'd pushed back and forth in the front porch swing, discussing her plans to attend the Grady School of Journalism. Those moments were as clear as a bell, but she couldn't find the one she was searching for.

She pushed aside the other memories and tried to focus on picturing her daddy in the *Snip 'n Save* office. In her mind, he'd said the magazine was his baby a thousand times, but this night she couldn't find a single instance. What she did remember was the weariness she'd seen in his face at the end of a long day.

57

Meghan Whitely

Last night, I barely closed my eyes. I couldn't sleep because I was thinking about that argument with Tracy. I kept trying to remember exactly what Daddy said to make me believe he loved the Snip 'n Save. *Before I sat down to breakfast this morning, I called Mama and asked if she could ever remember him talking about how much he loved the magazine.*

She laughed like I'd just told a real funny joke, so I asked why.

"Your daddy didn't love things," she said. "He loved people!"

I told her I was well aware Daddy loved people but distinctly remembered him saying how proud he was of having built up the Snip 'n Save *and making a success of it.*

"Isn't that the same as love?" I asked.

"It most certainly isn't." Then she reminded me about all the times Daddy had bragged about how his girls were what made him proud.

"Why didn't you tell me this back when I was working so hard to keep the magazine up and running?" I asked.

Mama took so long to answer that, for a minute, I thought we'd been disconnected. She's the most loving person in the world, but she's not quick to share her sadness.

"Are you still there, Mama?" I asked.

"I'm still here," she said, and when she finally started to talk, her voice was shaky and sad like it had been back then.

"When your daddy died, you were hurting so much it nearly broke my heart. The only thing that made you the least bit happy was working on the Snip 'n Save like you used to do with George. Only God knows why, but you found a little bit of your daddy in that magazine, and it gave you a measure of peace."

She gave a long deep sigh, then said, "After you lost your daddy, I wasn't going to take away that last bit of comfort you had."

Hearing Mama's words, I knew she was telling the truth, but I didn't want to believe it.

I wish I could say the conversation made a difference in how I feel about keeping the Snip 'n Save as part of our family, but it doesn't. No matter what anybody says, I still believe Daddy loved it. Maybe not the same as he loved Mama and Tracy and me, but all the same, he loved it, and I owe it to him to make sure it stays alive.

If the Snip 'n Save shut down, it would be like Daddy dying all over again, and I'm not willing to let that happen.

I think if I talk to Tracy and explain what I'm feeling, she'll be more likely to understand. Maybe we can both work at it—me do part, and her do part. At least until this ugliness with Dominic is over and done with.

58

The Snip 'n Save **Problem**

Three days later, Prescott Anderson called Tracy.

"Your case has been assigned to Judge Kingston," he said, "and the court has appointed a psychologist to interview you, Dominic, and Lucas."

Tracy's heart started racing. "But why? I thought you said this was a nuisance lawsuit, that it would never amount to much of anything."

"It pretty much is, but—"

"Then why are they doing these interviews?" she asked, her voice rising a pitch.

"It's standard procedure. Once a lawsuit is filed, it goes through the process regardless of whether or not the case has merit."

"But what if I say something wrong?"

"Don't worry." Prescott's voice was steady and reassuring. "All you have to do is tell the truth. Let the psychologist see what kind of an environment you're raising Lucas in, and that'll be the end of it."

"Are you sure?"

"Nothing is one hundred percent, but I'm willing to wager we'll find out what Dominic's really after long before the case goes to court."

When there was nothing more to say, Tracy hung up the phone. Her heart had slowed, but it was still beating faster than normal. She sat there for a long while thinking back on Prescott's words. She wanted to believe everything would be as he'd said. Trying to refocus on the task at hand, Tracy shook her head to clear her thoughts, then turned back to the ad she was working on, slid the headline into place, and closed the file without ever noticing how the graphic was sitting at an odd angle.

The truth was that Dominic could be extremely likable when he wanted to be; she knew that for a fact. He could charm a person into believing black was white and render them blind to his faults.

On the other hand, she knew she could come across as difficult and argumentative. Hadn't her mama said so a dozen times? Just a few weeks earlier, when she'd wrinkled her nose and refused to even taste the brussels sprouts, Lila had asked why she had to be *so very difficult*. She even argued with Meghan, her own sister and best friend! They had always been so close, but now, she bristled at the least little thing. Just last night, she'd sat there stating her opinion as if it were law, not once taking into account that Meghan was trying to help her. If that wasn't being argumentative, then what was?

The more Tracy thought about the upcoming interviews, the more worried she became. It seemed everything was coming down on her all at once.

She finished up the third ad and emailed Sheldon the folder. She'd promised him five, but three would have to do. There was simply no way she could focus, and it would be better to wait a week than to mess up the ads entirely, wouldn't it? Sheldon could use filler ads for the empty spaces, and she'd make sure those other two were the first ones she did for the next issue.

Pushing back from the computer, Tracy hurried into the kitchen where Lila was watching a cooking show.

"Mama," she said, "do you really think I'm difficult and argumentative?"

Lila snapped off *Rachael Ray* and turned. "What on earth would make you say a thing like that?" She reached across and put her hand to Tracy's forehead. "Are you coming down with the flu or something?"

"No, I'm fine. But I'm worried about this thing with Dominic. Mr. Anderson says it's just a nuisance lawsuit, so why would they send someone out here to check on me?"

"Sit down and have a cup of tea. You've obviously been working too hard."

Before she could say no, Lila pulled out a chair and eased her into it. As Tracy tearfully explained her fear that she would alienate the interviewer by not saying or doing the right thing, Lila assured her she was not the least bit difficult or argumentative.

"If anything, you're too easygoing," she said.

"But when I didn't eat the brussels sprouts, you said—"

"Oh, for heaven's sake. I should think you'd know better than to get worked up over a little thing like that. I just wanted you to test out my new buttered-sprouts recipe."

As Tracy sat there with her fingers wrapped around a mug of chamomile tea, her heartbeat slowed, and the throbbing behind her eyes eased. She was about to tell Lila of her conversation with Meghan, but before she had the chance, the *Snip 'n Save* phone rang. When Tracy started to get up, Lila placed a hand on her arm.

"You really don't have to answer that," she said. "The machine can get it."

Tracy dropped back into the chair, but moments after the *Snip 'n Save* phone stopped ringing, Tracy's cell phone started. She snatched up the phone before Lila had a chance to see the screen.

"Hello?" she said with the phone to her ear.

"What's going on over there?" Sheldon asked, sounding more than a little upset.

"What do you mean?"

"Those ads you sent over are full of mistakes! There's a baby picture in the ad for the shooting range, and the Border Café coupon is missing!"

Tracy's shoulders sagged. "Send them back. I'll redo them."

"Make sure you proof them, okay?"

"Okay."

She pressed "End" and slid back from the table. "I've got to go back to work, Mama. When Lucas gets up from his nap, would you keep an eye on him for me?"

"Sure," Lila replied. As she watched Tracy disappear down the hallway, she shook her head and grumbled, "It's time for me to do a lot more than just keep an eye on Lucas."

Without waiting, she dialed Meghan's cell phone, and when the voice mail came on, she said, "Meghan, this is Mama. Your sister is having a hard time, and you need to get over here right away."

Minutes later, Meghan called back. "What's wrong?"

"Tracy's sick with worry over this thing with Dominic, and she's not able to keep up with the *Snip 'n Save*." Lila's voice was curt, and she didn't bother with conversational niceties. "We've got to do something."

"Do what?"

"I think maybe it's time the three of us sat down together and talked about—"

"I'm not interested in selling the magazine," Meghan said flatly.

"That decision is not yours to make. I can appreciate how close you were to your daddy, Meghan, but the *Snip 'n Save* belongs to all three of us. Up until now, I saw the need for keeping the magazine, but given the way things are—"

"I'll take it over. I'll do it by myself."

Lila did not back off. "As I said before, Meghan, this decision is not yours or mine. The three of us need to talk it through."

Meghan gave a great thunderous sigh. "You've already made up your mind, haven't you, Mama?"

"No, I haven't," Lila replied. "And I don't plan on doing so until I know that whatever decision we reach is in the best interests of everyone in this family."

Meghan heard the decided emphasis that was placed on the word *everyone*.

59

Family Meeting

The following afternoon, the three Briggs women gathered at the kitchen table. George's sister, Phoebe, had taken Lucas to the park, and Meghan had rescheduled her appointments, so there was nothing that could interrupt the meeting. Lila was determined they would sit there until the problem was out on the table and she'd had her say. She set out a platter of sandwiches and a bowl of potato salad, but no one reached for either.

Meghan's chin was dropped down toward her chest, and her brows were so tightly knitted together they had the look of one.

"I really don't want to be doing this," Meghan said.

Lila poured three glasses of sweet tea and set one in front of Meghan. "I know you don't, honey, but it's something that's long overdue."

Tracy's expression was no less apprehensive than her sister's, but for a different reason. When the phone rang, she jumped as if she were stung by a bee.

"No one is answering the phone today," Lila said firmly. "Whoever it is can wait until we're finished here. Meghan, did you bring the reports I asked for?"

Meghan nodded. "Yes."

"Give Tracy and me a copy so we're all looking at the same thing."

Meghan handed each of them a thin packet of profit/loss statements for the past three years.

"This just shows the actual income generated by the *Snip 'n Save*. It doesn't take into account savings on homeowner's taxes, commuting cost, and, of course, the convenience of working from home."

Lila eyed the figures. "So after expenses and Tracy's salary, the *Snip 'n Save* only had a net profit of six thousand dollars last year, right?"

Meghan gave an almost imperceptible nod. "But it was over eight thousand the two years before that."

Lila lifted the first sheet, read through the other reports, then lifted an eyebrow. "The magazine pays Tracy thirty-six thousand dollars a year. That's a good salary, but other jobs could match that."

"I'm happy with that amount," Tracy said defensively. "I'm not looking for more."

"You might be happy with what you're being paid, but I'm not happy with you being so stressed out. You're a mama, and you need time to take care of Lucas. Before you can blink an eye, he'll be grown up and gone." Lila's eyes saddened. "Trust me, I know."

"I can take over most of the workload," Meghan offered. "That'll lighten the burden and give Tracy more time with Lucas."

"And just how do you plan to find the time?" Lila asked.

"I won't see patients in the afternoon, and I'll work evenings."

"Oh? Aren't you and Tom building a business? Now that you have your technician's license, he'll be counting on you to be an equal partner, the kind who shares the load instead of dumping it off on him."

"I do my share."

"Now, maybe, but if you go back to handling the *Snip 'n Save*—"

Meghan's eyes grew misty. "I can do both."

"Maybe so, but you won't be doing either job well."

"Tracy's not going to quit; she'll still be helping out."

"Tracy and Gabriel are getting married in a few months, and she'll want to move to Barrington. What then?"

"I'll take the laptop and do the design work from Barrington," Tracy offered.

"If you can't keep up now, what makes you think you can do it when you're married and have additional responsibilities?"

"Gabriel can take Lucas to school, and I'll stay home to work."

"Really?" Lila said with an air of cynicism. "I thought Gabriel just asked you to work at the—"

"Mama! I told you not to say anything about that."

"Wait, what?" Meghan asked.

"Girls, things change," Lila said, not answering Meghan for the moment, "and people have to change with them. There was a time when we needed the *Snip 'n Save*, but that time has passed. You girls are grown up now and both blessed with men who will love you and care for you the way your daddy did for me. You can hang on to the sweet memories you have of your daddy without letting them weigh you down like an anchor."

Tears rolled down Meghan's face. "Please don't say we've got to sell the *Snip 'n Save*. I can't lose that part of Daddy."

Lila reached across the table and took Meghan's hand in hers. "I know you think your daddy loved the *Snip 'n Save*, but the truth is he didn't. He cared for it the same way he cared about his black dress shoes. At times they pinched and were uncomfortable, but they served a purpose. The magazine also served a purpose. It allowed your daddy to work from home and be close to his family."

A faraway look of sadness settled on Lila's face. "After George died, I kept those black dress shoes for almost three years, because I couldn't bring myself to let go of them. I felt like they were a part of your daddy I needed to hold on to . . ."

"Do you still have them?" Meghan asked.

Lila shook her head. "When Tracy came home from Philadelphia, I cleaned out the closets to make room for her and Lucas. I took the shoes and a bunch of clothes I'd been keeping to Goodwill. The woman at the counter told me George's things would make some needy soul very happy."

"But didn't you feel sad losing that last little bit of Daddy?"

Lila gave a bittersweet smile. "Yes, I did, but the thought of somebody else being happy to have those things helped me feel better. And then after a while, I got so caught up in the happiness of having your sister and Lucas around, I forgot about them altogether. Well, maybe not altogether, but the thought of them went from being a weight I carried to a sweet memory."

"But, Mama, those were just shoes. It's different with the *Snip 'n Save*."

"It's not all that different," Lila said. "The shoes were to me what the *Snip 'n Save* is to you."

Meghan gave a deep sigh, pulled up from the bottom of her soul.

"I know how difficult this is for you," Lila continued, "but if you keep the past in there, crowding your closet, you won't have room for what you need for the future. Tom and the veterinary practice are your future, Meghan."

"But, Mama—"

"Letting go of the *Snip 'n Save* isn't the same as letting go of your memories. You'll always have those. Even when you're an old lady with snow-white hair and grandbabies in college, you'll still remember how much your daddy loved you."

"Keeping the *Snip 'n Save* isn't just because of memories," Meghan argued. "It provides an income for you and pays Tracy's salary."

Lila chuckled. "The income I get from it isn't enough to keep me in cookie dough. And Tracy already has a job offer from the school. The only reason she didn't take it was because of the promise she'd made to you."

Meghan turned to Tracy. "Is that true?"

Tracy gave a reluctant nod. "Knowing how you feel about the *Snip 'n Save*, I wouldn't feel right about going back on my promise. If it weren't for you, we might never have discovered that Lucas . . ." Her voice faltered, and the rest of the thought was left unspoken.

Lila reached across, squeezed Tracy's shoulder, then moved on to talking about the possibility of selling the *Snip 'n Save*.

"I'm not saying we have to come to a decision right this minute," she said. "But you need to think about it, Meghan. Maybe there's someone out there interested in owning a magazine, and they might be as happy to get the *Snip 'n Save* as that needy person was to get your daddy's shoes."

After a long moment of silence, Meghan said, "I'll think about it," but the words coming from her mouth felt as sharp and cutting as razor blades.

60

Lila Briggs

You might think this decision is easy, but it isn't. I cried a bucket of tears the day I took George's things over to Goodwill, so I understand how Meghan is feeling. If on that day someone had told me that a year later I'd be all the happier for having done it, I'd have laughed in their face.

The thing is, I'm a mama with two girls, and I can't allow one to suffer because I'm humoring the wants of the other. Tracy deserves to live her own life, and she can't do it sitting at that computer. She's got a mama's heart. I can see it, and I know Gabriel can, too. She'll be an asset to the school if for no other reason than she loves working with children.

I know Meghan can't see it now, but she'll be better off, too, once the Snip 'n Save is gone. She loves Tom, and she's happy to be working with him. Sometimes she'll stop by, bubbling over with stories of the animals she's treated or with the general happiness of being married.

I could insist we just go ahead and sell the magazine, but I won't do that. I've given Meghan enough to think about, and I believe, in the end, she'll make the right decision. She loves Tracy as much as I do, and I'm trusting she won't choose her own happiness over her sister's.

61

As Days Moved On

Matthew McGinley hadn't taken a vacation in three years. The law practice had more than doubled in that time, and he'd worked long into the night more often than he cared to remember. This year, he vowed it would be different. This year, he was taking a full three weeks off for the family trip to Ireland. He had a great-grandmother about to celebrate her one hundredth birthday, and relatives he'd never met were planning a party to end all parties.

For two solid months, he'd stayed late at the office and worked from home on Saturdays so he'd be caught up enough to take the time off without worrying about this, that, or the other thing waiting to be done. Before he left, he'd given his assistant, Pamela, the phone number where he could be reached but suggested she use it only in the direst circumstance.

"I know you can handle anything that comes up," he said.

Matthew, his wife, and his two girls were boarding the plane when Charlie Barnes called Pamela to notify him that Alice DeLuca had passed away.

Pamela offered her condolences, promised they'd get right on it, and hung up the phone. She sat there for a few seconds considering whether or not this was the direst of circumstances and decided it was not. The probate filing of Alice DeLuca's will was one of those things that could wait. Probate usually took several months and in some cases a year or more, so three weeks hardly made a difference. She typed a memo with the necessary details and slid it into the in-box on Matthew's desk.

Kathleen Miller had been with Child Welfare Services for less than a month when she was assigned to the *DeLuca vs. Briggs* case. For her first two cases, she'd worked alongside another psychologist, but this one she was handling alone. Excited to be cut loose so early, Kathleen was determined to make her assessment of both parties spot-on, sharp in even the minutest detail, with nothing questionable or left to chance. As soon as she got the assignment, she set up the interviews: Tracy first, then Dominic later in the afternoon.

The morning she was scheduled to interview Tracy started out with a blue sky and bright sun, but before Kathleen turned onto Baker Street, the rain began. At first it was just a few large splashes against the windshield, but moments later, the wind picked up and the granddaddy of all storms rolled in. It was almost impossible to see out the windshield, so she missed the Briggses' driveway and had to back up. When she did make the turn, she came within an inch of taking down the mailbox.

Lila saw the car pull into the driveway and opened the garage door.

"Come this way, it's shorter!" she yelled.

It was not much more than ten feet from where she parked the car to the garage, but by the time Kathleen made it inside she was soaked. Leaving a trail of water behind, she followed Lila back to the kitchen.

"You're Tracy Briggs?"

"Heavens, no, I'm her mama," Lila said with a smile. "Wait here, I'll call Tracy."

She disappeared down the hall, and moments later returned with Tracy and two fluffy white towels. She spread one across the seat of the chair and handed the other to Kathleen. "You might want to dry off a bit."

"Thanks."

Kathleen had taken special care to look the part on her first day as an independent; she'd worn her new wool suit and was now regretting it. She removed her jacket and hung it on the back of the chair, but no matter how much she blotted and dabbed at the skirt, it remained wet and was starting to take on the smell of a wet dog. Trying to move past her discomfort, Kathleen sat across from Tracy and pulled out her notepad.

"Now, if you can just tell me a bit about yourself."

Tracy said she was a single mom presently working at the *Snip 'n Save*, a family business, but her situation would likely be changing soon.

"Oh, and why is that?"

"Well, Mama would like to sell the magazine, and once Gabriel and I are married, I'll move to Barrington—"

"Married?" Kathleen flipped through the pages in her folder. "Hmm. There's no mention of that in here. If your fiancé is going to be part of Lucas's life, then I'll need to interview him, too."

She scribbled *fiancé* on the top of the last page, then started over. "This fiancé, did you have a relationship with him before you left Philadelphia?"

"No, definitely not! He operates a school for deaf children here in Georgia; I met him just before Lucas had his cochlear implant."

A rather confused look settled on Kathleen's face. She again opened the folder and flipped through the pages. "Does Lucas have a hearing problem?"

"Yes, we believe he was born deaf, but because he wasn't tested until he was almost fifteen months old, we don't know for sure."

Kathleen twitched her mouth to one side, looking perturbed. "Odd; there's no mention of that in the file, either."

She turned back to the first page and recapped the complaint.

"Mr. DeLuca claims he came home from work one day to discover you and the child both missing. He says it was months before he finally tracked you down here, and when he did, you refused to let him see or speak to Lucas."

"That's a flat-out lie!" Tracy heard the anger in her voice and tried to dial it back. "What I mean is, that's not what happened."

Kathleen closed the folder. "Why don't you tell me your version of the story?"

Tracy explained how she'd come home from work to find Dominic in bed with the babysitter and Lucas toddling around the apartment with no supervision.

"He was fourteen months old! He could have pulled something over on top of himself or wandered off. I was horrified."

"And then what?"

"I left the next day and came home where I had family to help out."

She continued, telling Kathleen how by that point Lucas hadn't started talking yet, and she was becoming more and more concerned.

"My sister set up an appointment with the pediatrician, but then that same week, Dominic canceled our health insurance."

"Did he know Lucas needed care?"

Tracy had to hold back from screaming, "You bet your ass he did!" The one thing she couldn't afford to do was alienate this interviewer.

"Yes, he did," she said. "I told him, but he seemed to not care."

"You must have been pretty angry about that," Kathleen said, throwing the thought out and waiting for her to respond. It was a tactic she'd watched her coworker Monica use on the first case they'd worked together.

"Of course I was angry!" Tracy said, a bit of testiness woven through her words. "Wouldn't you be?"

"So because you felt angry that he'd canceled the insurance, you didn't allow Dominic to see or talk to his son?"

"No, no, that's not it at all! He never even tried to see Lucas!"

"Wasn't that because he didn't know where you were?"

"He knew exactly where I was. He sent his goon friend here to tell me he wanted his car back."

Kathleen nodded knowingly. "Yes, the file does say you stole his car."

Tracy's cheeks grew red, and her jaw stiffened. "I didn't steal it," she said. "I borrowed it to bring Lucas back here where I could get help and find out why he wasn't talking. I shipped the car back to Dominic a few days after I got here, and I can prove it."

"Prove it how?"

Tracy excused herself, hurried into the office, and returned with the transport company's receipt.

"Can I hang on to this?" Kathleen asked.

Tracy nodded. "Yes, it's a copy."

At that point, they moved on to talking about Lucas. Tracy explained how Meghan put her and Lucas on the *Snip 'n Save* insurance policy, helped find the resources for having Lucas tested, and ultimately introduced her to Gabriel.

"It's a great school, and Lucas loves it there. He still has trouble with a few sounds, but that's normal for his condition. In about a year, he'll be able to speak as well as any other six-year-old."

"Wonderful," Kathleen said, giving what might have been the first smile Tracy had seen since they sat down. "I'd like to chat with him if you don't mind."

Tracy went to the hallway and called up the stairs for her mama to bring Lucas down. Kathleen spent a half hour talking to both Lila and Lucas. Then she asked if she might speak to Lucas alone.

Tracy and Lila stepped out of the kitchen, and Lucas stood there, looking apprehensive.

"Why do Mama and Gwandma have to go away?" he asked.

Kathleen smiled. "Because sometimes little kids feel they can't tell the truth if their mama or daddy is watching."

"Oh." He hesitated a second, then his face brightened. "Mama says I gotta tell the twuth all the time."

"She's right, kids should always tell the truth."

After a few questions about his favorite toys and storybooks, Kathleen moved on. "Lucas, have you ever met your daddy?"

He shook his head. "I meeted Gwammy Awice."

"Who's Grammy Alice?"

He grinned. "Daddy's gwandma, but she's my gwandma, too." Without being prodded, he continued on. "I miss Gwammy Awice. She buyed me toys, and we pwayed games."

"Oh?" Kathleen's left eye twitched, a sure sign there was more to this than she'd been told. "So where's Grammy Alice now?" she asked suspiciously.

For a moment it seemed as though Lucas wasn't going to answer, then he slowly lifted his arm and pointed a finger upward. "Gwammy's in heaven wif a Gwampa I never meeted."

His little-boy sadness tugged at Kathleen's heart. "I'm so sorry," she said. Then she scribbled a margin note to ask Dominic about his grandma, underlined it twice, and continued. "What about your daddy? Has your mama told you anything about him?"

He shook his head. "My daddy lives faw away and is busy."

"Did your mama say if he was a nice man or a bad man?"

Lucas stood there thinking, then shook his head again.

Once she ran through her list of things to ask about, Kathleen asked Lucas if he could go and get his mama. He darted out of the room and returned with Tracy.

"I need to get Gabriel Hawke's phone number," Kathleen said.

She jotted down the number, said it had been a pleasure, and left.

Tracy began to worry the moment the door shut behind Kathleen. In the whole two hours she'd been there, she'd smiled maybe three times. Tracy had hoped the interviewer would be a man or at the very least an older woman, someone who'd be less vulnerable to Dominic's charm.

She gave a weary sigh and dropped into the chair.

Kathleen carried her jacket from the house and tossed it into the back seat. The sky had turned blue again, and the sun was back, but the wet-dog smell of her suit was making her nauseous. There was no way she could spend the rest of the day in these clothes. She had to go home and change, and by then, it would be too late to conduct another interview.

She called Dominic and rescheduled for the next morning. Gabriel, she scheduled for the afternoon.

62

The Interviews

Dominic had been sitting around waiting for Kathleen Miller for a good hour before she called. He'd cleared the magazines from the table, brewed a fresh pot of coffee, shaved, then dressed in a sport shirt and his good slacks. He'd thought through what he wanted to say and planned on using the unassuming laugh that women found irresistible.

When she said she had to reschedule, it had thrown him off his stride, and he'd given a snap-back answer, which was precisely what he'd hoped to avoid. Aggravated with both himself and Kathleen, he figured he could use a drink and headed down to Murphy's. One thing led to another, and it ended up being well after one in the morning when he returned home. At that point, he was so exhausted he never even made it up the stairs to his bedroom.

When the doorbell *bonged* at nine o'clock the next morning, Dominic had all but forgotten about Kathleen Miller. She stood there for a full five minutes before he opened the door, and when he finally did, he looked like he'd slept in his clothes—which is precisely what had happened.

"Are you okay?" she asked.

Dominic ran his fingers through his hair. "I've been better." Trying to salvage the impression he was making, he added, "What with losing my grandma and all, I haven't been myself. Losing her was just . . ." He let the rest of the sentence trail off as if there weren't enough words to describe the terrible pain.

Kathleen placed her hand on Dominic's arm.

"I'm so sorry," she said. Leaving her hand in place, she asked, "Your grandma, was she Lucas's Grammy Alice?"

Dominic nodded. He hadn't counted on this and wasn't prepared, so he had to wing it.

"Yes," he said, giving a deep sigh. "She loved Lucas almost as much as I do."

Kathleen nodded and pulled her hand back. Thankful she'd spent two weeks working alongside Monica, she'd found it was prudent to be suspicious of what certain people offered up freely and worthwhile to dig deeper and find the things they hadn't intended to tell. When Dominic dropped down on the sofa, she sat in the club chair opposite him and took the folder from her bag.

"This won't take long," she said and smiled. "Your grandmother sounds like she was a wonderful woman," she went on, acting as though the interview hadn't yet started. "Were the two of you able to visit Lucas together?"

Dominic shook his head. "Afraid not. With her declining health, it just wasn't possible. I asked Tracy if we could bring Lucas here for a visit, but unfortunately . . ." He spread his hands in a gesture of helplessness.

That's when Kathleen first began to be suspicious. She thought about the questions she'd asked Lucas. Lucas didn't know his daddy, but he knew the grandma.

It's possible for an adult to look you in the eye and tell a barefaced lie, but it's less likely a child will do it.

After fifteen minutes of back and forth with not a single answer falling into place properly, Kathleen figured that was all she was going to get. She closed the folder and reached for her bag.

Seeing the deadpan look on her face, Dominic gave a mournful groan and dropped his head into his hands.

"It's no use," he said. "I can't go on pretending. The truth is I've never actually spent time with Lucas. Tracy won't allow it. I've parked down the street hundreds of times and watched him from the car, but that's it." With his voice quivering as if he'd been pushed to the brink of tears, he added, "Seeing my boy grow up without me is what made me realize I had to ask for guardianship."

Kathleen reopened the folder and started to write. "Can you recall the first time you tried to see Lucas and were turned away?"

"It's been so many years, it's almost impossible to say exactly . . ."

———— ☙❧ ————

Gabriel Hawke was Kathleen's last interview of the day. She arrived at the school late in the afternoon, thinking maybe she could wrap it up in an hour or so. She wasn't prepared for a half-hour tour of the school and the detailed description that went along with it. As they walked from room to room, Gabriel told of how it was when Lucas first came there and explained the progress they'd made.

"The first time he ever heard the sound of his mama's voice was in our audiology studio. Michelle worked with him." Gabriel pushed open the office door and stuck his head in. "Michelle, Miss Miller has a few questions about Lucas Briggs; can you spare a few minutes to talk with her?"

Gabriel smiled and stepped back, allowing Kathleen to enter.

"I have a phone call to make; Michelle will bring you up to my office when you're ready."

As soon as she sat, Kathleen whipped out her notebook, copied down Michelle's name, and began making notes. For the first few minutes, she scribbled as fast as she could, but Michelle was impossible to keep up with. After a while she simply sat and listened. In the end, she wrote that it was only the Briggs family involved in Lucas's treatment.

Once she finished with Michelle, Kathleen rejoined Gabriel in his office. She learned that although Dominic had never visited the school, his grandmother had.

"Barrington's close to fifty miles from Magnolia Grove," Kathleen said. "My understanding is that Alice was sickly, so how did she get here?"

"Charlie Barnes drove her, and we met them with a wheelchair." He told her about their lunch in the conference room and what a fine time Alice had had that day.

"It was one of her last good days," he said sadly.

"This Charlie Barnes, he lives in Magnolia Grove?"

Gabriel nodded, and Kathleen wrote the name in her notebook with a question mark alongside it.

"Do you know that Alice's grandson, Dominic, has petitioned the court for joint custody and guardianship of Lucas?"

Gabriel again gave a nod. "Yes, Tracy told me."

"Why do you think he did that?"

Gabriel sat silent for a long moment before he answered. "I don't know that anyone can say why another person does something, but since Dominic has never made an effort to have a relationship with Lucas, it surprises me."

"Have you ever known Tracy to deny Dominic access to Lucas?"

"Once. Four years ago. It was Thanksgiving Day, and he showed up at the Briggses' house drunk. I wasn't outside, but even inside the house, you could hear him cussing and screaming."

"What did Tracy do?"

"As I said, I wasn't outside with them; I was at the dinner table with the other guests. If you want to know exactly what happened, ask her sister, Meghan. She was there."

Kathleen wrote "ask Meghan about Thanksgiving" in her notebook, then thanked Gabriel for his time and left.

In the days that followed, Kathleen interviewed Meghan and Tom, and they corroborated Gabriel's story. Meghan told how Tracy had pushed Dominic off the porch after he'd grabbed her, and Tom shared with a sheepish look the incident of punching Dominic because he wouldn't leave Tracy alone. When Kathleen finished with them, she found Charlie Barnes, and he told the whole story of how Alice had struggled with Dominic's behavior and begged him to take responsibility for his son.

"I guess she'd be pretty glad to know he finally has," he said sadly.

A look of doubt swept across Kathleen's face. "I don't know if I'd say that."

When she asked if he knew of any other reason why Dominic would have taken a sudden interest in the boy, Charlie shrugged.

"I can't say what's going on in his mind, but I suspect it's because of the will."

"She had a will?"

Kathleen copied down the name of the lawyer who'd drawn it up, then thanked Charlie for his time.

"You've been helpful," she said. "Very helpful."

The following day she called McGinley & Hudson only to find out that Matthew McGinley was in Ireland and not due back for another nine days.

63

Meghan's Decision

In the days following the family meeting, Meghan did as she'd promised her mama. She thought about what they might do with the *Snip 'n Save*. There were times when she reasoned her mama's logic was sound and other times when the thought of letting go of that one last piece of her daddy brought on a loneliness not even Tom could fill.

On Sunday morning, she sat across the breakfast table from him, her shoulders slumped and her mouth downturned as she ignored the platter of eggs growing cold and sprinkled salt into her coffee.

"What's wrong?" Tom asked, but she shrugged.

"Nothing."

The sound of happiness in her voice had all but disappeared, and Sox, it seemed, sensed it. He remained by her side night and day, following her from one room to another. Rubbing against her leg, offering up a ball, or pleading to be noticed with a soft, melancholy whine. In the evening, when she moved about the kitchen preparing dinner, he lay beneath her chair, his body flattened to the floor, but his eyes following her every movement.

On evenings when that faraway look settled in Meghan's eyes, the dog would jump onto the sofa and snuggle alongside her, but she hardly noticed. After a while, he'd paw her hand, a signal that he was waiting to be petted. She'd lift her hand onto his back or tummy and leave it lying still as a stone as though she'd forgotten what it was there for.

After nearly two weeks of watching her mope around as sorrowful as a person who was already dead and buried, Tom insisted she needed to take a break. He closed the office early, and they went to the lake.

"We'll have supper here," he said as he set the picnic basket down and stretched a blanket across the grass. After they sat, he took a bottle of wine from the basket and poured them each a glass. For a while they simply sat there, watching Sox frolic along the edge of the lake but never getting close enough to touch the water.

Meghan gave a barely perceptible chuckle. "It's been years since he almost drowned, but he's still afraid to get close to the water."

Tom turned, and his eyes connected with hers. For a moment, he held her gaze; then she blinked and turned back to looking out over the lake.

"Sox isn't the only one who's scared," he said.

Tilting her head to the side, she eyed him with a curious expression. "Meaning what?"

"I'm scared, too. Scared you don't trust me enough to share what's bothering you."

Meghan gave a soft sigh and leaned her head against his shoulder. "It's not about you, Tom. It's about the *Snip 'n Save*."

"Anything that affects you has an effect on me too, Meghan. Joined as one, remember?"

She slid her hand into his, and he squeezed it just as he always did. That was one of the things she loved about Tom; he was dependable, always there for her. He was the touchstone she could return to when anything went awry.

They stayed that way for several minutes; then she said, "Mama says maybe we should sell it. She thinks it might be better for everybody."

"And what do you think?"

There was a heavy silence before she answered. "I can't help feeling it's the only part of Daddy I can still hold on to."

As they sat and talked, the sun dropped behind the roofs on the far side of the lake and the sky turned dusky. Sox curled on the blanket and dozed as Meghan explained her mama's reasoning and told how she herself was torn between wanting to keep the life she now had and preserving the life she'd once known.

"I never thought I'd have to deal with this kind of situation. When Tracy came home, I gave her a job working with the *Snip 'n Save*, and she promised to run it forever. Now she seems to think forever is too long."

"Maybe it is," Tom replied. "It definitely seems a lot longer if you're stuck in a place that doesn't make you happy."

The thought settled in Meghan's heart with a heavy thud. She had never considered working at the *Snip 'n Save* as being stuck. For her, it had been a labor of love, and she'd always believed it was the same for Tracy. "I guess you're right," she replied sadly. "Anyway, Gabriel has offered her a job at the school. It's what she enjoys doing, and I think she wants to take it."

"You think?"

Meghan gave a smile tinged with sadness. "Okay, I *know* she wants to take it."

"What about you?" Tom asked. "What would you rather be doing?"

"Well, of course I'd rather be working at the clinic." She listed the reasons, then said, "This may sound strange, but when I'm taking care of an animal and they look at me with those big trusting eyes, I feel like I'm exactly where God wants me to be. Like this is what I was always meant to do. Yes, it's special to be working alongside you, but being at the clinic is so much more than that."

"What about your mama? Do you know what she wants?"

"Mama's never said exactly, but I can tell you one thing for sure. She doesn't want to have anything to do with the *Snip 'n Save*. She made that clear right from the start."

"Do you think it's because she loved your daddy less than you did?"

"No way! Mama adored Daddy. She said they were soul mates, that they knew each other's thoughts even before the words popped out of their mouths."

"So she must have a pretty good idea of what your daddy would say if he were still here, right? Remind me again what she thought about selling the *Snip 'n Save*."

Meghan slid him a sideways glance, and the corner of her mouth curled. "Mama said I should quit imagining I'd be letting Daddy down. She claims he liked the *Snip 'n Save* well enough as a job, but the thing he loved was his three girls."

She allowed her mama's words to linger at the edge of her thoughts before continuing. The answer was there; it had always been there. She'd just failed to see it until Tom shined a light on it.

"I guess Mama and Daddy both want the same thing. They want their girls to be happy."

"For what it's worth, Meghan, I'll support you in whatever decision you make, whether it's staying at the clinic or going back to the *Snip 'n Save*. But the truth is I hope you'll stay. You have a unique way with animals; it's as if they know you love them, and they respond to that. If you left, our clients would really miss you." He pulled her closer and tilted her face to his. "And so would I."

He eased her onto her back, then covered her mouth with his.

That night, Meghan made her decision.

The following day, Meghan called Sheldon Markowitz and asked if he was still interested in buying the *Snip 'n Save*.

"Depends," he said. "How much are you asking?"

"Thirty thousand, and you take over everything."

"I'm not arguing about the cost, but I don't have that much cash. I can do fifteen down and pay off the balance in installments."

They talked through the terms of a three-year payout, and Meghan said that seemed acceptable, but there was one more stipulation. Sheldon listened to what she wanted, then agreed.

"I would have done it anyway," he said, "just because it's good business."

After they'd gone back and forth on a few sticky points, Meghan told him this didn't mean they had a deal.

"I'm just feeling out the market," she said. "Mama's already said this isn't just my decision, so the only thing I can do right now is promise to talk it over with her and Tracy. Give me some time, and when I know more, I'll get back to you."

"Trust me, you won't regret this," Sheldon said.

"Hopefully not," she replied.

64

Meghan Whitely

You might think that once I'd reached a decision my mind would be at rest, but it's not. The truth is I feel like all our memories of Daddy are about to be flushed down the drain and Mama wants me to be the one to do it.

She says this decision about the Snip 'n Save *isn't mine alone, but it feels like it is. It feels like it's always been mine.*

Even though I've already talked to Sheldon and he's agreed to buy the magazine, I keep thinking maybe there's another way out. There isn't. I know that. If there were, I would have come up with it days ago. I've looked at this situation a million ways from Sunday, and what it always boils down to is that either Tracy would have to give up her life or I'd have to give up mine.

I can't do that, because Tom needs me to help him build a business. And it's not fair to ask Tracy to do what I won't do myself. She wants to do something more meaningful with her life by working with kids and building places where children with hearing disabilities can learn. Her life has changed, and she's changed, I understand that. My life changed when I found Sox. In rescuing him, I rescued myself. The same thing happened to Tracy. She found herself in finding a voice for Lucas. Now she wants to work with kids, and she wants it just as much as I want to work at the clinic.

The bottom line is that I'll do what I have to do. I just hope Daddy can find it in his heart to forgive me.

65

The Way It Is

On the surface, Kathleen Miller's first case seemed to be a simple "him versus her" analysis, but once she got involved, she found it was far more complicated. When she sat down to write her report, there were a dozen different questions picking at her mind.

She'd expected to interview two people, then make a judgment, but a number of other factors crept into the story. First there was Tracy's fiancé. With an impending marriage, she couldn't discount the effect Gabriel Hawke might have on the boy's life. Then there was the fraternal grandmother, dead and buried, taking the truth of what was or wasn't along with her. Alice DeLuca was the one person who would have known whether Dominic actually pursued a relationship with his son.

Meghan swore Dominic came to the house only once—that Thanksgiving Day when he was drunk and abusive. But after hearing it was her husband, Tom, who pulled Dominic off Tracy and knocked him to the ground, that story also had scraps of doubt clinging to it.

As if the waters weren't muddy enough, a will had suddenly surfaced. Charlie claimed Matthew McGinley of McGinley & Hudson drew it up, but she'd called his office only to discover McGinley was out of the country and no one could speak for him.

The only person Kathleen could absolutely trust was the child: Lucas.

She read through the notebook of testimonies a second and then third time. Each time she found another niggling little detail worthy of concern. She flipped the pages back and forth for well over an hour, then pulled a packet of index cards from her desk and wrote the name of each person on a card. Beneath their names she wrote the facts in black ink. Opinions and observations she pushed to the bottom and wrote in blue ink. The glaring questions she wrote in red, and on Dominic's card she circled the one word that presented the biggest question of all: Why?

Spreading the cards across the kitchen table, Kathleen could compare the testimonies of one person to another and as she did so, a premonition settled in her chest.

It was the same feeling she'd had three years earlier in New York City. She'd been attending Columbia at the time and headed home for the weekend. As she'd neared the Port Authority Bus Terminal, she saw someone up ahead. Despite the drizzle of rain in the air and the dusky sky, he wore sunglasses and a baseball cap pulled low over his forehead. For a full block, he followed a white-haired woman who was moving slowly. When she neared the corner, he broke into a run, knocked her over, snatched the purse from her hand, and disappeared in a flash.

Kathleen had sensed it was going to happen. If she'd called out, he might have run away or perhaps some other bystander would have been at the ready to grab him before he could flee. But she hadn't called out. She'd done nothing. A trickle of blood ran down the woman's face as Kathleen helped her to her feet.

"I didn't see that coming," the woman said tearfully.

Kathleen had, but she'd said nothing for fear of seeming foolish.

She wouldn't let that happen again. This time, the premonition of wrongdoing would factor into what she said.

After nearly two hours of studying the cards and weighing one fact against the other, Kathleen sat at the computer and typed up her report, including both the hard facts and her gut feeling. She started with a review of Dominic.

"Although the plaintiff claims he has been denied access to the boy," she wrote, "I have reason to doubt the truth of his statement." She went on to say that Dominic's now-deceased grandmother had a relationship with the child and during the last few months had visited often.

"In view of this, I find it difficult to believe the child's mother would prevent the birth father from visiting unless she had substantial justification." She then detailed the Thanksgiving Day incident.

The next two paragraphs were about Tracy and Gabriel. After stating that Tracy was possibly an overly protective mother, she claimed that it was understandable given Lucas's medical situation. Of Gabriel, she said he was extremely fond of the boy and had expressed hope to one day legally adopt Lucas.

"Through Gabriel Hawke's testimony, I learned Charlie Barnes, a family friend, often drove Alice DeLuca to visit her great-grandson. When interviewed, Mr. Barnes was a cooperative witness with no apparent reason to color his testimony in either direction."

She went on to say Charlie Barnes knew for a fact attorney Matthew McGinley had recently prepared a will for Alice DeLuca.

"I have called Mr. McGinley three times but was told he is out of the country and no one can speak on his behalf. Although this is speculation, I believe the will may have a codicil, which might be the impetus behind Mr. DeLuca's request for guardianship."

At the end of her five-page summary, Kathleen concluded that, in her opinion, the child would be best served if guardianship was denied and supervised visits allowed.

Kathleen Miller's report arrived in Judge Kingston's box on Tuesday morning. When he first received Hiram Selby's appeal for guardianship, Judge Kingston had thought the problem was a negligent mother, but after reading over the report, it appeared otherwise. He read it through a second time, then phoned Hiram.

"Have you read the psychologist's report on the parties involved in this case?" he asked.

"Yes, I've read it," Hiram said, "but the report has a rather biased slant, don't you think?"

"In what way?" the judge asked.

"It favors the defendant based solely on the basis of motherhood. Plus, these allegations of a will providing some ulterior motive are ridiculous. My client is Alice DeLuca's only heir. The fact that he will most certainly inherit the residence and farm only increases the legitimacy of his claim to have the child's best interests at heart. I would think it's obvious he would like to pass the property on to his son one day."

"I'll be the one to decide what's obvious," the judge replied sharply.

When Judge Kingston hung up, he sat there drumming his fingers on the desk, trying to remember if he'd ever before heard a plea from Hiram Selby. Then it came to him: he'd known this lawyer back when he'd worked civil law. The guy was an ambulance chaser who'd filed an endless stream of nuisance lawsuits, which inevitably settled out of court.

"Not this time," he grumbled and rifled through the pages of Kathleen's report in search of the lawyer who'd failed to return her calls.

Matthew McGinley was at the office early Monday morning. He'd arrived back in the US on Sunday, but with the time difference, he was bleary-eyed and exhausted. By three o'clock, the endless pile of documents awaiting him began to blur, and he found himself nodding off. Deciding to take the remainder of the afternoon off, he promised himself he'd plow through the remainder the next day.

When Judge Kingston called on Tuesday morning, Matthew had yet to reach the death notification put there by Pamela.

"Why hasn't Alice DeLuca's will been filed for probate?" the judge asked.

Just the fact that Alice DeLuca was dead came as a surprise to Matthew, and beyond that, he couldn't imagine why the will hadn't gone to probate.

"I'll check into it and get back to you," he said.

"Make it today!" Kingston said and hung up.

"Pamela!" Matthew yelled. "Why wasn't the DeLuca will sent to probate?"

A second later she was standing in front of his desk, her hands set squarely on her hips. "In case you don't remember, you told me not to disturb you on vacation unless it was critical."

"Submitting a notarized will for probate is a routine matter," he said sharply. "Why didn't you just go ahead and send it?"

She narrowed her eyes and gave him a petulant glare. "You have a note in the file indicating you want to handle this personally because of Mrs. DeLuca's letters!"

"Gosh, you're right," he said, sounding apologetic. "I'd forgotten about that." He thought back to the afternoon Alice gave him the letters to be handed out at the reading of the will. She'd said there was bound to be anger over some of the decisions she'd made, and hopefully the letters would clarify things. He'd promised to see to it personally, and that's exactly what he was going to do.

Before the hour was out, Pamela had called everyone and told each of them the reading of Alice's will was scheduled for Wednesday afternoon at two o'clock.

"Tomorrow?" Dominic exclaimed. He'd been hoping to first be awarded guardianship so he'd be ready regardless of what Alice had decided. "I can't make it that soon," he said. "Hold off for a few weeks."

Pamela informed him that Mr. McGinley said regardless of who was there, the reading would be held at the scheduled time.

Once the meeting was set, Matthew called Judge Kingston back. He informed him that the will was to be read the following afternoon and before end of business would be submitted for probate.

"Send me a copy," the judge said. Almost as an afterthought, he asked, "Is there anything in the will that would make it more advantageous for whoever was the guardian of her great-grandson?"

"No," Matthew said earnestly. "Nothing."

The judge's next phone call was to Hiram Selby. Without mincing words, he said, "This appears to be a frivolous lawsuit with little justification. My understanding is that the defendant will agree to supervised visitation, and I think your client would be well advised to accept that compromise and move on."

"With all due respect, Your Honor, my client will never go along with that. He is prepared to be flexible on shared custody but adamant about the guardianship issue. He feels it's imperative he be involved in decisions regarding the boy's future."

Running low on patience, Judge Kingston cut to the chase. "I don't suppose the terms of his grandmother's will have anything to do with Mr. DeLuca's sudden need for guardianship. Or do they?"

"Absolutely not, Your Honor. My client's pursuit of this is only in the best interests—"

"Yes, I know," the judge said cynically. "In the best interests of the child. We'll see about that. I'll have a copy of the will on my desk tomorrow, so on Thursday morning, I want to see you and opposing counsel here in my office."

"Of course, Your Honor."

As he replaced the receiver, Hiram Selby suspected he had a problem.

That same afternoon, Hiram called Prescott Anderson and made one last plea for a settlement.

"We're willing to drop shared custody if your client will go along with guardianship."

"No deal," Prescott said. "Judge Kingston has advised that it would be better for all concerned to wait until after the will is read."

66

Reading of the Will

When Gabriel got the call from Pamela asking that he attend the reading of Alice DeLuca's will, he questioned it.

"I think there's been a mistake," he said. "The person you're probably looking for is Tracy Briggs, Lucas's mom."

Pamela bristled. After having been chastised for not bringing immediate attention to Alice's death notice, she was none too anxious to have another mistake laid at her feet.

"Mr. McGinley specified you should be there, and I most certainly have not made a mistake," she said curtly, then hung up before Gabriel could ask a question.

He sat wondering about it for a few moments, then called Tracy.

"Alice's lawyer just called and asked for me to be at the reading of her will tomorrow afternoon. Do you know why?"

Sounding almost as confused as Gabriel, Tracy said, "I got the same call, and they asked me to bring Lucas. After being so snippy with the psychologist, I'm worried that . . ." Her voice trailed off as if the thought was too painful to finish.

"This lawyer has nothing to do with the custody issue," Gabriel assured her. "This is about Alice's will, but I can't imagine what."

Tracy gave a weighted sigh. "I'm sure Dominic will be there, and I'm not looking forward to seeing him. The last time we saw each other, he tried to yank Lucas out of my arms."

"I don't think you have to worry about that happening again. We're meeting in the lawyer's office, so he'll behave himself."

Tracy started to say that even Dominic's best behavior was questionable, but she held back. Hopefully Gabriel was right and things would go smoother than she anticipated.

That night, Tracy found sleep almost impossible to come by. As soon as she dismissed the thought of one worry, another cropped up. Knowing Dominic as she did, she couldn't help but wonder if this meeting was some kind of ploy to give him a say in Lucas's life.

The thought brought tears to her eyes. Moments later, a tear rolled down her face, and she tasted the salt of it. Regardless of the cost, she had to make certain this didn't happen. Letting Dominic back into Lucas's life meant he'd be back in hers. He was clever and skilled at gaining an advantage. Dominic could take a single word and turn it into an argument. Sooner or later he'd find a way to cause friction between her and Gabriel.

Dominic could afford to gamble, because he had nothing to lose. She had everything.

After a night of sleeplessness, Tracy woke weary and with red-rimmed eyes. She dressed in black slacks and a matching sweater, which made her skin appear even paler than it was. Skipping breakfast, she went into the *Snip 'n Save* office, booted up the computer, and for the next fifteen minutes just sat there, staring at the screen.

Finally, she opened the filler ad for the Chamber of Commerce and tried moving some type around. She added a panoramic photo of the shops on Main Street, then decided it didn't look right and deleted it. After almost an hour of achieving nothing, she powered down the computer, went into the kitchen, and sat across from Lila.

"I'm worried, Mama." Her words were small and as helpless sounding as they'd been when she was a child.

"About what?" Lila asked.

Tracy shrugged. "Dominic, I guess. He's going to be there today, and I have no idea what he'll do. You know he always had a way of . . . of manipulating . . ." Her eyes welled up again.

Lila stood, came around the table, and hugged her daughter from behind. She leaned forward and pressed her cheek to Tracy's.

"You've got to stop believing that," she said. "Dominic has no power over you. Maybe he did at one time, but you're not the same person you were back then. You're a woman now. A mama. The love you have for your son has made you way more powerful than Dominic; you just haven't realized it yet."

Tracy turned and looked into her mama's face. "Really?"

Lila nodded. "Really."

Before Gabriel came to pick them up, Tracy had changed into a rose-colored silk dress and brushed a stroke of blush across her cheeks. Once she and Lucas were dressed and ready to go, they sat together on the front porch swing, and she explained they would be meeting his daddy.

"Last time was different, because I was surprised at him showing up," she said. "But this time, we know he'll be there, so when he talks to you, you need to be nice. Even though Dominic hasn't been around for a long while, he's still your daddy."

"But . . ." Lucas sat there, looking confused. "You said Mr. Gabwiel—"

"Gabriel will be your second daddy. So, just like you had two grandmas, you'll have two daddies. One who will live with us and be there every morning to take you to school, and one who was there when you were first born."

"I don't wemember a first-bown daddy . . ."

"That's okay. You need to be nice anyway."

Lucas still looked bewildered when Gabriel pulled into the driveway.

Charlie Barnes was sitting in the reception room when they arrived for the meeting. It was the first time Tracy had seen him since the funeral. She wrapped her arms around him and whispered, "We've missed you."

"I've missed coming over," he replied. "Being without Alice is hard."

Remembering the tales Alice told of how Charlie had handled the repairs around the farm, Gabriel said, "If you're looking for something to keep you busy, we can always use a handyman at the school."

Charlie gave a grin and nodded. "I just might take you up on that."

Dominic walked in a few minutes later, and the conversation came to an abrupt halt. Before he had both feet through the door, he spied Gabriel sitting next to Tracy with Lucas on his lap. The sight of Tracy with her shoulder leaning against his made their relationship obvious.

Looking across with his brows hooded and his jaw clenched, he asked, "What's *he* doing here?"

"Alice wanted Gabriel to be here," Tracy replied.

"Why?"

She felt the color rising in her cheeks. Without even trying, he could still get her riled.

"How would I know?" she answered sharply.

That old feeling of anger was still there, just beneath the surface of her skin. One wrong word, one heckling remark, one dig from the past, and it would break loose. Suddenly she felt Gabriel's hand on her arm, firm, reassuring, holding the anger in check.

Dominic flopped down in the chair directly across from her. He sat with his legs stretched out and splayed as if he were claiming the territory and warning her not to encroach on it. When Tracy ignored him, he turned to Gabriel.

"You wanna let go of my boy so he can come talk to his real daddy?"

Gabriel glanced over at Tracy, and she gave a nod of approval. It was the behavior she'd expected, and she'd forewarned Gabriel. It was true Dominic was Lucas's daddy, but it was a painful truth neither of them wanted to accept. Gabriel reluctantly lifted Lucas from his lap and stood him on the floor. "It's okay, Lucas. Go say hi."

Lucas looked up, wide-eyed, and shook his head.

"Don't be frightened," Tracy said. "Remember we talked about this at home? Dominic is the daddy who was there when you were born. You should go say hello."

Lucas wrapped his arms around Gabriel's leg and again shook his head.

Dominic's face darkened. "You got him trained, huh? Well, we'll see—"

Before Dominic could finish, Pamela stepped into the waiting room. "Mr. McGinley is ready to see you."

She led them back to his office, then pulled the door closed as she left. It was what Matthew had suggested she do.

McGinley stood and gave a cordial nod.

"Please, have a seat." He motioned to the semicircle of chairs facing his desk. Still standing, he said, "I am truly sorry for your loss. Alice was a wonderful woman, and I know she was dear to each of you."

He lifted two envelopes and handed one to Dominic and the other to Gabriel.

"Alice left these for you, but before you open them, I'd like to go over the bequests and stipulations of her will."

Matthew sat and opened the file folder atop his desk. He cleared his throat and began. Reading through the document, he said, "Alice has left her car and whatever cash there is in her bank account to her grandson, Dominic."

Dominic glanced at Tracy and gave a snide smile of satisfaction.

Matthew continued. "Alice wanted Lucas to have Daddy DeLuca's gold pocket watch in the hopes he would remember her side of his family." Matthew flipped a page.

"The remainder of the estate," he read aloud, "including the farm, land, and house will be given to the Hawke School with the stipulation that it be used to create a recreational camp for children with disabilities."

Dominic was out of his seat in a flash. He leaned across the desk and stuck his nose in Matthew's face. "Are you shitting me?"

Matthew, a good head taller than his opponent, stood and leaned forward to meet the angry glare. "I'm not finished! Sit down, or I'll call security."

Dominic dropped back into his chair with a heavy thud.

"Lastly, Alice requested that Charlie Barnes be the executor of her estate, and she has included a second stipulation that if anyone challenges him, his decisions, or the decisions set forth in this will, they will ultimately forfeit anything previously designated for them." Matthew leaned back in his chair and nodded. "Now go ahead and open the envelopes."

In Dominic's envelope there was a single sheet penned in Alice's shaky handwriting. He sat and read in silence, sharing nothing of what she said.

"All these many years, I have loved you," she wrote, "and nothing you have ever done has changed that. A grandmother's love is not given or taken away because of merit; it simply is what it is. A simple unadorned thing meant to last forever.

"Yes, I sometimes pushed you to do things, but it was only because I thought they would bring you happiness. Now that I am nearing my final hour, I realize it was never up to me to find your happiness; that's something you must do for yourself.

"I pray I have chosen wisely in leaving you the car and the money. I thought long and hard about this decision, but in the end felt it best not to burden you with the farm since, for you, it has always been a symbol of being left behind. Now it's time to start anew, Dominic. Forget your mama. Just go forth and be a better person than she was. Hopefully this bit of money will help you get on your feet and set you up with a fresh start. Find a place where you can be happy, and always remember I loved you dearly."

When Dominic finished reading, he slid the letter back into its envelope and tucked it into the breast pocket of his jacket. He blinked back a tear, then folded his arms across his chest and sat with his face turned to the side.

Matthew then gave Gabriel a nod, and he opened the envelope in his hand. It was addressed to Tracy and himself. Unfolding the pale-blue paper, he read the letter aloud.

"Dearest Tracy. They say that the good Lord makes things right in His own way and time, and surely that is true. For as I lost a daughter when Dorothy disappeared from my life, I found one when you allowed me to be part of yours. I can never thank you enough for giving me the joy of knowing my great-grandson. Lucas is a child filled with love and grace; I have only to look into his sweet face to know he will one day be a man like Daddy DeLuca."

Gabriel's eyes flitted ahead to the next sentence, and his voice cracked as he read the words.

"And Gabriel, what joy knowing you has brought. I am an opinionated old woman who was at first prepared to dislike you. I considered you the stumbling block that kept Dominic from being with his child. Watching you and Tracy together, though, I soon came to realize I was wrong. Far from being a stumbling block, you are the glue that is strong enough to hold this family together."

A tear sprang to Tracy's eye, and Dominic gave a disgruntled snort.

Gabriel sucked in a heavy breath, then continued reading. "You are not of our family, and yet you have a heart like Daddy DeLuca. I know I can trust that you will take the farm he so dearly loved and turn it into a place where children like Lucas will bring new life to the land with their happiness and laughter."

She went on to say because she had great faith in Gabriel's judgment, he was free to subdivide the property and sell off parcels to fund the construction of the camp if he deemed it necessary.

"Trust Charlie," she advised. "He is a wise man who will stay by your side to help and guide you in moving forward. He has been a good friend to me, and he will be a good friend to you, also."

As Gabriel read her final words, his eyes filled with tears.

For several moments there was only silence in the room.

Dominic's left eye twitched, and he continued to jiggle his foot as he'd done the entire time Gabriel was speaking. When no one else spoke, he gave an impatient huff.

"This is bullshit!" he said with a snarl. "I'm not gonna just sit on my hands and let some do-gooder take over."

Matthew glared across the desk. "Do I need to remind you that by challenging Alice's will, you forfeit whatever she has given you?"

Dominic leaned back in his chair, his jaw quivering and his brows so low his eyes seemed hidden beneath them.

With his arms stiff and his hands braced against the desk, Matthew leaned forward and looked at Dominic. "So do you intend to challenge this will or not?"

After a moment, Dominic asked, "How much money is in the account?"

"Eight thousand three hundred and forty-two dollars."

Dominic sat there with his chin jutted forward and sparks of anger bristling about him. As much as he believed the farm should have been given to him, he could ill afford to risk the money and a car that ran without problems.

"This is so wrong," he said and looked at Gabriel. "You stole that farm from my grandma! I don't know what line of bullshit you gave her, but—"

"Enough!" Matthew shouted. "The only question on the table is whether or not you intend to challenge this will. I want a yes-or-no answer, and that's it!"

Dominic's shoulders slumped. "I guess Grandma made up her mind," he said. "Nothing I do is gonna change it."

"Yes or no?" Matthew repeated.

After a long moment, Dominic said, "No. Once I get my money, I'm out of here."

Matthew took a large manila envelope from the folder and handed it to Tracy. "Alice also left this for Lucas. She asked that you hold on to it and give it to him when he is old enough to understand."

With a wan smile curling the corner of her lips, Tracy nodded.

67

Tracy Briggs

When we left Mr. McGinley's office, Gabriel and I were in a state of shock. We rode down in the elevator with Dominic and Charlie, but no one said a word. As we stepped out onto the street, I noticed the look on Dominic's face and couldn't help feeling sorry for him.

He turned off in the other direction and was halfway down the block when I called out to him.

"Hey, Dominic," I said. "If you want to come and visit with Lucas the way your grandma did, it's okay with me."

He gave me that look of disgust he's so good at, then turned away, shook his head, and kept on walking.

Now that his grandma is gone, I doubt we'll ever see Dominic again. He hates this town, and Lucas and I seem to be a part of the same package.

Maybe I should feel sad about Lucas not knowing his birth daddy, but the truth is, I don't. There are some people you're better off not knowing. Dominic's one of them. First, he makes you feel sorry for him. Then that leads to loving him. Once you start loving him, you're trapped. He drags your love across the floor like a mop, and if you try to leave, he threatens to kill himself because he can't live without you. So *you stay, caught in his trap, too miserable to enjoy life and too intimidated to leave it behind.*

Thank God for Lucas.

Loving him is what gave me the courage to walk away. There are a million things you can forgive a man for doing, but being uncaring about his own child is not one of them.

I guess it's like Alice said. Everything works out in its own sweet time. I may have given Lucas a terrible birth daddy, but I'm more than making up for it with the daddy he'll soon have.

68

Fair Trade

After Dominic learned what was in the will, he called Hiram Selby.

"My grandma gave the farm to the school. That kills the deal," he said. "There's nowhere to go from here."

The one thing Hiram hated more than being referred to as short was losing money, especially money he'd been counting on.

"We've still got a case," he replied. "We can argue that Grandma was off her rocker, incapable of making a decision. We'll claim she was an old lady taken advantage of by conniving money-grubbers."

Dominic drew in a labored breath, then let it go. "Not gonna work. She had the damn thing notarized, and they've got witnesses."

"That's nothing. We'll argue undue influence. Say they made her believe that's what she wanted to do."

Dominic thought about the money and the car that would be taken away if they argued the case and lost. "What do you think the odds are of us getting the decision changed if we made that argument?"

"Fifty-fifty. Higher if we can prove she was mentally unstable."

For a moment Dominic wavered, thinking of how much he could end up with if he sold the farm and pocketed the profit—or at least half of the profit, because Hiram would take half before he handed over a nickel. Then he remembered the clause in Alice's will. If Hiram argued the case and lost, he got nothing; Dominic would also get nothing, and he'd lose the money and car he already had. The question was, did he trust Hiram enough to risk the eight thousand dollars?

"Fifty-fifty isn't good enough," he said. "Let's just forget about the whole thing."

Knowing that a piece of something was better than nothing, Hiram asked, "What about shared custody of the kid? You're gonna go through with that, right?"

"Nah. What good is it at this point?"

"Wait a minute! You're pulling out of everything? I put time into this. Tomorrow I'm scheduled to meet with Judge Kingston. We could still—"

"Forget about it. Without the farm, I don't need the kid."

"So that's it?" Hiram grumbled. "Okay, I'll let Kingston know we're dropping the lawsuit, but I still expect to get paid."

"Really? How are you gonna get paid if I don't have any money?"

"Your money problems aren't mine. If you don't come up with the money, I'll sue you and take whatever you've got." Hiram pictured the black Chrysler he'd seen Dominic driving. "If there's no cash, I'll take your car."

Dominic laughed. "That's it? I give you my car and we're square?"

With him giving in so easily, Hiram grew suspicious. "Your car's not on a lease or something, is it?"

"No lease," Dominic said. "I own it outright."

"You got the papers to prove it, right?"

"Yup."

When Hiram agreed to the deal, Dominic said he'd have the car over to him within the week and hung up.

That evening, Dominic called Charlie and asked how long it would be until he could get the money Alice left him.

"Probate takes a while," Charlie said. "I'm guessing a month, maybe two."

"Any way to get it faster?" Dominic asked. "I don't think I could stand to stay at the farm, knowing it's about to be taken away from me."

Having promised Alice he'd watch out for Dominic, Charlie mentioned he had a spare bedroom.

"You can stay here for a while," he offered.

"That's not quite what I'm looking for. I'm pretty anxious to leave town and get going on that fresh start Grandma wanted me to have."

Charlie couldn't point a finger at exactly what it was, but the way Dominic spoke led him to believe there was more than what was being said. As they went back and forth about one thing and another, he grew increasingly suspicious. He considered the facts a dozen different ways. Knowing Alice's money had to come through him for distribution, he figured it was safe to spot Dominic an advance.

"I can let you have two thousand," he said. "I'll send the rest once the estate is settled."

"That'll work," Dominic replied.

A few days later, with twenty crisp one-hundred-dollar bills in his pocket, Dominic slid behind the wheel of the beat-up old Buick that still had one blue fender and drove to Aldridge. Broom followed behind, driving Alice's Chrysler.

When he rounded the corner of the street where Hiram Selby lived, Dominic coasted to a stop alongside the curb. The sky was black overhead and the street as silent as a cemetery. He climbed out of the car, closed the door quietly, and then started up the walkway with the title for the Buick in hand. Tiptoeing onto the porch, he held the papers against the front door, then pushed a thumbtack through them.

As he hurried back down the walkway, he gave a snarky laugh. By the time he got back to the curb, Broom had moved into the passenger's seat. Dominic slid behind the wheel of the Chrysler, and they headed back to Murphy's.

"You don't figure this lawyer guy's gonna come after you when he finds out that's the car you're giving him?" Broom asked.

Dominic curled his upper lip and shook his head. "No way. He's a chickenshit to begin with, and I'm gonna be long gone before he can come looking."

———— ❧❧ ————

That night, they had three beers and then swung by the boarding-house where Broom lived. Having decided to leave town with Dominic, Broom tossed his things in a duffel bag and left the landlady a note saying he'd moved out. Neither of them knew where they were headed. They only knew it would be north of Georgia.

"We'll know where we want to be when we get there," Dominic said.

———— ❧❧ ————

By the time Hiram discovered he was the new owner of the beat-up Buick with one blue fender, Dominic and Broom were well into Tennessee.

69

A Unanimous Decision

For several weeks, Meghan held off on having another family discussion regarding the fate of the *Snip 'n Save*. She'd been hoping against hope that some miracle would happen, the kind of miracle that would enable her to hang on to the magazine. But once Alice's will had passed through probate, it was understood that the school would be building a children's camp, and Tracy wanted to be part of it. When Gabriel asked that she take over as full-time director of the camp, her eyes had sparkled with delight, yet she'd said she'd have to wait until a decision was made about the *Snip 'n Save*. Although she'd held the answer in abeyance, she was already talking of craft classes and campfires where the children could toast marshmallows.

When Lila suggested it was time for the family to make a final decision, Meghan knew there could be no more delaying. Until now she'd said nothing about her conversation with Sheldon. Her first choice had always been to keep the *Snip 'n Save*, but since that was no longer possible, selling it to Sheldon would be less painful than handing it over to a complete stranger.

As soon as they were settled at the kitchen table, Lila came right out with it. "Have you given any more thought to the problem at hand?"

Tracy saw Meghan's downturned expression and said nothing. Yes, she wanted to be free to work at the camp, but a promise was a promise. Meghan had stepped in to help when she needed someone, and she was determined to do the same. If Meghan insisted on keeping the *Snip 'n Save*, Tracy wouldn't argue the point.

Lila waited a moment and then said, "Well?"

Without lifting her eyes or looking square into her mama's face, Meghan said, "I've already talked to Sheldon, and he wants to buy it."

"Sheldon?" Tracy said, her voice airy and light, the sound of happiness threaded through the name. "Why, that's perfect! He knows everything about the magazine!"

Without giving credence to it being "perfect," Meghan interrupted with the details of what she and Sheldon had discussed.

"Fifteen thousand now and a three-year payout for the rest of it."

"How soon can we get the deal done?" Lila asked.

Meghan looked up, wide-eyed. "Is there some kind of rush?"

"Yes, there is," Lila answered. "Your sister's wedding is only three months off, and it would be nice if she could get herself settled ahead of time."

Tracy reached across and covered Meghan's hand with hers. "Take as long as you need," she said. "Gabriel and I will have the rest of our lives together. A month or two doesn't matter."

Meghan turned to Tracy with a melancholy smile. She thought back to the days before her own wedding, how thrilling it was and how excited they'd been. She didn't want to rob Tracy of that same joy.

"He's ready to make the deal," she said. "It's a cut-and-dried transaction, so I think we can wrap it up by next week."

"Wonderful!" Lila said. Knowing the sacrifice Meghan had made, she looked over and smiled. "I think your daddy would be very proud of you right now."

With her chin tilted toward her chest, Meghan gave a shrug. "I just hope he can find it in his heart to forgive us for selling something he worked so hard to build."

Lila stood, came around the table, and hugged Meghan's shoulders.

"Sweetheart, you worry about the most foolish things. If George were here sitting at this table, he'd say exactly what I'm saying. The *Snip 'n Save* was nothing more than a business. The only thing your daddy and I ever wanted was to see both of you girls happy."

Meghan forced a smile and said, "Thanks, Mama."

A week later, Sheldon Markowitz signed the papers and became the new owner of the *Briggs Snip 'n Save*. Although he was now the owner of the magazine, it would forever be called the *Briggs Snip 'n Save*, which was the final stipulation Meghan had requested and Sheldon had agreed to.

That evening, Meghan cleaned out the office and packed up any last remaining bits of information for the new owner. She was wearing dark jeans and a black T-shirt that, if not for her blonde hair, would have made her seem a shadow floating around the room.

"Want some help?" Tracy asked.

Meghan shook her head. "No, thanks. This is something I need to do myself."

She went through the file folders one by one, saving every scrap of paper and discarding nothing. Things such as dried-up ballpoint pens and pencils with chewed erasers she set aside; those she planned to take to the clinic and keep in her desk. She scoured the computer for the family pictures her daddy had kept, and after she'd gathered them into one folder, she uploaded it to her flash drive. Rubber bands, paper clips, a key chain puzzle, a miniature flashlight, a Rubik's cube—all of it went into the pile of things she would carry home.

She was in the midst of cleaning out the center pencil drawer, the one containing all types of novelties and memorabilia, when she came across the piece of folded notepaper. It was tucked into a 2008 pocket calendar, wedged beneath a handheld calculator that no longer worked.

Tugging it loose, she unfolded it carefully; then she saw the familiar handwriting. At the top of the page was a heading: "George Briggs's Bucket List."

Meghan dropped down into the familiar chair, and as she read the words she could almost hear her daddy speaking them aloud. She thought back to the day they'd talked of a bucket list, and he'd said everyone should have one.

"Why?" she'd asked.

She could picture the way he'd turned to her and smiled.

"Because then you'll have pinpointed the things you want most from life, and you won't waste time worrying about the less important matters," he'd said.

At the time, Meghan had thought about making her own bucket list, but she'd never gotten around to it. Holding the paper now, she read through the list of things her daddy had hoped to accomplish. Several items were crossed off, but a number of them were not.

A single line was drawn through "Spend a week at the beach with Lila and the girls." Another line was drawn through "Quit smoking." After that, there were a number of items crossed out; most she remembered, a few she did not. "See a World Series game" was crossed out, as was "Family visit to Disney World."

Further down the list was "Get Meghan another dog. Settle Tracy in a profession she enjoys. See both girls happily married. Have grandbabies." The last three items on the list were "Sell the *Snip 'n Save*. Retire. Move into a condo with Lila after the girls have left."

For a long while, Meghan sat there with tears rolling down her cheeks. One splashed onto the note, and her daddy's condo wish became blurred. She grabbed a tissue, blotted the stain, then wiped the tears from her face.

As she sat there with the note in her hands, she could feel the truth of every word. It was just as her mama had said. The *Snip 'n Save* was never a piece of her daddy. The memories of him she carried in her heart—those were the pieces she could hold on to. Those pieces had been there all along. They were something she would never lose.

With her eyes still teary, she pushed the chair back, stood, and turned toward the kitchen.

"Mama," she called, "there's something here you need to see . . ."

Although the hour was late, Meghan sat at the kitchen table with her mama and Tracy as she read the note. This time, there was no distance between the women. They sat shoulder to shoulder, leaning on one another as they shared memories and laughed. They spoke of the week at the beach and the Disney trip. Lila told of how George and three friends had driven to Philadelphia to see the Phillies defeat the Tampa Bay Rays to win the World Series.

"He claimed seeing that game was the thrill of a lifetime," Lila said with an echo of fond remembrance threaded through her voice.

Meghan handed the note to Lila. "Here, Mama, I think you should be the one to hold on to this."

Lila looked at the note for several minutes. Then she stood, grabbed a pen from the cabinet drawer, and drew a line through "Get Meghan another dog."

Meghan gasped. "Mama, what are you doing?"

"I think your daddy would be pleased to know we're still working on his list," Lila said and smiled.

70

Meghan Whitely

I told Tracy I felt silly holding on to the Snip 'n Save *when it wasn't at all what Daddy wanted, but she just laughed. She said that Alice had written in her letter that the Lord orders things to happen in His own sweet time, and that His time isn't always the same as ours.*

"The Snip 'n Save *was there when you needed it, and it was there when I needed it," Tracy said. "Maybe that was our daddy's way of watching over us."*

I believe there's a lot of truth in what Mama said. It seems as if Daddy is still watching over us. When I needed something to love, he sent me Sox, and now he's given me his bucket list so I can let go of the Snip 'n Save *without feeling guilty. It's possible those things were coincidence, but in my heart of hearts, I'll never stop believing it was Daddy.*

Even though he's still in my heart, I can't help wanting to keep a more tangible piece of him around. I asked Mama if I could have his office chair, and she said yes, although for the life of her, she couldn't imagine what I'd want with such a ratty-looking thing.

She's right; it is kind of ratty-looking, but it still has Daddy's smell. I brought it to the clinic and gave Peggy the fancy new swivel chair Tom bought me. She whirled around in that chair and acted like being the receptionist was the most important job in town. As for me, I'm happy to be sitting in that old chair of Daddy's. I think after all these years, the seat cushion has kind of hollowed itself out to match my behind.

Mama says she's going to keep crossing things off Daddy's bucket list. I looked at the list, and there are only a few things left. One is "have grandbabies." I told Mama now that she's got Lucas, she could go ahead and cross that one off, but she shook her head.

"Uh-uh," she said. "Grandbabies is plural."

She was looking me square in the eye when she said it. I told Tom, and he grinned so wide I thought his face would split in half.

"Your mama has a point there," he said and walked off whistling.

Of course, nobody knows what the future holds, but I can tell you this much: I'm feeling pretty good about it.

71

Wedding Bells

On a crisp November day, after the leaves had turned red and gold, then fallen and scattered themselves across the lawn and walkway, Lila climbed up into the attic. It was the first time in years she'd been up here, but she knew what she was looking for and exactly where to find it.

When they'd moved into the house, George had wrestled the huge trunk up the stairs and pushed it to the far side under the eaves.

"We won't be needing this anytime soon," he'd said with a laugh.

That was the year before Tracy was born.

Lila pushed aside a box of books and two cartons of baby clothes. Then, using an old T-shirt, she wiped a layer of dust from the top of the trunk and lifted the lid.

On the top was a quilt George's grandma had made decades earlier; beneath that, the curtains from their first apartment. She set those things aside and pulled out the box she was looking for.

She lifted the lid, and there, packed in reams of tissue paper, was the wedding dress she'd worn the day she and George were married. Lila had thought about offering it to Meghan, but hers had been a summer wedding and the velvet dress would have been too warm. Anyway,

Meghan was tall and willowy like her dad. The floor-length dress would have risen above her ankles.

Tracy was like Lila—shorter, a bit broader in the waist, and with shoulders that wouldn't be dwarfed by the heft of velvet. And for a January wedding, the dress was perfect. Lila removed the bundles of rolled tissue, unfolded the dress, and held it up for inspection. It was just as the dry cleaner had promised: perfectly preserved.

She closed the trunk and carried the dress downstairs. Although the day she'd worn the dress was over thirty years ago, she remembered it as if it were yesterday. They were so young, so much in love. It was long before gray strands threaded George's hair, long before her waist became thick and tiny lines settled at the corners of her eyes.

Glancing in the mirror, Lila held the dress in front of her and remembered it all: the kiss at the altar, the first dance, the promise he'd whispered in her ear. Tears welled in her eyes as she placed the dress on a hanger and hung it on Tracy's bedroom door, the silky velvet shimmering in the sunlight and the train pooling on the floor.

That afternoon, Tracy slid the dress over her head as Lila watched.

Turning to catch herself in the full-length mirror, Tracy gasped. "It's beautiful, Mama!"

The dress was almost perfect. A row of lacy flowers circling the neckline had turned yellow and would have to be replaced, and the train needed to be cut back so it was not quite so cumbersome, but that was it.

Lila pulled her sewing machine from the back of the closet where she'd stored it after she turned her sewing room into Lucas's room. All that month, she and Tracy worked on the dress. They browsed the fabric shops until they found a scalloped lace border that was the exact shade of ivory as the gown. After Lila stitched the new lace into place, she sewed tiny seed pearls around the edge of each seashell-shaped scallop. The train that once stretched out three feet behind Lila as she walked down the aisle was trimmed to less than twelve inches, and a loop was added to the underskirt so Tracy could lift it and hook it to her wrist as she danced.

By then, Tracy's time was her own. Sheldon had taken over full production of the *Briggs Snip 'n Save*, and Meghan was happy to spend her days working alongside Tom at the animal clinic. After years of having the responsibility of being a mother, Tracy now had the luxury of being a prospective bride. In time, she and Lucas would move to Barrington and she'd work at the school until the camp was built, but for now, it was only two or sometimes three days a week. The other days she spent leisurely, browsing through bridal magazines, addressing wedding invitations, selecting favors, and shopping for the event.

Meghan was to be the matron of honor, so on an otherwise uneventful Tuesday, the two of them went downtown and browsed through the shops. At Bridal Elegance, they selected three dresses, and Meghan carried them off to the fitting room. Moments later, she stepped out in an off-the-shoulder burgundy taffeta, and Tracy grinned in delight.

"Oh, my gosh, you look amazing!"

Meghan grinned back. "And the best part is I can wear this dress again." She could already imagine Tom whirling her around the dance floor at the Starlight Room as they celebrated their next anniversary.

Although the sisters had grown up close, over the years, time, lifestyle, and responsibilities had slid little slivers of separation between them. That space now began to grow smaller and smaller until, a few weeks before the wedding, it disappeared completely, and neither of them could remember it ever being there.

"It's nice to see you two together and getting along so well," Lila said.

"We've always gotten along," both girls answered.

Lila smiled and said nothing. It was satisfaction enough just to see them as they now were.

December flew by. Christmas came and went with everyone at the house and Lila cooking up a storm. Cakes and pies were lined up along the counter, and the refrigerator was filled to overflowing. In the living room wrapping paper and ribbons were scattered about, and Lucas's shrieks of delight could be heard clear to the end of the block. Lila reveled in each moment knowing that, in the days to come, it would be different. Not bad, just different.

As much as she loved having the family here, she knew that was destined to change. Just as she had left her mama's house and moved into a life of her own, so would the girls. Sure, they would come to visit, but little by little they would drift into their own responsibilities just as she had.

She couldn't help but wonder what she'd do with so much room after they were gone. More than once, she eyed George's bucket list and focused on the part where he'd thought of retiring to a lovely little condo. And more than once, she'd also recalled the adorable condo his sister, Phoebe, had in an adult living complex.

Not such a bad idea, she thought, but held off saying anything.

As the wedding drew closer, Tracy worried that low clouds—or, worse yet, an icy-cold rain—might hover over the Good Shepherd Church and spoil everything. On the dreariest day of December, she looked up at the steel-gray sky and pictured herself walking down the aisle trailing puddles of water in her wake.

None of those things happened. In fact, the second Saturday of January dawned with a sky as bright as a blue diamond and equally as clear.

Though the chill of the previous evening had not yet burned off, Tracy threw open the window and sucked in a deep breath. Downstairs she heard the rattle of pots and pans; Mama had invited Charlie, Meghan, and Tom for breakfast and was already cooking. Gabriel would be there also.

She thought back on how her mama had at first been reluctant to include Gabriel, claiming it was bad luck for the groom to see the bride before their wedding.

Tracy'd laughed and rolled her eyes. "Mama, we're not exactly kids!"

Everyone else laughed along with her, and Gabriel said he'd love to come for the wedding-day breakfast.

"Don't worry, Mama B, nothing in this world can stop me from marrying Tracy, especially not a sneak peek at my lovely bride the morning of."

"Mama B," that's what Gabriel now called her. He'd slid into the family as seamlessly as Tom had, and apparently Lila couldn't be happier.

The wedding jitters that had plagued Tracy the month before vanished that morning as she sat at the table with a cup of hazelnut coffee and a cinnamon bun so sweet the taste of sugar lingered on her tongue for hours.

The invitation said five o'clock, but people started arriving at the Good Shepherd Church before four thirty. They strolled through the courtyard, greeting one another and marveling at such a day for a wedding. And such a day it was: warm for January with not a cloud in the sky and sunlight slanting through the nearly bare trees. Ladies needed nothing more than a lightweight shawl around their shoulders, and men left topcoats hanging in the closet at home.

When the time grew close, friends and neighbors began to scuttle inside, each vying for a spot near the center aisle, a spot where they would get a firsthand glimpse of the bride. Before long, every seat was taken, and latecomers stood shoulder to shoulder along the back wall.

Once the others were seated, Charlie escorted Lila down the aisle and sat her next to Phoebe, George's sister. Moments later, the bell in the steeple chimed, and the organist stomped down on the foot pedals. The song Gabriel and Tracy had chosen was "A Thousand Years." It was how long they'd promised to love one another.

First down the aisle were Meghan and Tom, walking side by side and wearing such a glow they could have easily been mistaken for the bride and groom. Meghan carried a small bouquet of stargazer lilies tied with a length of ivory velvet, a piece of the fabric trimmed from Tracy's gown.

Following behind was Lucas. He carried a small pillow made of the same velvet with the two gold bands on top held in place by a narrow ribbon. With a crisp bow tie snapped onto the collar of his shirt, he marched up to the altar, then turned back to watch his mama and Gabriel.

A hush fell across the room when Tracy and Gabriel started down the aisle together. Women smiled, and a number of the men looped their arms around the women next to them.

Phoebe gave a gasp and leaned into Lila. "Good grief," she whispered. "She looks exactly like you did."

"She's wearing my gown," Lila whispered back.

Tracy's hair was swept off her neck and caught in a delicate pearl clip. Wispy tendrils hung loose and framed her face. She had chosen not to wear a veil. It was a symbolic decision that no one could argue.

"When I left town with Dominic, my eyes were covered with a veil of foolishness," she'd said. "But I'm entering this marriage with nothing veiling my eyes."

As they walked slowly down the aisle, Tracy's left arm was looped through Gabriel's. In her right hand, she carried three calla lilies tied together with the same ivory velvet as her gown. When they reached the altar, they turned to Pastor Dale, Gabriel standing to the left of Tracy and Lucas standing on her right.

Pastor Dale's voice echoed throughout the room. "Ladies and gentlemen, we are gathered here today to unite Tracy Briggs and Gabriel Hawke in holy matrimony and to establish a family bond no man can break . . ."

When Pastor Dale asked if they were prepared to enter into such a bond, they both answered yes and turned to one another. The pastor reached down, took the velvet pillow from Lucas's hand, and loosened the ribbon.

Gabriel spoke first, his hands clasping hers, his eyes focused on her face and seeing nothing of the surroundings.

"Tracy Briggs, I've loved you for longer than you could possibly know, and today I rejoice in knowing we'll become a family. I want you to know that for as long as I live, your feelings will be my feelings; your sorrows will be my sorrows; your joys, my joys; and your son, my son. Our son. My love for you is unshakable. My devotion to you endless. From this day forward, I swear you will never walk alone. My heart will be your shelter, and my arms will forever be your home, so help me God."

He held her trembling hand in his and gently slid the ring on her finger.

Tracy's eyes were brimming with tears of happiness, and her voice shook a bit as she began to speak.

"Gabriel Hawke, on this our wedding day, I pledge you my unconditional love and deepest devotion. I promise that no matter what the future might hold, I will be by your side to love, honor, respect, and cherish you for all the days of our lives. I want your face to be the last thing I see before I fall asleep at night and the first thing I see when I wake in the morning. At this moment, I feel all my prayers have been answered. I believe our love has been heaven-sent and will endure for all eternity. You will have my faithfulness, love, and devotion for as long as we both shall live."

Pastor Dale handed her the second ring, and she eased it onto Gabriel's finger.

At that point, Tracy expected the pastor to pronounce them man and wife, but instead, he turned to Gabriel and gave a nod. It was time to proceed with the secret only the two men knew would happen. Gabriel stepped in front of Lucas and squatted down.

"Lucas, thank you for sharing your mama with me and allowing me to love you with all my heart. I wasn't there when you took your first steps, but I promise that now I'll love and support you in every step you take for the rest of your life. Please accept this gift as a symbol of my love for you."

Gabriel had searched for months trying to find the most appropriate gift to include Lucas in the celebration. For girls, a locket or bracelet was usually suggested, but for boys there was nothing. Finally, he'd made the decision on his own. He reached into his pocket, pulled out a gold key chain with an engraved fob, then offered it to Lucas. "Will you allow me the honor of being your daddy?"

Wide-eyed, Lucas looked up at Tracy, who beamed. Then he looked back at Gabriel and nodded.

Gabriel smiled, gave him a hug, and stood, but before he could move back to Tracy's side, Lucas reached up and tugged the tail of his jacket.

"Wead it to me," he said.

Gabriel squatted again, and the room stilled as his voice softened and he read the words aloud.

"You will forever have the key to my heart." Gabriel's voice quivered, then cracked as emotion threaded his words. He sucked in a breath, then continued. "My love for your mama made us a family, but my love for you makes me your daddy."

Lucas grinned. "Mr. Gabwiel, does this mean you're my weal daddy?"

Gabriel nodded. "Yes, Lucas, I'm your real daddy." He pulled the boy into his arms again and kissed his forehead.

Quickly swiping at his eyes, Gabriel moved back to stand beside Tracy, and Lucas followed along. A twitter of laughter ran through the audience as Lucas positioned himself in between the bride and groom. Pastor Dale's lips curled, and he could no longer hold back the grin.

"By the power vested in me, I now pronounce you husband, wife, and family. You may kiss the bride."

Lucas stood looking up as Gabriel wrapped his arms around Tracy and covered his mouth with hers. The kiss was long, sweet, and filled with passion. When it ended, the organist again stomped on the pedals, and the joyous sound of "Signed, Sealed, Delivered" filled the room.

Gabriel scooped Lucas into his arms, and the three of them started back down the aisle.

Tom leaned into Meghan and whispered, "Well, that was certainly an extraordinary moment."

Meghan turned with a smile. "It's been a year of extraordinary moments."

Lila overheard her daughter and gave an imperceptible nod. Truly it had been a year of extraordinary moments. Sisters coming together, love finding a way, and, perhaps most importantly, letting go of the past.

With George's sister, Phoebe, on one side and Charlie on the other, Lila followed Meghan and Tom back down the aisle.

That night Lila returned to the house alone. She brewed a cup of chamomile tea and sat at the kitchen table recalling the events of the day.

If only George could have been there.

That thought triggered another one. She crossed the kitchen and opened the drawer where she now kept his bucket list.

Returning to the table, she unfolded the yellowing paper, smiled as she read through the items on his list, and then crossed off "See both girls happily married."

It had been a year of extraordinary moments, and George had not missed a one. He'd planned for them all, and in the end, he'd left a note telling her so.

The moon was already high in the sky when she climbed into bed and remembered the last item on George's list: "Retire and move into a nice little condo."

"I'm still working on it." She sighed and snapped off the light.

Epilogue

Although no one can see it now, Lucas will open Alice's envelope on his sixteenth birthday. Inside, he will find a seven-page letter written on pale-blue stationery. In it, Alice will tell of the DeLuca family and how the farm once rang with laughter and happiness and how she had known him for such a short time and yet loved him so completely. Along with the letter, he'll find pictures, some so faded you can barely make out the farmhouse. On the back of each picture is the family history Alice has penned in blue ink.

After so many years, Lucas can hardly remember Alice's face, but in the pictures, he will see her as a young woman sitting alongside Joe with their baby girl in her arms. She is smiling as if she expects only the best of life. There are other pictures also: Daddy DeLuca standing proud in front of the Magnolia Grove courthouse, a field of peanut plants stretched out for as far as the eye can see, and countless photos of Dominic as a boy, then a young man, his shoulders pushed back and his head held high.

Of all the photos, the one that will be Lucas's favorite is the one where he is sitting at the dining room table with Alice. In front of them is a board game, Chutes and Ladders, he thinks. Even though many of his childhood memories have faded, he remembers those afternoons of being together. He will tuck that picture into the frame of the mirror that hangs above his dresser, and whenever he catches a glimpse of it, he will smile.

Just as Alice has hoped, it will be a memory that lasts forever.

Acknowledgments

When a reader holds a finished book in hand, they see only the face of the author, but in truth, many people contribute to the successful making of a novel. I consider myself blessed to have had the wonderful team at Lake Union working with me on the development of this book.

I am truly grateful to my agent, Pamela Harty, for introducing me to Lake Union and continuing to provide day-to-day support with such unending grace and wisdom.

I am extremely fortunate to have been paired with Alicia Clancy, my editor. She goes above and beyond what might be expected and comes to know my characters as well as I do. Her advice is both wise and insightful. I am delighted to have her as my partner on this exciting journey.

I also owe a debt of gratitude to Lindsay Guzzardo, my developmental editor, for forcing me to dig deeper and find the treasure trove of emotions hidden beneath the surface.

My utmost thanks also goes to Karen Brown, my copy editor, and Nicole Pomeroy, my production manager, for their attention to detail and thoughtful edits. Also to my author relations manager, Gabriella Dumpit, for carefully following up on each and every detail, answering my endless questions, and seeing this project through to completion.

A sincere note of thanks to Ekta Garg, fellow author, beta editor, adviser, and friend.

I would be lost without Coral Russell, the do-everything person who keeps my blog on target, organizes fan events, and steps in to help when I need a third hand. Thank you for all these things and the thousands of others you do.

And to the ladies in my BFF (Best Fans & Followers) Clubhouse, I am eternally grateful. They read my books, share them with friends, review them on Goodreads, and eagerly await each new release. Loyalty such as this is something to be treasured.

For things too numerous to count, I thank my husband, Dick. He is, and will always be, my greatest blessing.

About the Author

Photo © 2017 Brian Adams Photography

Bette Lee Crosby is the *USA Today* bestselling author of nineteen novels, including the first Magnolia Grove novel, *The Summer of New Beginnings*. She has been the recipient of the Royal Palm Literary Award, Reviewer's Choice Award, FAPA President's Book Award, International Book Award, and Next Generation Indie Award, among many others. Her 2016 novel, *Baby Girl*, was named Best Chick Lit of the Year by *Huffington Post*. She laughingly admits to being a night owl and a workaholic, claiming that her guilty pleasure is late-night chats with fans and friends on Facebook and Goodreads. To learn more about Bette Lee Crosby's work, visit www.betteleecrosby.com or check out her Amazon Author Page.